Chasing Checkers
ACCELERATION

Christopher Hinchcliffe

Christopher Hinchcliffe / Morgandale Press
contact@christopherhinchcliffe.com
www.chasingcheckersbook.com

Publisher's Note: This is a work of fiction. Names, characters,
places, and incidents are a product of the author's imagination.
Locales and public names are sometimes used for atmospheric
purposes. Any resemblance to actual people, living or dead, or to
businesses, companies, events, institutions, or locales is completely coincidental.

Edited by Rachel Small (Faultless Finish) and Maya Berger (What
I Mean to Say.)

Cover Design by Damonza

Chasing Checkers: Acceleration / Christopher Hinchcliffe. --
1st ed.
ISBN 978-0-9952415-2-7

That which we manifest is before us; we are the creators of our own destiny.

—GARTH STEIN, *The Art of Racing in the Rain*

Chapter 1

Teddy twitched in his seat. His knees quivered. His hands clenched. With each passing moment his heart pumped a little faster, a little harder. He tried to focus on his breath, to calm himself. But all he could think about were the seconds counting down.

The bell rang.

Teddy jumped up from his chair, startling his best friend Richard, who was sitting beside him, half-asleep. Richard ran a hand through his floppy brown hair and smirked at Teddy.

"Your first essays are due on Monday," Mrs. Gottlieb said, from the front of the room. She raised her voice over the scraping chairs and chattering students. "Have a nice weekend."

Teddy barely listened as he stuffed his books into his backpack.

"Easy there, Teddy," said Richard. "What's the hurry, man? It's Friday."

Exactly, thought Teddy. He zipped up his bag and grinned at Richard.

"Practice."

Richard laughed.

"Oh, right. 'Practice.'" He made air quotes. "You mean you haven't beaten that thing yet?"

Teddy shuddered but tried to play it off as a shrug. On Monday, he'd bought the latest racing game, *GP Pro 7*. He'd already beaten every course on the highest level except for one—Laguna Seca. Grand Champion status eluded him. It was driving him crazy.

"Just taking my time, savouring the victories," he lied. "Besides, a lot of homework this week." He gestured towards their teacher and slung his backpack over his shoulder. It felt heavier than usual. *Do incomplete assignments weigh more?* he wondered.

"Skipping the gym, then?" asked Richard, as they pushed their way into the teeming hallway, merging with the weekend traffic.

Teddy hesitated. "Yeah. But I tweaked my shoulder last week so it's probably better anyway." As he spoke, Teddy could almost feel this imaginary pain flare up. He rotated his arm stiffly for effect.

"Sure, Teddy." Richard smiled and punched him in the shoulder. Teddy blushed, and they both cracked up.

After a quick stop at their lockers, he and Richard headed outside to wait for the gang. They stood on the sidewalk just beyond the school's designated smoking area: "the Pit." It was an ugly patch of hard-packed dirt in the perpetual shade of a tall oak tree. As the crowd of students filtered out, the boys kept their eyes open for their friends.

Teddy spotted Ben and Justin first. Ben was half-walking, half-sidestepping alongside Justin, chatting away.

His football jersey, two sizes too big, flapped around him. Justin walked with his head down, fixated on his smartphone, oblivious to (or uninterested in) whatever Ben was saying. His button-down shirt was tucked neatly into his dark jeans, his black hair parted to the side, holding in stiff defiance of any breeze that might attack it. Teddy tried to guess how much gel Justin went through in a week.

"Guys, over here!" Teddy called, waving them over.

Justin glanced up and adjusted his course. Ben moved with him like a shadow, not even pausing to look at Richard and Teddy.

"And then he was like, 'Oh no you don't,' and I was like, 'Oh really?' Hand grenade. Boom." Ben fanned his arms over his head and made a garbled sound effect. "Game over, sucka. Hey. *Hey!* You aren't even listening."

"Ten points, Gryffindor," Justin said. "Afternoon, gents."

Teddy and Richard smirked. Ben turned his attention to them.

"Guys, guys, you gotta hear about this epic *Call of Duty* game I played last night."

"Ben, you already told us. At lunch. Remember?" Richard nudged Teddy with his elbow.

"What? Oh, yeah," Teddy said, catching on. "Epic, Ben."

Teddy didn't like teasing Ben as much as the others did, but he was such an easy mark. Besides, Teddy had heard so many *Call of Duty* stories he pretty much knew what Ben would have said anyway.

Ben squinted and looked up, cocking his head. "Did I? Oh."

Teddy looked over Justin's shoulder and noticed Leah and Zana approaching them. He was still getting used to Zana's new haircut—her frizzy black hair was cropped almost to the scalp. Leah, as always, had her dark brown hair pulled back in a ponytail. She wore a simple white tank top and faded blue jeans. As she turned back towards the door to wave at a friend, Teddy couldn't help but notice how well those jeans fit her. He buried his hands in his pockets.

Leah coughed as she passed the smokers, waving a hand in front of her face.

"Why are you standing here of all places?" she asked. "Hey, you," she said, sidling up to Teddy and giving him a playful hip check. She leaned in and kissed him behind the ear. Teddy felt a warm pulse flow through him. "No training today?"

He glanced at the ground then back at Leah. He was about to speak, but Richard piped up first.

"Poor boy's got a bum shoulder. Ain't that right, champ?" He punched Teddy again, harder this time. His shoulder actually was getting a little sore now. He rubbed it.

"I did something to it last week. Thought a bit of rest might be good." He hated lying to Leah, especially after the summer they'd just had. *But hey, what's one more secret?* he thought. He looked into her eyes and could tell she wasn't buying it.

"Well, that doesn't surprise me," she said, after a pause. "The series really has you working hard."

Teddy cringed and looked away. He thought about the spreadsheet. Placing third in the Formula Firebrand National Shootout two months ago had come with all sorts of goodies. There was a trophy, naturally, and a bunch of branded swag—hats and shirts and bags and things. Of course, the real prize was a ride in the brand-new Formula Firebrand series next year. But with that came the spreadsheet. Teddy hadn't thought much of it at first. It had seemed so simple: a list of exercises, a column of numbers, and some empty cells to record his progress. All of the drivers had been given one to help them stay in shape during the off-season.

It was a recipe for torture.

Teddy knew that drivers at the top levels had to be in peak physical condition. But he was totally unprepared for what the series was asking him to do. The only time he'd seen the inside of a weight room before then was during a module on strength training in ninth grade. He'd had to ask Dr. Wilmoe, the gym teacher, to show him how to do all the exercises. Brutal intervals on the treadmill and stationary bike. Endless curls and presses with the dumbbells. Gruelling floor exercises meant to strengthen his core. Teddy felt sore just thinking about it.

"Man, that's nothing," said Ben. "You should see what we have to do for football and rugby. Teddy's little racer's workout is like our warm-up."

The others groaned.

"The difference is, Ben," said Justin, "that Teddy actually *needs* to be in shape. He's got a professional racing career on the line. How fit do you have to be to sit on a bench all season? Or does the cardio help you keep up with fetching water for the *real* players?"

Everyone laughed—except Ben, of course.

"I'll show you fit," he said, lunging at Justin and putting him into a headlock. This only made everyone laugh harder. Ben was a full foot and a half shorter than Justin, and he had to jump awkwardly to land the move. Justin practically bent over to help him out, like a tired parent tolerating the roughhousing of his overexcited child. Teddy was surprised Justin wasn't more concerned about his hair getting messed up.

"Seriously, though," said Zana. "Why are you loitering in cancer central? Is something up?" She dropped her backpack to the ground and knelt to unzip it. She rummaged around and pulled out a wrinkled navy blue polo shirt. "I've got to be at the pet store in, like, ten minutes."

"Oh, it's nothing serious," said Richard. "I just wanted to catch you all before you went home. See if anyone wanted to hit the movies or something after rehearsal."

When Richard and Tom announced in July that they were starting a band, Teddy hadn't thought they'd get much further than giving it a name. It took them the rest of the summer, but they'd managed to convince Ben, Zana, and Leah to join them. They'd been practicing almost every day since school started two weeks ago. They'd even signed up for the school's talent show in the spring.

Teddy's lips tightened. *A movie will eat into practice time.*

"And your thumbs are broken? You could have texted," said Zana.

"And miss this chance for some real human connection?" Richard winked. "Nah, my phone died in third period."

Teddy snorted. "More like you sat on it and cracked the thing."

Richard ran a hand through his hair and turned away. "Tomato, tom-ah-to."

Zana rolled her eyes. "Well, whatever you decide, I can't do anything before nine. Leah, let me know, OK?"

"Sure thing."

Zana darted off up the street.

"What about Tom?" said Ben. "Where's he?"

"You didn't see?" Leah giggled and nodded towards the smoke-wreathed crowd behind them. Everyone looked. Teddy spotted Tom chatting up a group of girls.

"Are those eleventh graders?" asked Justin. "The man is shameless."

"Hey, Tom!" Leah shouted. "Are you trying to make me jealous?"

Tom glanced back, looking for the source of the voice. Teddy thought he saw a look of anger flash across Tom's face as he spotted them, but then he just made a flourish with his hand and did a little bow. The girls he was with laughed and walked away. He took a step after them then apparently changed his mind and jogged over to the group.

"I'm disappointed in you, Tom," said Richard.

"Can I help it if I'm an attractive senior now? Can you believe they'd never met an Englishman before?"

"I can believe they've never met anyone like *you* before," said Leah, smiling.

"Why thank you. Why is it you and I never dated?"

Teddy straightened his back. "Ahem."

"Oh, you're too much man for me, Tom." She winked.

"Hey now," said Teddy, leaning away from her.

"And you're the perfect amount," she said, grabbing him back in a hug. Teddy warmed again.

"Whatever. I'm on to you."

"Anyway, Tom," said Richard, "that's not what I'm talking about. I mean hanging around the Pit. It's bad for your lungs.

"Aw, you care. How sweet." Tom reached in to pinch Richard's cheeks. Richard swatted his hands away.

"I *care* about your voice, man. You're no good to us if you're wheezing up on stage."

"Maybe he's going for a Leonard Cohen vibe?" suggested Justin. "Or late Bob Dylan?"

Leah laughed. "Not sure Dylan is really the sound we're going for."

"Fine, fine. OK, well, what is this, detention? Why are we still standing around? Let's get rehearsing already."

"That's my cue," said Justin. "Unfortunately, I can't come to the movies tonight, sorry. I've got a meeting with the City Youth Leaders. Next time."

"No problem, man," said Richard. "Take it easy."

As Richard, Ben, and Tom headed towards Leah's house, Leah reached out and grabbed Teddy's hand. "I'll text you after, OK?" She gave his hand a quick double-squeeze.

"Sounds good," he said.

Teddy stood for minute and watched them leave. He felt a twinge of jealousy as they started to sing a song he didn't recognize. They were almost out of earshot when Ben stopped singing. He couldn't be sure, but Teddy thought he heard Ben ask, "Bob who?"

Once he was sure he was out of sight of the others, Teddy broke into a trot. Then a jog. By the time he got to his driveway, he was sprinting. He bent over outside the door to catch his breath.

Whew. There. Workout accomplished.

The door opened.

"What the heck's wrong with you?"

Still bent over, Teddy craned his neck to look his dad in the eye.

"Just" . . . pant . . . "a little" . . . pant . . . "cardio."

His dad frowned. "Keep running, son."

"You heading out?" Teddy asked.

"Yup. Got three showings this evening. Won't be back until eight at the earliest. You're on your own for dinner."

Teddy straightened, composing himself. "No problem. Good luck."

"Thanks. What do you have planned?"

"Oh, nothing much." Teddy was already booting up the game console in his mind. "Might catch a movie later." His fingers started to itch.

"Oh yeah? Can I come?"

"Sure, Dad. I think that new Disney movie you're so desperate to see is out."

"Well count me in! See ya."

His dad walked to his car, whistling something from *The Lion King.* Then he paused. "Oh, I almost forgot. Some mail arrived for you."

Mail? Teddy only ever got mail around his birthday, in July. *Something from Firebrand, maybe?*

"What is it?"

"You'll see." His dad chuckled and opened the car door. "But I can tell you that your mother is anxious to talk to you about it on Sunday." He got in the car and pulled out of the driveway.

Teddy frowned and his shoulders slumped. "Oh," he said to the empty driveway. He stood that way for a minute or two before turning to face the open doorway.

He knew exactly what was waiting for him inside.

Chapter 2

"So there I am, with no pants, reading the newspaper, and this old woman comes up to me and asks me where I got my socks. She liked the pattern and wanted to buy some for her grandson!"

Matt leaned back into the sofa, grinning. Teddy snickered. His mom's expression remained unchanged, as if she were still waiting for the punch line.

"I'm not sure I understand the point," she said. Her voice was serious. "How does riding the subway without pants improve your acting?"

Teddy's snicker graduated to a giddy laugh. He looked at his brother, who just shook his head, still smiling.

"It's about breaking down barriers, Mom. Getting comfortable with being uncomfortable. Plus, it brightens people's day. Gives them something amusing to talk about at work instead of what happened on *Game of Thrones* last week."

"Oh, did you watch it?" Teddy almost gasped.

"Right?!" Matt leaned forward, sliding to the edge of the cushion.

Almost in unison, they each slapped a knee with one hand and then collapsed backwards into their seats. Without saying a word, Teddy knew what his brother was thinking. He loved it.

"But surely there's a way to do that without exposing your skin to every germ, virus, and fluid . . ."

Teddy made a loud gagging noise.

"Fluid, Mom? Really?" said Matt.

"Well, I just mean, have *you* seen what happens to skin that's been in contact with—"

"I'm gonna stop you right there, Mom," said Matt. "That is, if you're still planning on us eating tonight."

"Or ever," added Teddy, shuddering.

It had been a while since the three of them had eaten dinner together. Teddy's parents had gotten divorced when he was eight, and since then, Teddy had visited his mom in the city almost every weekend. At least during the school year. During the summer racing season, things were a little less structured, of course. Sometimes he'd visit Matt at his place downtown. He'd stay over and they'd watch movies and order pizza. Matt rarely joined Teddy at their mom's.

They chatted as they ate. Matt did most of the talking. He told them about work, and their mom grilled him about his girlfriend, Beth. Teddy slurped his spaghetti, content just to listen. The fixture hanging above the table cast a soft light that seemed to wrap them in a warm, homey cocoon.

"How's the sauce?" she asked.

"It's like a party in my mouth, Mom," said Teddy. His words were garbled by half-chewed noodles and meatballs. Next to pizza, his mom's spaghetti sauce was easily Teddy's favourite food.

"Oh grow up, would you, please?" she said, laughing.

"Hey," said Matt, "remember when Brian was over for dinner and we offered him five bucks to eat the whole plate with his hands?"

They all started laughing.

"And then Mom took a picture of him with his fingers and lips all red and noodles hanging out of his mouth?"

"He looked like a zombie devouring intestines."

This sent their mom into hysterics.

"Oh, no," said Teddy. "We're losing her."

"And Mom threatened to publish the picture in the local paper on his eighteenth birthday?" Matt continued.

Their mom heaved with laughter. It wasn't the first time Teddy and his brother had made her lose it like this. It had become a kind of sport for them. When she got going she made a sound that Matt compared to a yak in heat.

Once she began to settle, Matt burst out in an imitation of her laugh, sending her into another fit. Soon they were all in tears.

Teddy couldn't remember the last time he'd felt this happy. He thought back to July, when he stood on the podium at Motown. He'd just won his spot in the Formula Firebrand series. He remembered the electric tingle of excitement and fear, of hope and uncertainty. It was like his past and his future had come together, stuffed into a single moment. This was the opposite. It was as if this dinner, this fit of laughter, was all there had ever been. A few minutes of pure delight had expanded and pushed out everything else.

Teddy looked around the table, taking it all in. The contorted faces of his brother and his mom. The sound of joy in their laughter. The smell of the food. It felt perfect.

Then Teddy's gaze wandered to the kitchen counter. He saw the barstool with his mom's white doctor's coat draped over the back. Peeking out from behind the coat was the stack of fat envelopes he'd brought with him. They seemed to be looking back at him, like rats lurking in the shadows.

And then the moment was gone. Punctured like a tire. A loud bang, a drop in the front end, and Teddy was struggling to keep control, to keep it on track.

His mother composed herself, dabbing her eyes with her napkin. "So, Teddy, have you given any more thought to your college applications?"

Teddy looked down at his plate and poked at the remaining noodles. They seemed less appetizing than they had just ten seconds earlier.

Matt wiped tears from his eyes. "Uh-oh, Teddy. Here we go."

"Hey, stop," she said. She arranged her cutlery neatly on her empty plate. "I'm just asking."

"Yeah, some," Teddy said.

"And?"

He could see there was no way of putting this off any longer.

"Look, I don't know, all right? I've got a lot going on right now. I've got school and training and the series to think about."

Matt cleared his throat, stood up, and started clearing the plates. When their mom wasn't looking, he gave Teddy a look that seemed to say, "Stay cool."

"I understand all that," she replied. "But you've only got a couple of months to decide and to get your applications in. You need to think seriously about what you're going to do after racing."

Teddy stared at his mom. The sound of plates landing a little too hard in the sink came from the kitchen.

"Whoops! Sorry!" said Matt.

"*After* racing?" said Teddy. He felt the room's warmth shift from cozy to stifling. "What do you mean 'after racing'?"

"Well," she said. Her calm tone sounded forced. "I mean after the series. I mean next year."

"You mean after I lose."

"Hey, who wants dessert?" called Matt. "I think I saw some ice cream sandwiches in the freezer." The others ignored him.

"Sweetie, that's not what I mean at all. But . . ." She hesitated. "You have to consider the possibility. And even if you win, I hope you don't think that means you aren't going to college."

Teddy pushed his chair back from the table and folded his arms. He could feel frustration building up inside him. He fought to keep his voice low and steady. "Actually, yeah. That's kind of exactly what I was thinking."

"Teddy, that's completely out of the question. You *are* going to college, whatever happens next summer."

Here we go.

Teddy had never been comfortable fighting with his parents. He'd never been the rebellious sort. But that part of him that stubbornly refused to accept defeat on the race-track had kicked in. He tried to work the problem like he would in a race.

I'm in P2. She's in front—an obstacle. Only a few laps to go. Think!

He took a breath and sat silently for a moment, holding his mom's stare, weighing his options.

Finally, Teddy pulled his chair back in and folded his hands on the table. "OK, Mom. Fine. Suppose I don't win. Suppose I do terribly."

"I'm not saying that—"

"I know, but just suppose. Even if I don't do well, even if I have no chance of making it to the next level, to AmRun Light, that doesn't mean I won't make it into another series. Even if I lose any chance of making it all the way to Am-Run, that doesn't mean I'm going to give up racing."

This time, it was his mom who leaned back and folded her arms.

OK. I've got her attention.

"Now, correct me if I'm wrong, but college students have a longer summer break than high school students."

She nodded.

"So, if I end up competing in a lower series, then I don't need to train as much in the off-season, and there's no reason I can't go to college and keep driving."

"I suppose that's right," she said.

Teddy felt in control now. He was right on the tail of the car in front, drafting it through the turns, preparing for the moment to pass.

"But if I do win, or do well enough to get a ride in Am-Run Light, or even just another chance at Formula Firebrand, then it's going to be really hard for me to do both."

"Yes, but Teddy, that's my point. You need to prioritize school, even if you do win."

The other car started to pull away.

Time to shift gears.

"Are you saying that I should give up on my dream, even when I have a shot?"

Teddy knew it was a cheap trick, but he couldn't let her gain any more distance.

She unfolded her arms and huffed. "You know I don't think that. But I won't let you gamble your whole future on it, either."

"So it's a question of priorities?"

"Yes, exactly."

He could feel himself gaining again. "OK, well, if I agree to take my applications seriously, will you agree to let me prioritize racing?"

Her eyes narrowed.

"I'm not sure what you mean."

They were barrelling down the straightaway now. Teddy was right up alongside the other car with the inside line for the next turn.

Here's my shot.

"What I mean is, I'll apply to college, but if I get a chance to move up again next year, I can put school on hold."

They were coming up fast to the corner. Teddy's heart raced. He gripped the wheel so hard he could feel his hands start to cramp.

"Oh, I see." She paused and looked away. "OK."

Yes!

Pass complete. The corner was all his.

"But," she said, looking back at him.

Crap. He'd hit the brakes too early. His advantage had shrunk to nothing. *But I still have the inside line.*

"You only get one shot. You can defer college for one year. They'll allow that easily enough. But if you don't make it to the next level *this year*, then school comes first after that. End of discussion."

Good enough! Teddy pulled through the corner on the inside. The position was his.

He took a deep breath, trying to hide his excitement. "That sounds fair," he said, with a thoughtful nod.

His mother turned to the kitchen. "Matt, could you—"

"Already on it."

Matt placed the stack of envelopes on the table, along with a plate of ice cream sandwiches. For the next hour, the three of them went through the glossy brochures and discussed Teddy's possible future.

"What about engineering?" suggested Matt. "That would make sense with the racing and all, right?"

Teddy recoiled. *Four years of math and science? No, thank you.*

"Yeah, maybe," he said.

"I see this one has a special pre-med-school program," his mom said. "What do you think? Take after me?" She winked and nudged him with her elbow.

"Hey, where's the one for Clown College?" asked Matt. He and their mother started giggling.

Teddy had stopped listening. He knew he'd made progress, but hearing them talk about what he might do *besides* race cars made his stomach turn.

Don't they get it? I don't want *to do anything else. I want to* drive.

He glanced up at his mom. Even though he'd gained a position, this race was far from over.

Chapter 3

"I think you and your mother came to a very sensible agreement," his dad said, as they drove back home.

"Yeah," Teddy replied, without much enthusiasm.

"Especially since you're going to crush it in the series." He reached over and slapped Teddy's knee. "Hey? Hey? Amiright?"

Teddy rolled his eyes. He knew his dad was trying to be supportive, but in the moment it was a little annoying.

And "crush it"? Ugh. He sounds like Ben.

"Sure, Dad. 'Crush it.'"

When they got home, all Teddy wanted to do was head to the basement and fire up *GP Pro 7*. The conversation at dinner had left him buzzing. He needed a distraction. Grappling with Laguna Seca felt like just the ticket.

Unfortunately, it was already past ten by the time they got back, and Teddy knew his dad wouldn't let him start a gaming session. Whatever Teddy said, they both knew that there was no such thing as "just a few minutes" once he picked up his controller.

Instead, Teddy went straight to his room and opened his laptop. An essay he'd written for school, due the next day, was open on the screen. He was about to print it but decided to give it one last proofread first.

Maybe this will knock me out.

He'd read as far as the title when a blue icon started to bounce at the bottom of the screen, accompanied by a chirpy *bleep-bloop*.

He opened Skype. Allison had sent him a link. Teddy smiled and clicked on it. It took him to an article about a new open-wheel series featuring all-electric race cars. He'd heard of the series already but read the article anyway.

Bloop.

"Possible career move?" Winky face.

Teddy felt his face flush. He typed back.

"You wish."

"How's that?"

"You just want to remove the competition."

"That's cute. You think you're my competition." Laughing-with-tears emoji.

Teddy leaned back and put his hands behind his head, grinning. As he tried to think of a witty comeback, he looked up at the corkboard hanging on the wall above his desk. Colourful plastic thumbtacks held together a patchwork of photographs, ticket stubs, and sticky notes. He scanned the photographs. The gang at Leah's cottage; he and Leah standing outside his house before last year's spring formal; sitting in his first go-kart, a yellow plastic square with his lucky number, 56, strapped to the frame with zip ties.

His grin grew into a smile. It was his first pole position. He couldn't take credit for it, though. In those days, starting positions were determined by lottery. He'd gotten lucky. Still, he'd felt prouder than he ever had before.

Then his gaze landed on the most recent addition to the photo collection: the podium ceremony after the shootout. Allison stood at the top, in first position. Her dirty-blond hair was matted with sweat and tied back in a loose ponytail, and she beamed at the small crowd gathered in front of the podium. She held her arms above her head, one hand clutching the first-place trophy, the other clenched in a fist of victory.

To her right stood Alexandre LeGuivre. The French-Canadian looked surprisingly well-groomed considering he'd just finished a race, not to mention the pretty serious wreck he'd survived to do it. He gripped his second-place trophy with both hands above his head, a tense, almost angry look on his face.

Teddy looked at himself standing on Allison's left. He hated how he looked in photographs. He always seemed much younger than he was, and cameras had a knack for catching his short brown hair standing up at funny angles. In this photo, he was looking up at Allison, cheeks red, a dorky grin on his face. His right hand held the third-place trophy a little above his shoulder. In the other hand, hanging by his side, was a pair of red driving gloves. Those same gloves now hung in a frame on the wall above his bed. A little brass plaque beneath them read: *Graham Thompson, 1968–1999*

Bloop.

"Dude, I'm kidding."

Teddy shook his head and panicked. *Crap. She must think she offended me.*

"Sorry," he typed quickly.

Yeah, that'll show her. Stupid.

"For what? Anyway, good time to call?"

Teddy checked the clock. It was almost eleven. He knew he shouldn't. His dad wouldn't be thrilled if he heard him on the phone this late on a school night.

He shook his head. *What am I thinking? I'm not five.*

"Absolutely," he wrote back.

Teddy scooted across the room to close the door and turn off the light. He returned to his desk and flipped on the lamp. He grabbed some headphones from a drawer and plugged them in just in time to keep the sound of Skype's ringing from filling up the room.

His picture popped up on the screen. He let it ring for a few more seconds as he adjusted the lamp and ran a hand over his hair.

Good enough, I guess.

He accepted the call.

Allison's face appeared, smiling. Her hair was tied in a floppy bun, and he noticed that she had two new studs in her right ear. He could feel his cheeks start to go red and tried readjusting the lamp to hide it.

"Gosh it's dark over there," she said, skipping past the "hellos."

"Yeah, well, it's late. It's night there too, isn't it? You're only a couple hours behind us."

"No, I mean it's dark in your room. I can't even see your face. I feel like I'm talking to your hands."

Reluctantly, Teddy moved the lamp again. It felt like a spotlight.

"Ah! There's my boy."

Teddy cringed.

My boy. Great.

He and Allison had been Skyping almost every week since the shootout. He couldn't understand why he was so nervous. It wasn't just tonight, either. It was all the time. He usually settled down after a few minutes. But whenever he first saw her face he felt like he was looking down from a hundred-foot diving board.

Allison chuckled. "Now it's like I'm interrogating you. Why is your room so dark?"

"I told you, because it's late. I don't want to disturb Dad."

"Is that why you're whispering?" she whispered.

Teddy couldn't help laughing a little.

"Yes," he replied, even quieter.

"O . . . K . . ." she said, grinning.

They stared into their cameras for a moment.

"So, you beat Laguna yet?" she asked.

"Not yet. Haven't had much time with school and stuff."

"Uh-huh. I don't miss those days. Well, don't worry. I promise I'll only remind you once tonight that I beat it in twenty-four hours. Did I mention I beat it in twenty-four hours?"

"I think you did, yeah."

"I'm just saying." She shrugged dramatically.

"Yeah, yeah. Some of us have lives."

"Oh I'm sure. All those extracurriculars of yours must keep you busy. How is Glee Club going, anyway? Or was it Student Council? You're just *so* busy it's hard to keep track."

"Hardy har. You know what I mean. Homework and training and stuff."

"I hear ya. I'm telling you, whoever wrote that fitness thing for us was a sadist. I nearly twisted an ankle doing sprints yesterday."

"Well, you were never very good at speed."

"Oooo. Bazinga."

Pleased that he'd finally got a joke off, Teddy started to relax. "Hey, let me ask you something."

"Shoot."

"Did you ever think about going to college? I mean, instead of racing?"

Allison raised an eyebrow and pursed her lips to one side. "I mean, I thought about it, yeah."

"And your aunt and uncle, did they try to pressure you?"

"Not really. They didn't go to college. Uncle Jim started fixing HVACs right out of high school, and now he owns the business. So they don't really see it as a must."

"Hm."

"Why? Are you thinking about going?"

"Sure. I don't know if it's what I want, but it's always sort of been expected, you know?"

"I guess. But doesn't the series change all that?"

Teddy told Allison about the conversation he'd had with his mother.

"Ah. Well, I guess that sounds cool. I don't know, Chex. Seems like you're making more work for yourself."

Teddy breathed in sharply. Allison rarely called him "Chex." It was a nickname only a handful of people he'd grown up racing with ever used. When he heard it in her voice, it was like remembering something he'd forgotten. As if Allison had been there with him from the beginning.

"I don't know what you mean," he said.

"I just mean, like—I'm one of those 'burn the boats' types. Don't leave yourself a safety net. It splits your focus. Just concentrate on your goal and, you know, jump."

Yeah, but what if I'm not cut out for my goal? What if I fall short?

Teddy realized his expression must have given away his doubts.

"Hey," Allison said. "You *know* you've got what it takes right? You know that *I* believe you can go all the way."

Teddy could feel his cheeks reddening again. The light from the lamp burned like the summer sun. He fought back a smile and looked away from the camera.

"Yeah, I guess."

"Hey—look at me."

Teddy turned back to the screen.

"I mean it."

He was about to thank her when he heard a faint *ding* in the background.

"Hang on a sec," she said.

Allison picked up her phone. Another *ding*. Then another. She started texting quickly. An anxious look crossed her face.

"Everything OK?" Teddy asked.

"Uh, yeah. Fine. Look, I gotta go. But remember what I said."

"Thanks, Allie."

"No problemo. All right, now hit the sack. It's way past your bedtime, kiddo."

Teddy watched Allison turn back to her phone before her screen went blank.

He slouched in his chair, away from the light. His eyes took a minute to adjust to the darkness.

Kiddo. Seriously? All that nice stuff and then KIDDO?

Teddy closed his computer and walked to the bed, stripping off his clothes along the way. He collapsed. He felt exhausted, but his mind was whirring.

Why do you do this to yourself? Teddy stuffed a pillow over his head. It didn't help. *You know you don't have a shot. She's older than you are. She lives across the country. What makes you think it could work? And besides, YOU HAVE A GIRLFRIEND. Stop dreaming, "kiddo."*

He flipped onto his back and stared at the ceiling. In the faint light coming from the streetlamp outside he could make out the checkered flags he'd painted on his ceiling as a kid.

Right. Enough. You're just friends. You have stuff in common. You both like racing. That's all there is to it.

He tilted his head back. The plaque on the frame hanging above him glinted. Graham Thompson. A Canadian racing legend. Two months ago, Graham Thompson had been one of Teddy's heroes. Two months ago, Teddy had been just another Graham Thompson fan. Two months ago, Teddy had learned the truth: Graham Thompson was his birth father. Besides Leah and his family, Allison was the only other person who knew.

He sighed. *That's not all there is to it, though. She knows my secret—she's part of my secret.*

Teddy took a deep breath in and exhaled. Once, twice, three times. By the eighth exhale he felt calmer. He pulled himself under the blankets and closed his eyes. He could feel sleep creeping over him when a thought murmured in the back of his mind, like a whisper from shadows. Something was bugging him.

Who was she texting?

Chapter 4

Teddy placed the orange plastic tray on the cafeteria table and sat down. He leaned forward and took a whiff of his food.

Ah. Heaven.

His fitness plan included some recommendations for an appropriate diet, but he'd thrown that page away the moment he read it. He didn't need a nutritionist to tell him that a deep-fried chicken burger, soggy fries bathed in ketchup, and a huge, warm chocolate chip cookie weren't the right fuel for an aspiring driver. But he figured he deserved some compensation for the workouts.

"Teddy, that's disgusting," said Leah, nodding at his plate.

"What? It's basically the same thing you guys got."

"Ha! I think she means the gallon of ketchup there, champ," said Richard.

Teddy looked at the others' plates. Instead of fries, Leah had opted for the "salad"—a plastic container of wilted pale-green lettuce and a few sad slices of tomato that were more pink than red. Richard never got any sides. His chicken burger looked lonely on its large white plate.

"Whatever," said Teddy, grabbing his burger and dipping it right into the goopy mess in front of him. He took a large bite and started chomping. "Mmmmm . . ."

Leah laughed. "You're disgusting." She gently lobbed a tomato at his face. "At least eat the real thing."

"Aw, aren't you guys just revoltingly cute?" said Richard, taking a nibble of his burger.

Teddy was relieved to be eating. It had been a long morning. He'd slept through his alarm and had only woken up because his dad started banging on his door. And thanks to his chat with Allison, he'd completely forgotten to print off his essay the night before. Naturally, the printer at home had been out of ink. He'd had to sprint to school without showering or eating breakfast so he could print it off in the IT lab before classes started. He'd barely made it to his first class on time.

While Richard and Leah were discussing their rehearsal schedule for the week, Teddy felt his phone vibrate in his pocket.

Allison had texted him. "Hey, I found something for you."

Teddy clicked on the link she'd sent. *The Derek Zoolander Center For Kids Who Can't Read Good and Wanna Learn to Do Other Stuff Good Too.*

Teddy snorted. Loudly.

The others stopped talking and looked at him.

"Care to share with the rest of class?" asked Richard.

"Who is that?" said Leah.

Teddy hesitated.

"Oh, it's nothing. Just Matt. Inside joke." He shoved his phone back into his pocket without replying. He felt it vibrate a few more times.

Richard shrugged and started talking to Leah about practice again. But Leah looked at Teddy for a few seconds with narrowed eyes. Teddy turned back to his food.

She knows I lied, he thought. *No. She doesn't. How could she? If I'd said it was Ben or Justin or Tom, sure, because they've got class this period.*

He poked at his fries.

Teddy and Richard were heading to class when Leah grabbed Teddy's arm.

"Can you wait a second?" she asked.

"Um, sure?" Teddy turned to Richard. "You go ahead. I'll catch up in a second."

Richard made a gun with his hand, winked, and clicked his tongue.

Teddy paused before turning back to Leah, trying to force his face into a neutral expression. He knew what was coming.

"So, are you ready for your meeting?"

Teddy stared at her blankly.

My what, now?

"What meeting?"

"With the psychologist."

Oh crap.

In his rush to get out of the house that morning he'd completely forgotten. Today was his first appointment with

Dr. Miller, the sports psychologist that the series had assigned to him. He checked his watch. His dad was supposed to pick him up from school in half an hour. Right in the middle of Mrs. Gottlieb's class.

He thought about just skipping the class altogether but then remembered the essay.

"You forgot?"

"I guess it slipped my mind."

"Well, are you nervous or anything?"

"To be honest, I haven't really thought about it. We made the appointment over a month ago. Before school started."

"Well, I'd be nervous," said Leah. She started to move towards a quiet corner of the hallway. "Won't you have to talk about, you know, stuff?"

Well now I'm nervous.

"What do you mean? What stuff?"

"I mean . . ." She looked around to make sure no one could hear her. "Personal stuff," she said, in a hushed voice. "Like about Graham."

Teddy clenched his teeth. Hearing Graham's name said out loud in a public place made him uneasy. Nobody else at school knew the truth about his birth parents: That his father had been a famous AmRun Pro driver who'd died in a crash. That when his mother, Susan, had found out, she'd rushed to the hospital and was killed in a car accident. That Teddy had been in the car when it happened. That his adoptive parents had hidden all this from him until the day he'd been invited to drive in the shootout.

He'd told Leah about it the same day and had sworn her to secrecy. He'd said then that he needed time to process everything before trying to explain it all to their friends. But time had only made things worse. Finding out that he was the son of one his driving heroes had raised questions he couldn't begin to answer—questions about who he was and what it meant for his own dream of a racing career. He hadn't even talked to Leah about it since the shootout. The last thing he wanted was to discuss it with a perfect stranger.

"Hrm. I hadn't thought of that. Maybe. I don't think he's that kind of psychologist. I figured he was just going to give me some breathing exercises, or teach me some fancy visualization techniques or something. Besides, if I don't bring it up . . ." His voice trailed off.

She frowned and exhaled sharply. "Well, OK. Let me know how it goes, though, all right?"

She leaned in and gave him hug. Caught off guard, Teddy stood awkwardly for a moment with his arms pinned to his sides before hugging her back. She kissed him on the cheek.

"I guess I was worried because you haven't talked about it since the summer." She looked at the floor. "It feels like we haven't really talked at all much lately."

Teddy felt awful. Here he was worrying about getting caught in a lie, and she was busy worrying about him. He put his hands on her shoulders.

"Hey, I'm sorry about all that. Let's do something this weekend. Just us. A movie or something. We can go to De-metres after and get waffles and ice cream."

She looked up at him and smiled. Teddy's skin tingled.

"We're going to the cottage this weekend. Man, your brain really is fried." She shook her head.

"Oh, right. Next weekend then."

She laughed and gave him another peck on the cheek. "OK, sounds good."

Teddy burst into Mrs. Gottlieb's class just as she started speaking. She paused midsentence. Avoiding her glare, Teddy headed straight for his desk. Richard leaned over.

"Don't worry, man. I got you covered. I told her you were talking with Mr. Larch about your trig homework." He winked.

"Excuse me, Teddy?"

Teddy's heart stopped. He felt his face go white.

"Yes, Mrs. Gottlieb?"

"Aren't you forgetting something?"

Am I?

"Your essay, perhaps?"

Right!

"Yes. Yeah. Sure. Right here."

He fished it out of his bag and walked to the front of the class.

"Here you go," he said, handing it to her. He turned to walk back to his desk and stopped short. "Oh, Mrs.

Gottlieb. I have to leave early today. For a doctor's appointment."

Her expression changed from one of mild annoyance to something resembling concern. "Of course. I hope everything is OK."

"Oh, yeah. Everything's fine. It's something for racing is all."

"I see." Teddy saw her look morph into one of impatience seasoned with a hint of disappointment. "Well, then you'd better be sure to borrow someone's notes."

"Hey, Mrs. G?" A boy in the front row raised his hand. His biceps looked eager to burst free of their cotton restraints.

"What is it, Scott?"

"Well, Teddy just reminded me—a few of us won't be here Friday. The football team's got an away game."

Mrs. Gottlieb's face brightened.

"How exciting. Go Devils!"

Teddy trudged back to his seat.

The waiting room was brightly lit and decorated in a modern minimalist fashion. Teddy sat on a sofa with thin grey cushions and a shiny metal frame. A glass table beside it held three artfully arranged magazines and an orchid in a small white pot. On the wall were photographs of people—athletes who'd been to the clinic, Teddy figured. One showed a woman playing tennis, her teeth bared as she brought her racket down ferociously on a ball suspended in the air in front of her. Another showed a man in full hockey gear standing next to a tall trophy. He cradled his helmet in one arm while the other rested on his stick. Teddy didn't recognize the trophy, but he was pretty sure it wasn't the Stanley Cup. He was fascinated by the two dark gaps in the man's otherwise perfect smile.

A tall man strode into the room from the adjoining hallway.

"Hi, Teddy? I'm Dr. Miller. You can call me Ronnie."

He extended a hand. Teddy stood up and shook it. The doctor's grip was intimidating.

Teddy was more than a little surprised. It wasn't that he'd expected Dr. Miller to be a middle-aged man with a beard and a cigar—not exactly. But this guy looked more like an Olympic wrestler. He couldn't have been older than thirty-five.

"It's nice to meet you," he said. He released his hand from Dr. Miller's grip and tried to shake the blood back into it in a way he hoped was subtle.

Dr. Miller turned and led Teddy down the hall. "I'm really excited to work with you. You're only my second race-car driver."

"Oh yeah?" Teddy said, distracted by the pictures on the wall. They continued all the way down the hallway. Figure skaters. Football players. Pole vaulters. *This guy's worked with some serious athletes.* Teddy swallowed. His forehead started to feel damp.

"Most of the people I work with compete international-ly, some of them since they were kids. Come on in. Have a seat." Dr. Miller waved a hand at a low sofa positioned against the wall next to the door. Teddy sat.

Wait, maybe I'm supposed to lie down? No, don't be stupid.

"Who was the other driver?" Teddy asked, trying to sound casual.

Dr. Miller stepped behind a desk on the other side of the room and grabbed a file folder. As he came back around he picked up one of the chairs that faced the front of the desk with one hand, swung it around, and placed it in front of the sofa as if it weighed nothing. He sat down and opened the folder, scanning its contents.

"Oh, another young guy. I think you know him. Alexandre LeGuivre?"

Teddy's heart stopped.

LeGuivre? You've got to be freaking kidding me.

"You guys will be racing together next year, right?"

No thanks to him.

Teddy huffed. "Yeah, I know Alex." He tried to keep the contempt out of his voice. He didn't try very hard.

"Uh-oh." Dr. Miller looked up from the file folder and smiled. "Bad blood there?"

Teddy looked away. "A bit, I guess. Yeah. We were at racing school together. And we both competed at the shootout this summer."

"Well, don't worry. It's not the first time I've worked with, shall we say, *competitors*." He smiled wryly.

I guess "nemeses" isn't very scientific.

"Sure. No problem." Teddy stared into his lap and clenched his jaw. Between the pictures on the wall and Dr. Miller's imposing physique, he'd already been feeling on edge. The last thing he'd needed was for LeGuivre to be thrown into the mix.

"The important thing to remember is that everything we say and do here is strictly confidential. And I'm not on anyone's side. My job isn't even to help you win."

Oh yeah? Then what's the point of all this?

"My job is to make you a better athlete."

Teddy's mind slammed on the brakes. He'd never been called an athlete before. He looked directly at Dr. Miller's face for the first time. The man was looking at him intently but kindly. Teddy saw in his eyes a strange kind of curiosity. It felt like Dr. Miller was trying to see what was inside of him, and what he might be able to bring out. He worried he was starting to blush, but the doctor had his attention now.

Teddy sat up and shifted to the edge of the sofa, resting his arms on his knees.

"Sounds good," he said. "Sounds real good."

"Excellent. I'm glad to hear it. Now, before we get started, I want to get a sense of your background. I understand you started karting when you were eight?"

"Seven, actually." Teddy felt a little a jolt of pride.

Dr. Miller smiled. "Seven, right." He jotted something in his folder. "And this series you're racing in next year, the Formula Firebrand series. This is a big step for you career-wise, isn't it?"

Teddy chuckled. "You could say that, yeah."

Understatement of the century.

"Great. And—you don't mind if I get personal for a second, do you?"

"Not at all."

"Your mother, she's a doctor at Toronto General?"

"A trauma surgeon, yeah."

"And your father is in real estate?"

"Yeah, he's runs his own little agency."

"Terrific. And you have one brother?"

"Matt."

"Right." Dr. Miller closed the folder and placed it on the floor beside his chair. He leaned in.

"Now, I wonder if you could tell me about your birth father. I gather he was a race-car driver too."

What the . . . !

Teddy felt his heart stop. It was like he'd been stabbed in the gut and all the heat in his body was rushing to escape through the hole.

How does he know about Graham?

Chapter 5

Teddy approached the car in front of him quickly. Too quickly. He considered braking to avoid rear-ending it. But his blood was boiling and he had no desire to slow down. He was going for the pass.

He flipped the indicator and checked his mirrors before moving smoothly, if a little aggressively, into the left-hand lane. The red Corolla was barely a blur in the corner of his eye as he passed.

"How could you have told him? Without even asking me first?" Teddy kept his eyes on the road. He rotated his grip on the steering wheel back and forth, as if he were wringing water out of a wet towel.

His dad shifted uncomfortably in his seat.

"Hey, watch your speed, please."

Teddy huffed but eased his pressure on the accelerator.

"You knew I wasn't telling anyone yet. You *knew* it."

"I'm sorry, OK? You're right. I should have told you that I spoke to Dr. Miller about Graham."

"No, you should have *asked* me."

Teddy kept his eyes on the road, but he could sense that his dad was taken aback by his tone. He'd only ever snapped at him once before—the night his parents had told him the truth.

"I don't know what you want me to say. It was weeks ago. Dr. Miller called me up to confirm your appointment. We started chatting. He wanted to know a bit about your history and it just came out."

"I don't get it. You kept the truth about Graham a secret for years. From *me*. And you just blurt it out to a complete stranger out of the blue?"

His dad turned to him. "Teddy, that's not fair. Dr. Miller isn't a complete stranger. He's a doctor. You'll be working with him for months, maybe longer. His whole job is helping you with your mental game. You don't think he should know that your birth father was also a driver? That he died during a race?"

Teddy grunted. He couldn't deny that his dad had a point. When he'd learned the truth about his birth parents, just two days before the shootout, he hadn't handled it especially well. In fact, he'd all but stormed out of the house. He relaxed his grip on the wheel and slouched down into the seat, feeling his anger start to dissipate. He looked for an opportunity to change back into the middle lane.

"I just wished you'd asked me. I was totally blindsided in there."

"You're right, Teddy. You're absolutely right. And I'm sorry."

They drove the rest of the way home in silence. Teddy spent the trip thinking about the shootout and the events leading up to it. The phone call from Greg inviting him to race. The conversation with his parents about Graham and Susan. And Allison. Allison and the one-two punch she'd delivered. Allison, who not only knew who Teddy's birth parents were, but whose own parents had been in the other car—the one that killed his mother. Allison. His fellow orphan. And now, his fellow driver. Their lives had collided with those cars and then ricocheted in opposite directions. Neither had known about the other's existence until Allison put it together sixteen years later.

Everything had changed for him that weekend.

When they got home, Teddy went straight to the basement. He turned on the TV and fired up his console. As he flopped down onto the sofa, he pulled out his phone. There was a message from Leah asking how his meeting had gone. Two messages from Allison. She was complaining about her workout and had sent a picture from the gym. Teddy started to reply to Allison's text, but changed his mind. He tossed the phone out of reach and picked up the controller.

"Dude, let's have some Stones. I can't handle any more of this sappy acoustic stuff." Tom reached for Richard's iPod, which was sitting in the car's ashtray. "Holy antique, Batman! This thing is ancient." He wiped his thumb around the circular pad on the front.

"It's retro, man. A classic."

After scrolling for a minute or two, Tom settled on "Gimme Shelter."

"No—*this* is a classic." He started pulsing his head to the beat. "Haven't you got your phone fixed yet?"

"No rush," Richard replied. "I threw my SIM into ol' faithful here."

Teddy watched from the back seat as Richard pulled a grubby-looking Motorola flip phone out of his pocket. It reminded him of the phone his dad used to have. He wondered where Richard had gotten it. He hadn't seen one like it in years.

Teddy was crammed in the back of Richard's fifteen-year-old Buick with Leah and Zana. Leah was in the middle. She held Teddy's hand in her lap. The warmth of her body seeped into him. He worried that his palms were starting to sweat.

The five of them were on their way to Leah's family's cottage for the weekend to help her parents close it up for the winter. He'd been looking forward to the trip all week.

"It's a shame Ben and Justin couldn't make it," said Leah.

"Is it?" asked Zana.

"Oh, come on," said Leah.

"What? Justin hardly ever comes out with us anymore. And I can't be the only one who's noticed how Ben is becoming more of a jock every day. I swear, if they ever actually make him first string he'll be a nightmare."

"Lucky for us that's about as likely to happen as Richard's pride and joy here making it to the cottage in one piece," said Tom, patting the dashboard lovingly. He belted out the song's chorus.

Richard took a hand off the wheel to punch Tom in the arm before he started singing along.

"I'm just glad we could both get off work this weekend," Leah said to Zana.

"Tell me about it. Did you hear we're getting a shipment of, like, a thousand hamsters on Saturday?"

Teddy felt his phone buzz in his pocket. He pulled it out. It was Allison.

"Big plans this weekend?"

Teddy looked at Leah, who wasn't paying attention to him, and gently pulled his hand back from hers.

"Sort of. Cottage weekend. You?"

"Nothing special. Helping Aunt Carol around the house."

She sent him another picture. This time, she was posing in front of a mirror, holding a broom. She'd used a filter that made her face look like a cartoon dog's. He stifled a laugh and wrote back.

"Did you change your hair or something?"

"No, it's a new face cream. *Eau de Chien*."

"Well, it's a huge improvement."

"Why thank you. Jerk."

"Who are you texting?" said Leah.

Teddy jumped.

"What? Oh." He wanted to lie, but he couldn't be sure Leah hadn't already seen who it was. He scrambled to put his phone back into his pocket. "It's Allison. Allison Reading? From the summer?"

"Sure. I didn't realize you guys kept in touch."

"A bit, yeah." Teddy felt his temperature plunge.

"What's she up to these days?"

"Oh, you know, same as me. Preparing for the season and stuff."

"She's not still in school though, right? I remember you saying she was older than us."

"What's that? Teddy's texting with an older woman?" Tom turned around to face the back.

"It's nothing. Allison. You met her at the shootout."

"Rings a bell. Cute blonde with lots of metal in her ear."

Teddy started to blush.

"Isn't she the enemy?" said Tom.

"Well . . ." Teddy stuttered.

"Hey guys, check this out. Justin posted a selfie with the prime minister." Zana started passing around her phone.

Teddy looked out the window and took a few deep breaths.

What is wrong with me? he thought. *So what if Allie texts me? There's nothing going on. I'm allowed to have friends.*

Unlike in the city, up at Leah's cottage autumn was in full swing. The air was crisp and cool, and the leaves were almost gone from the trees—the gang spent most of Saturday raking them into piles while Leah's father collected them in a trailer attached to an old three-wheeled Honda ATV. The "Big Red," they called it.

It was Teddy's favourite time of year to be at the lake. He loved how the sun sat low in the sky, making it feel like late afternoon even in the middle of the day. He even enjoyed the yard work, the way the warmth his body generated seemed to push against the cold air on his skin.

Teddy had left his phone inside. The conversation in the car the day before had rattled him. He'd kept it in his pocket until they'd reached the cottage, and had only taken it out then to let his dad know they'd arrived safely. He'd ignored the new messages from Allison.

He'd just finished raking a rather large pile and was pausing to admire his work when he felt a shove from behind. He stumbled forward and toppled into the leaves. He rolled over just in time to see Leah dive in after him, laughing. He grabbed a handful of leaves and threw them at her face. Most of them missed their target and drifted harmlessly back into the pile. A few wet ones hit the mark.

"Ew!" Leah cried.

She retaliated. Now they were both on their knees, hurling volley after volley. Teddy felt like he was eight again. He loved it.

After a few minutes they collapsed on their backs, panting. Teddy gazed up through the naked branches at the long wisps of cloud streaking across the pale blue sky.

"This reminds me of third grade," he said.

Leah laughed. "What?"

"When you saved me from that bully."

"I have no idea what you're talking about."

"Really? These fourth graders pushed me into a pile of leaves at recess. They were holding my face down. I was practically choking on them when you came over and started talking to them."

"I don't remember that at all. What did I say?"

"No idea. I was too busy being used as a human mulching machine. All I know is that after that day, they never bothered me again."

"You're making that up."

"Why would I make a story like that up? You think I'm proud that I was rescued by a girl?" He turned his head to look at her. Her face was speckled with mud. Her dark hair blended into the leaves. "I had a crush on you after that."

"What? You never told me that."

"Uh, hello? Girls had cooties back then. Still do, probably."

She lobbed another handful of leaves at him.

"Missed me."

"Oh yeah?"

Leah rolled over until she was almost on top of him and kissed him. Teddy moved his hands to her waist. When she pulled back he looked into her eyes, breathless.

"Didn't miss you that time," she said.

Leah's dad told them to call it a day around four. The light was already fading, but he said they could take the Big Red for a spin before they came in. Teddy didn't even have to ask to be the one to drive it. The others were more than happy to ride in the trailer.

Teddy was surprised by how wiped out he was. *Four days a week in the gym and I'm defeated by a rake and some leaves.* But once he'd thrown his leg over the Big Red and fired it up, he caught a second wind. The engine's vibrations massaged his muscles, sending sparks through every nerve in his body, feeding a new energy into him. The accelerator was a trigger underneath one of the handles. He pressed it a few times while the engine was still in neutral, getting a feel for its responsiveness. The others laughed as the engine revved. "Show-off!" they yelled.

Teddy stomped on the pedal that engaged the gears, and they set off.

It occurred to him that he'd never driven anything like the Big Red before. And driving with a trailer was a new experience entirely. It was thrilling, trying to work it all out—how it handled, how it braked, how the trailer affected the machine's balance. He was making a new friend, learning what it liked and what it didn't, what it wanted and what it gave back. It was nothing like a car, or even a go-kart. Sitting on top, he felt totally exposed but also in control. He recalled his mother's terror of motorcycles and her stories of all their wrecked drivers she'd treated in the ER. But Teddy wasn't afraid. Not a bit. He hadn't felt this alive since the last time he was in a race car—since the shootout.

Teddy drove them along the gravel road that connected the cottage to the highway, all long bends and gentle hills. As he grew more confident, he started to play around. He'd squeeze the handle brakes when the others weren't expecting it, giving them a sharp jolt, or take them full speed into a corner. He understood better what the machine could handle than they did, and he took advantage of it. The engine was too loud for Teddy to hear what they were saying in the trailer, but it sounded like they were having a good time.

They crested a hill that descended into a wide turn.

Teddy grinned.

This'll get 'em.

Rather than braking, or even coasting down the hill, Teddy accelerated. He knew he'd have time to slow near the bottom, before the apex of the turn. He heard his friends half-scream, half-laugh behind him, as if they were riding a roller coaster.

As they approached the bottom, he gripped the handle brakes and squeezed, gently at first. Then harder. He realized they weren't slowing down fast enough. The Big Red's large, heavily treaded tires had almost stopped rolling, but they continued to slide down the loose gravel, pushed by the weight of the trailer.

Teddy panicked. He knew if he tried to turn at this speed he'd risk flipping over, trailer and all. He had no choice but to release the brakes and take his chances steering through the corner.

They hit the apex at the bottom of the hill. Someone screamed as the trailer swung around. Now that gravity was no longer working against them, he squeezed the brakes. The Big Red came to a stop, but the momentum of the trailer was too great. It continued to push the back tires out to the side, until the trailer and the Big Red formed a *V*.

Teddy's heart thumped in his chest. He fought to keep from hyperventilating.

I can't believe that worked.

He turned to the others. Their faces showed a mixture of fear, relief, and confusion.

"How about that?" he said, between breaths.

Tom clapped and hooted. Teddy smiled widely and laughed, hoping it was enough to mask the shame and embarrassment burbling up inside.

It was dumb luck they hadn't rolled over—and Teddy knew it. He remembered one of the lectures Greg had given at the academy. "A driver's job is to stay in control. Control the vehicle. Control yourself. Take a small piece of the world and completely master it for an instant. Then let it go and move on to the next piece. Everything is fighting against you, trying to take control away from you. Other drivers, the weather, the laws of physics—each claims dominion over the space the driver struggles to rule." Showing off like that had been reckless—an invitation for catastrophe.

He only prayed the others didn't realize what had happened, or how badly things could have gone.

Chapter 6

Teddy and his dad craned their necks. His dad let out a whistle.

"How'd they get them up there, you think?" Teddy asked.

"Dunno. A crane, maybe?"

"Right. Sure."

Teddy had seen the tower a hundred times before, but only from the highway. Never this close. It reminded him of one of those glass elevators he'd seen in fancy office buildings downtown. There were four levels, stacked like boxes. The back walls were white and illuminated by colourful lights emanating from the floor. On each level, in each box, sat a brand-new car: BMW M5, Mini Cooper S, BMW M3, Mini Countryman.

"It's like a vending machine," said his dad.

"Got any change?"

"You know, I left it in my other pants."

They stood there another minute or two, before the cold December breeze encouraged them inside.

It was the most impressive car dealership Teddy had ever seen. It was impossibly clean, every surface gleamed, and the aroma of new leather and polish seemed to drape itself around him, pulling him in. The high ceilings made him want to shout just to hear the echo. The cars on display were spaced out neatly but irregularly—plenty of space to wander between them. One or two were even cordoned off with maroon velvet ropes. *Like holy relics.* Teddy suddenly felt dirty, contaminated, as if he needed to brush off the residue of his dad's fifteen-year-old Ford Taurus before he could dare step off the welcome mat.

A short, middle-aged man approached them. He was stocky, but not fat, and his broad smile displayed a set of unnaturally white teeth. Teddy was pretty sure this man wasn't the owner, but everything about his manner seemed designed to create the opposite impression.

"Good afternoon, gentlemen. How can I help you?"

So I'm a gentleman, now, am I? Something about the man made Teddy uneasy. His dad, on the other hand, appeared to warm right to him.

"Hi there. Steve Clark. We're just looking around, thanks."

"Of course, Mr. Clark, by all means. Anything in particular?"

"Not especially. I'm looking to upgrade. Maybe a 3 Series?"

Teddy wouldn't have thought it possible, but the man's smile got a little wider.

"Well, the new Z3 M has just arrived. They're only available for preorder now, but I'm happy to arrange a test drive if you're interested."

The man stepped forward, reaching one hand behind Teddy's dad while gesturing with the other towards the front corner of the showroom.

Teddy's dad laughed affably.

"I'm sure I'd fall in love instantly. But I think I need something a little more practical. Tell me, what do you have in the preowned department?"

The man dropped his arms. Teddy could almost see him shifting gears in his mind. He glanced at his dad and smirked.

Can't sell a salesman.

"I see. Well." He gestured to a corner in the back. "We've got one or two vehicles that might suit you. Feel free to wander around. If you have any questions, just ask for Raymond."

"Thanks, Raymond." Teddy's dad smiled. "Will do."

The pair of them ambled towards the back corner. His dad paused to look at the sheets of paper stuck to the windshields, studying each car's specs, options, and pricing. Teddy circled each vehicle slowly, deliberately. He dragged his index finger along the bodies, careful to keep his hand low and out of sight of the sales staff. He didn't know if there was a rule against touching, but that wasn't why he was hiding it. He wanted the privacy, to make a connection with the machines. Just a little contact, that was all, and Teddy could feel the weight of each car and the power of each engine reverberating up through his arm.

He was halfway around a gorgeous sky-blue M5 when he spotted it. He hadn't noticed it at first, tucked in behind a much larger sedan. A Mini Cooper with a classic red body and white roof. Without thinking, he walked over and opened the door on the driver's side. He stopped short and looked around. No one seemed to be paying him any attention, so he ducked in.

He wiggled around in the seat and put his hands on the wheel. Of course, he knew this was nowhere near as powerful as the BMWs that his father was inspecting. But this car seemed to have more character. It felt familiar.

It's like a go-kart. He smiled.

"I'm not too sure I can subject my clients to that back seat, sport."

Teddy jumped.

"What? Oh, yeah. I know. I was just thinking it would be fun to drive."

"You know, I always wanted one of these. *The Italian Job* was a big movie back when I was your age. The original, of course, with Michael Caine. Not that awful remake with what's his face. Hamburgler."

"Mark Wahlberg."

"That's the one. Well, maybe when you're fully licensed we'll pop in for a cheeky test drive. Just for fun."

Teddy's heart rate doubled.

"Yeah?"

"Why not? Now, where's Raymond. I want to talk to him about this 330i. I think it might be just the thing."

The bell rang and students flooded the hallway. Teddy pushed his way through the crowd to his locker. The chatter was louder today than usual. Everyone was excited about Christmas vacation and busy making plans before leaving. Teddy kept his head down. He couldn't afford to get sucked into small talk with anyone right now. He had a date to keep.

Teddy swapped his backpack for his gym bag and fought the flow of warmly dressed bodies pouring towards the exit. By the time he'd reached the boys' changing room, the school seemed deserted.

Right on schedule.

Teddy had bet that no one else would be hanging around to use the gym on the last day before vacation. When he entered the weight room and found the lights off, he smiled. *Perfect.* After switching them on, he walked over to a stack of blue mats piled against the wall. He dragged the pile next to the rack of free weights and placed his phone on top. Then he turned on the camera to check the angle and lighting. Playing with his hair a bit, he sighed.

Ah well. Good enough.

The phone started to *bleep-bloop*. Incoming Skype call.

Teddy answered.

At first the screen showed only white. As the picture adjusted, Allison's face appeared. Her hair was pulled back in a ponytail and her earrings and studs glittered in the fluorescent lights of her gym in Edmonton. She grinned.

His heart got a head start on the workout.

"All right, bud. Ready for this?"

Teddy grinned back.

"Bring it."

It had been Allison's idea. The Formula Firebrand series was holding its first off-season practice the following week in Florida. She'd thought it would be fun if they did a workout together beforehand. "You know, to *pump* each other up."

At first Teddy hadn't loved the idea of having a workout partner—even Allison. He was embarrassed enough about his fitness without an audience. But he had a hard time saying no to her. He told himself it was because she was his best driver friend, because of the secret they shared. Deep down he knew he just liked hanging out with her, even virtually.

"Here, try this." Allison stepped out of view. After a moment Teddy heard the music of AC/DC blasting through the phone.

"Woah! Turn it down."

"Sorry." She disappeared again. "Now?"

"Better. OK, now, try to keep up."

For the next hour they went through an intense circuit of jump rope, push-ups, sit-ups, squats, plyometrics, and a variety of dumbbell presses, flys, raises—everything Teddy had been doing all term. It had always felt like a chore before, a necessary evil. Now he was having a blast.

"Come on, Chex. One more round." Allison clapped her hands.

Teddy hunched over, panting. He searched for his water bottle. "You've got to be kidding me. We've already done two more than the sheet says."

"What! You're still sticking to the sheet? And here I thought you were a winner."

"Ha. I seem to recall losing to you."

"And I plan on continuing the streak. But I don't want to take candy from a baby. Seriously, you Toronto kids."

Teddy wasn't sure if it was the dig at Toronto or the word "kids," but he felt a fresh surge of energy.

He straightened up and took a deep breath in. "Fine. But let's make it interesting. Last one to finish buys Tim Hortons."

Allison laughed. "Dude, they don't have Timmy's in Florida."

"Whatever. Dunkin' Donuts then."

"Gross. Make it Dairy Queen and you've got a deal. I haven't had a Blizzard in months." She looked down and rubbed her stomach.

Teddy salivated imagining a fresh, cold Smarties Blizzard.

"Deal."

"I bet they taste even better when they're free."

"Too bad you'll never know. Go!"

By the time they'd finished, Teddy's T-shirt was drenched with sweat. He couldn't remember ever working so hard. Even so, he felt charged up, like he could still run a marathon—if only his legs would stop shaking.

Allison approached her phone with her palms facing the camera. "High-ten!"

Teddy stepped towards the stack of blue mats, leaning forward with his hands up.

"Teddy?"

At first, Teddy thought the voice had come from the phone.

"Allison?" he said, doing his best Allison impression.

"Um, yeah?" Allison's hands dropped. She had a confused look on her face.

Teddy realized his mistake. He spun around. Standing in the doorway was Leah.

"Oh. Hi. Hey. Hey there." Teddy smiled awkwardly, his lips quivering at the edges.

"What are you doing?" asked Leah.

"Teddy? What's going on? Who is it? Tedddddd-yyyyyy?" Allison's voice seemed to fill the room.

"I was just working out."

Leah crossed her arms. "You know what I mean."

"Yeah. I just—" He raised a finger to Leah and turned back to the phone. "Hey, Allie, I gotta go. I'll call you later."

"Wait. Wha—"

Teddy ended the call.

"So it's 'Allie' now."

"Leah, we were just training."

Teddy was grateful his face was already red from the exercise. His body seemed suddenly eager to expel what little sweat he had left.

"I see. So this is what you've been doing all term. 'Training.'"

"No. It's not like that. This was the first—" Teddy stopped. He could see from Leah's expression that she wasn't going to believe him, whatever he said. He'd never seen her look so angry. No, not angry, disappointed. It felt like a sledgehammer to the gut.

This isn't fair. If I could just explain. He crossed his arms. His initial shock started to dissolve. *But why should I explain? I wasn't doing anything wrong.*

He tried to deflect. "Anyway, why are you still here?"

"We were rehearsing in the auditorium. I told you about it at lunch. Maybe you weren't listening?" Her tone was sharp, almost mean.

Crap. She's right. Teddy stayed on the defensive. "Well there you go. We were both just practicing. What's the big deal?"

Leah uncrossed her arms and stepped into the room. The door closed itself behind her.

"The difference, Teddy, is that you knew what I was doing, and who I was doing it with."

Teddy saw an opening. He spoke without thinking. "Yeah, Richard." The words felt like bile on his tongue.

"I'm sorry?"

"You heard me." Teddy glared at her. He couldn't help it. He knew it was wrong. But he'd lost control. Something inside of him, something ugly and cruel, had taken over.

Part of him wanted to drop to his knees. To explain everything. *Of course I feel a connection with Allison. She gets me in ways no one else possibly can. She's a driver. And she was there! The day my whole life changed—she was there. She knew who I was before I did. But nothing is going on between us. How could it? She lives a million miles away. Besides, I'm just a kid to her.* But that part of him was being muzzled, forced not to its knees but facedown into the floor.

"What are you trying to say? That me and Richard—"

He cut her off. "Well aren't you? You guys sure have been spending a lot of time together."

"For the *band*, Teddy. The competition. I can't even believe this."

"Well," Teddy said.

Leah stared at him, silent. Teddy could see that he'd hurt her. His expression remained stern, but he felt himself cracking inside.

"This isn't about me, Teddy. I know you've been lying to me about Allison. The texts, the calls. I'm not stupid. I just didn't realize how much it was happening."

It's not what you think! I'm sorry!

Teddy tried to speak, but it was like screaming into a hurricane. The words were there, but they were swept away the second he opened his mouth. He fought it.

"Leah, I—" He faltered.

"It's fine, Teddy. I understand. I'm not part of that world. I get it. I just wish—" She paused.

Teddy could see her eyes start to well up. The down-turned corners of her mouth trembled.

"I've tried so hard, Teddy."

Teddy was struck dumb. He could feel tears gathering in his eyes. He struggled desperately to hold them back. Unable to speak, he raised his hand.

"I have to go," she said.

She turned, opened the door, and left. The door slowly closed behind her.

Teddy's legs finally gave in. He dropped to one knee, then both knees. His head fell to his chest and he began to sob quietly.

What just happened? What have I done?

Chapter 7

A warm breeze greeted Teddy as he stepped out of the rental car. He'd only been in Florida for a few hours, but the gentle heat and thick humidity had already seeped into his bones. Every trace of the dry winter chill he'd left behind had vanished. He wished he'd changed when he and his dad had dropped their bags off at the motel. A thin film of perspiration coated his skin. He doubted the weather was the only cause, though. His nerves were on high alert. He took off the spring jacket he'd worn on the plane and tossed it onto the front seat before closing the door.

"We should step to it," said his dad. "We're a bit late."

They strode through the parking lot. Bright yellow lines popped against the deep black asphalt. The smell of tar wafted up like the steam from a fresh loaf of bread.

They approached the building adjacent to the lot. It had two distinct parts. The first part, a three-storey block of concrete and corrugated metal, stretched almost the width of the property. The sunlight reflected aggressively off the clean white paint. Teddy was grateful that his dad had reminded him to bring sunglasses. At one end of the wall facing the lot were two large triangles: one red, one black. They met in the middle, creating a sort of arrow that drew the eye to the other part of the building—a cube of tinted glass and dark steel. And right in the middle of the cube, above the double doors on the ground floor, was the Formula Firebrand logo.

Teddy's dad opened the door. Icy air rushed out at them.

Teddy halted. For a moment he felt dizzy, disoriented.

"Everything all right, sport?"

"Yeah, fine. It's just . . . nothing."

"Don't worry. You'll do fine. Just gotta shake a few hands. Don't let them intimidate you."

Yeah. Sure. Easy peasy.

Teddy stepped across the threshold and into a spacious lobby. The walls were lined with photos of race cars in action. He could tell who was driving them from their livery. One car in particular caught his eye: a blue-and-white Am-Run Pro storming down the straight at the Indianapolis Motor Speedway. His heart stopped.

It's my . . . It's Graham.

Then he noticed the car's number, 25. Graham's number was 99—same as Wayne Gretzky.

Teddy shook his head, relieved. Graham's picture on the wall would have been a reminder of what he was hiding from everyone, of the expectations they would have if they knew the truth. He turned to his dad, who seemed to be reading his mind. Neither said anything.

They walked up to the reception desk. A woman in a white polo shirt with the Firebrand logo was typing at a computer.

"Teddy Clark and Steve Clark. We're here—"

"For the orientation, yes. Welcome to Sebring."

"Thanks. Loving the weather."

"I'll bet. Y'all must enjoy getting out of them igloos once in a while."

Teddy couldn't tell if she was joking or not. Once, at a go-karting tournament, a kid from Minneapolis had asked him if it was true that Canadians drove dog sleds to school. "Minneapolis is actually farther north than Toronto," Teddy had replied. "And a lot snowier."

His dad took the joke in stride. "Can you believe we haven't seen a bit of snow yet this year? Must be global warming." He chuckled.

She started laughing. "Global warming. That's a good one."

Teddy was again puzzled. *Is she laughing at the joke? Or the idea of global warming?* he wondered.

"Well, if y'all just head down that hallway and through those doors, you'll end up in the shop with the others."

"Cheers."

"And good luck to you," she said, looking at Teddy.

"Uh, thanks." He forced a smile.

They headed in the direction she'd indicated. At the end of the hallway was a set of heavy-looking double doors. They pushed them open and walked through.

"The shop." Right.

The room was cavernous. Teddy imagined that his whole high school could fit inside of it. He counted at least twenty work stations, arranged in two rows down the middle. They were like miniature garages. In each station, tall rolling tool chests and high tables littered with parts and electronic equipment were arranged around an empty space about the size of a Formula car. Along one wall were racks full of pristine tires, wings, and nose cones. A row of offices stuck out from the opposite wall, creating a loft space above them. This space was stacked haphazardly with used parts and what looked to Teddy like a few wrecked chassis.

I wonder if any of those were destroyed at the shootout, he thought, remembering the crash that had secured him his spot in the series.

But none of the stations contained a car. Even so, at least thirty people milled about. They tinkered with things on the tables and huddled around computer screens. They paid no attention to the newcomers.

Teddy turned to his dad. "Where is everyone?"

"Teddy! Good to see you again." A tall man wearing black slacks and the same branded polo shirt as the receptionist came out of one of the offices and walked over to them. He extended a hand. Teddy shook it.

"Hi, Dan. How are you?"

"Splendid, thanks. Steve? How's things? Good flight?"

"Aside from a little hiccup at the car rental place, smooth sailing, thanks. Sorry we're late."

"Not at all. We're only just getting started." He gestured for them to follow. "You've missed the introductions, but you'll have plenty of time to get to know everyone. And of course, you already know some of them. I'm sure Alex and Allison are looking forward to seeing you again."

Oh, I'm sure they can't wait.

"Right."

Teddy had no trouble believing that Allison was anxious to see him. He'd all but ignored her since their gym session the week before. He'd avoided every call and sent only abrupt replies to her text messages. Even if he'd wanted to explain what had happened with Leah, he wouldn't have known where to start.

But Teddy was certain that he was the last person Alexandre LeGuivre wanted to see. The feeling was mutual. Teddy would rather find a pack of ravenous hyenas waiting for him on the other side of the door than the French-Canadian.

They walked past the door that Dan had come out of. The windows in the room were covered with blinds. Teddy tried to peek through the slats as they passed but couldn't make anything out.

"We'll just sneak in the back," whispered Dan.

He opened another door slowly. They entered a long room with a couple of pop-up tables lined up in the middle. On the wall were whiteboards covered in colourful scribbles. At the head of the table stood a man with leathery, sun-beaten skin and a thick grey moustache. He was dressed the same way as Dan was. The man was saying something, but Teddy didn't hear it. He was fixated on the fifteen young men and two young women who sat around the table. The drivers.

The man stopped talking and everyone turned to the back of the room.

Teddy's stomach contracted. He scanned the faces. Most of them he'd never met, though he recognized them from photographs. He knew only two of them personally. Allison, who sat at the corner farthest from Teddy, and Alexandre, who sat opposite her.

So much for sneaking in.

"This must be our wild card. Teddy, right?" The man's voice was gruff. Scolding.

"Uh, yeah. Yes. Hi." His voice cracked.

Alexandre smirked. Teddy glared at him. His hands clenched into fists by his sides.

"Don't let us interrupt, Mike. Carry on." Dan pulled out an empty chair at the end of the table for Teddy. He indicated another chair in the back corner of the room for Teddy's dad, and then joined Mike at the front.

Mike resumed speaking. He was in the middle of a speech about how the drivers were rising stars, talented individuals with lots of potential, etc. Mike's tone was harsh, serious, almost mean. Teddy frowned a little. He felt as if he were back in third grade getting a lecture about bullying or staying away from drugs.

The others lost interest in him and turned back to Mike, but Allison kept looking at him. "Hey," she mouthed.

Teddy smiled tightly and nodded. She gave him a puzzled look before turning back to Mike.

"Obviously, tomorrow is the first day of work. The only thing on the agenda this afternoon is a quick tour of the shop, and you'll all meet your teams. As you know, you've each been assigned a mechanic and an engineer. They're all excited to meet you."

Mike paused and looked at Teddy. For a split second, half of his face scrunched up a little. He seemed to be half-grinning, half-winking. Teddy had no idea how to read it, but he felt uneasy.

"All right," Mike continued. "Let's go."

Everyone filed out of the room behind Mike and Dan. Allison tried to hang back but started causing a bit of a jam. She left the room and Teddy did his best to compose himself before reaching the door.

She was waiting for him when he exited.

"Hey," Allison whispered. She punched him in the arm. "Where have *you* been?"

"Hi," he said. "You know. Just busy."

"Well if it isn't Miss Reading. How are ya?" Teddy's dad had come up behind them.

"I'm good, Mr. Clark. Thanks."

"You here alone?"

"Not exactly." She glanced at Teddy. "I mean, my uncle and—"

"Shh. We should listen." Teddy crossed his arms and followed the crowd, trying to look more interested than he felt.

Allison huffed.

Mike was talking again, highlighting some of the features of the shop as they walked. Most of it was too technical for Teddy to really understand. There was lots of talk of "telemetry" and "computer modelling." Teddy thought of the fat binder he'd received back in the summer.

I guess scanning the pictures isn't gonna cut it.

When they reached the centre of the room, Mike stopped. "All right, I'm going to call out your name and a number. Head over to the appropriate station and meet your team."

Dan handed Mike a folder. He started reading aloud.

"Reading. One."

Allison gave Teddy an anxious look as she walked towards the far end of the shop. Teddy shrugged.

That'll buy me some time.

Teddy waited nervously as Mike ran through the rest of the drivers. He'd only ever worked with the mechanics at the Rock Point Racing Academy in Morton Falls—"Motown," they called it. They were easygoing guys, trainees themselves, mostly. Teddy knew that if the building he was standing in now was any indication, he was about to meet some serious professionals. One by one the other drivers wandered off to join their teams. Finally, Teddy found himself standing alone with Mike, Dan, and his father.

"And last but not least—eighteen. Clark." Mike closed the folder and eyed Teddy. "Go get 'em, Wild Card."

Teddy lowered his head to hide his scowl and headed for his station. His dad slapped him on the back.

"Look at that," he said cheerily. "You've already got a nickname."

Yeah. I'm not so sure it's a good one.

Most of the drivers had been invited to join the series because of their experience and achievements. Only three drivers had made it in because of the shootout.

"I don't see why *I'm* the wild card. Why not Allie? Or Alex?"

"Hey, you're the underdog. Like Rudy, from that movie. Everyone loved Rudy."

Teddy rolled his eyes. "You sound like Matt."

As they walked, Teddy thought about the comparison. Rudy had been entirely out of his league physically and athletically. Everyone had been rooting against him. He'd succeeded through sheer force of will. Teddy was hardly in the same boat. He'd trained his whole life for this. Dozens of people had supported him along the way. And his birth father was practically a legend in the sport.

I should be anything but *the wild card. If people knew the truth, they'd think I was a crown prince or something.*

The thought made him sick to his stomach. After all, even with all his advantages, he'd still only made it into the series by the skin of his teeth. It was literally because of an accident that he was here at all.

Maybe it's better this way. Keep everyone's expectations low.

Teddy and his dad arrived at station eighteen. Two men stood where the car would normally be, their hands clasped in front of them. Their black pants were made of a heavier fabric than Dan's and Mike's and didn't have creases. And instead of white polo shirts, they wore charcoal-coloured short-sleeved button-downs. The shirts featured the Firebrand logo on one side and their names on the other: Stewart and Trevor.

Stewart, the taller of the two, had light, short-cropped hair and rimless glasses. He stepped forward and offered a hand.

"You must be Teddy. I'm Stew, your engineer. Nice to meet you."

As the introductions were made, Trevor made no effort to join in. Then Stewart looked back and cocked his head slightly and Trevor moved forward, extending his hand. Teddy hadn't thought it was possible to trudge a distance of only two feet, but Trevor accomplished it flawlessly.

"A real pleasure," Trevor said.

Teddy could see it clearly wasn't. He was taken aback. This was teenage-level sulk from someone who was at least twenty-five—and, he assumed, a professional mechanic. He felt a sudden urge to be extra polite, just to compensate for the man's sour attitude.

"So I hear you trained at Rock Point," said Stewart.

"I did, yeah. Great place. Greg Godwin's an excellent teacher."

"That's what I hear. I've known quite a few mechanics who came out of there, too. All good guys."

Trevor coughed and quickly brought a fist to his mouth.

"Isn't that right, Trev?" Stewart glared at his colleague.

"You bet. Great guys."

What's this guy's deal? It was becoming increasingly obvious to Teddy that he was going to have to battle with more than just the other drivers this year. *Is it possible to request a new mechanic? If only Maxim were here.*

The four of them chatted for a few minutes. Trevor didn't say much, just stood behind them looking bored. Stewart gave them a little tour of the station and explained his role.

"Basically I crunch the numbers from your onboard computer and suggest adjustments to the car that will match your driving style to the course. Between the telemetry and the feedback you give us during practices, Trevor and I can do a pretty good job of customizing the car for you."

Teddy knew all about this aspect of racing from watching the pros, of course. But hearing it explained like this, when *he* was the one who would benefit from it—it sounded like magic. He started to tingle with excitement.

"Wow. That sounds . . . just . . . awesome." He glanced at his dad, who looked almost as giddy as Teddy felt.

Stewart smiled. "It's pretty cool. We just want you to have the best shot possible."

"You can't always count on accidents to win."

Teddy's head snapped around. Trevor was leaning casually against a tool chest behind him. Stewart and his dad were looking too, their eyes wide.

"Right, Wild Card?" he added, with a cocky grin.

The other shoe had dropped. Now Teddy understood. Trevor didn't want to be saddled with him—the underdog.

Teddy's enthusiasm evaporated. His mood sank fast. All the anxieties and fears he'd had from the moment Greg called him, back in July, came rushing up. He looked the smug mechanic in the eye.

Wait a second. Who does this guy think he is? I may not be the best driver here, but dammit, I'm here, aren't I?

He straightened his back and crossed his arms.

"Right, Trev. Absolutely."

Trevor shifted his weight. His grin faded.

"All right, everyone, gather 'round." Mike was back in the centre of the room waving for the others to come over. "That's pretty much it for today. We expect to see everyone at the track tomorrow at 8:00 a.m. sharp. Sleep well, boys and girls."

The crowd headed for the exit. Allison grabbed Teddy by the arm. He jumped.

"Oh, hey," he said.

"Hey. What's going on with you? You're acting . . . I dunno, weird."

"Probably just nerves." He was in no mood to explain.

"Well, that makes two of us. Have you seen who's here?"

"I missed the intros, remember?"

"Yeah, but, I mean, you looked everyone up before, right?"

"Sure. A bit." In truth, Teddy had spent hours researching his competition. He could recite most of the other drivers' careers by heart. He also knew they'd probably done the same.

Mike's probably not the only one calling me "Wild Card."

"Did you talk to *them*?"

"Who?"

"The twins, Teddy. Obviously."

"Oh, them. No. I haven't talked to anyone."

Allison gestured behind Teddy with her eyebrows. He stopped walking and glanced over his shoulder. Kyle and Kayla Tusk. They were supposed to be prodigies or something. They'd started racing even younger than Teddy. They'd topped almost every series they'd raced in. But some years they hadn't raced at all. He'd never heard of anyone like them.

Fraternal twins, they didn't look much more similar to each other than Teddy and Matt. They were a little shorter than he was, though he knew they were a couple of years older. They looked fit and trim but had unusually blocky frames. Their ribcages seemed to extend in a straight line from their armpits to their waists. Kayla's face was rounder than Kyle's, with fuller cheeks and a softer jawline. Their skin looked pale, almost translucent. *Like something that escaped Area 51*, Teddy thought.

Only two things really made them look like twins. They both had the same straw-coloured hair cut in the same style. Short, loosely parted, and slightly dishevelled—a pixie look on Kayla, a surfer look on Kyle.

And they had the same eyes.

Those eyes.

Large, dark, opaque. Like pieces of coal stuck on a snowman.

"Well, I tried to talk to them before we got started," Allison said. "They are so freakin' weird. Stop staring!" She nudged him in the ribs. They resumed walking.

"Weird how?"

"Like, I asked Kyle if he'd been to Florida before. He said he'd once gone jogging in a hurricane."

"OK, that's a little strange."

"But it's not just what he said. He and Kayla kept looking at each other. Like they were having a private conversation the whole time without saying anything."

"Maybe they're just trying to get into your head. You know, psych you out."

"Yeah, maybe."

Allison seemed to give this possibility some serious thought.

When they reached the atrium, Allison stopped and faced Teddy.

"So, look. I need to tell you something."

Her hands started to fidget.

His mind flashed back to the shootout, to the back of the cube van—the last time she'd had "something to tell him." *I was in the other car, Teddy,* she'd told him. *The day Graham Thompson was killed. The day Susan Thompson was killed. I was in the other car. The one that hit her.*

Allison was about to speak when Teddy's dad interrupted.

"So Allison, is someone picking you up? Can we give you a ride?"

"Uh, no thanks. My uncle is probably waiting outside."

"Well, I'd love to say hi. I don't think we were properly introduced in the summer."

His dad all but pushed them out the door.

A dark-blue sedan idled by the sidewalk. The passenger-side window slid down. Teddy saw two men inside. He recognized the driver as Allison's uncle.

Allison shot Teddy a look and then sped up to reach the car first. She said something to the guy in the passenger seat. Then he and her uncle got out of the car and came onto the sidewalk.

Allison's uncle was a round, balding man in his late forties. Teddy guessed the other guy was in his early twenties and probably had a collection of lettered jackets in his closet. The kind of guy Ben aspired to be and Teddy resented. He thought about Mrs. Gottlieb. *Go Devils.*

"Guys, this is Teddy, who I told you about. And his dad, Mr. Clark."

"Steve. Hi."

"And, uh, this is my uncle Jim. And Chet, my . . ."

Cousin. Trainer. Dog-walker. Anything but—

"Boyfriend."

Vertigo. Ears ringing. World spinning.

"Well, isn't this a treat? Say, why don't you join Teddy and me for dinner?"

I think I'm going to vomit.

Chapter 8

"Good morn—woah. You all right there, Teddy?" Stewart adjusted his glasses, as if Teddy were simply out of focus.

Teddy dropped his gear bag. He knew how he looked. He'd spent the night on the edge of the motel room's bathtub counting the tiles on the floor. Every so often he'd look at himself in the mirror. Each time his eyes were a little puffier, a little more bloodshot. The harsh blue light of the cheap wall fixture seemed to suck all the colour out of his skin. By the time the sun had risen, he looked like an extra in *The Walking Dead*.

"Where's your dad?" Stewart asked, when Teddy didn't respond to his first question.

"I sent him to the hospitality area. The man can't resist free coffee."

"Kindred spirit." Stewart smiled and nodded towards a coffee thermos sitting next to a laptop perched on a toolbox. It was shaped like a barrel and looked like it could hold a gallon of coffee.

"Rough night, Wild Card?"

Teddy glanced at Trevor and shrugged. He had zero interest in letting the mechanic know how much his smugness was getting under his skin.

"Something like that."

"Rough" wasn't nearly the right word. He'd have preferred a massage from a steamroller. The worst part was that he hadn't seen it coming. Any of it. It wasn't just that Allison had a secret boyfriend. He'd been totally unprepared for his reaction. He'd been trying so hard to contain his feelings for her, he'd almost tricked himself into believing they weren't there. Almost. But Chet had kicked open the door, and his brain wouldn't shut up about it.

Dude, you need to let it go. It's not gonna happen!

Oh yeah? Then why was she keeping him a secret?

Because you're a dopey-eyed kid, and she knew you couldn't handle the truth.

I'm *dopey-eyed?* You're *dopey-eyed!*

Thankfully, Allison's uncle had declined the dinner invitation. But then the texts had started. Every fifteen minutes his phone would ding. "Hey, you OK?" "What's going on?" "Helloooo?" It was like water torture. Still, he couldn't bring himself to turn it off, or even put it on silent. He'd read every single text but never replied.

"Well, here." Stewart went over to a small fridge with a glass door. "I know it's early, but this might help."

He handed Teddy an energy drink.

Teddy looked at the can, all shiny aluminum and primary colours. He'd only ever tried one once before. It tasted like sweetened battery acid. His stomach had burned for an hour afterwards.

Teddy took the can, cracked it open, and guzzled it down. The combination of carbonated water, sugar, and industrial-strength stimulants singed his throat.

He shuddered and scraped his tongue on his teeth a few times. But he couldn't deny that it helped. The pounding in his head subsided. The fog he'd been plodding through all morning lifted. The garage finally came into focus.

He stood in one of two dozen bays opened onto a wide strip of cracked asphalt. Each was about the size of a standard single-car garage. The cinder-block walls were scuffed with rubber and grease. Teddy usually liked the smell of oil, gasoline, and concrete. He found it energizing. Now, in his tender state, it was making him queasy.

Or is that the energy drink?

He tried to shake it off.

Come on. Harden up. There's work to do.

He focused on the car sitting in the middle of the bay. The engine compartment in the rear was open, and Trevor was tinkering with its insides. Teddy could see it was just like the one he'd driven in July. Only the livery was different. The main body was all white, adorned with the logos of various companies that were contributing parts or safety equipment to the series. The sidepods had overlapping triangles of red, white, and black that reminded Teddy of the Firebrand headquarters. "FIREBRAND" appeared in bold lettering along the outside of both sidepods and across the large wing at the back of the car. The nose cone was bare except for a large number in black: 56.

Teddy spun around. Stewart was watching him inspect the car. The engineer smiled.

"We thought you'd like that."

"That's my old go-karting number."

"I know. All the teams did a little digging to find numbers that might mean something to the drivers."

Teddy was touched. He started to feel a little better about the day's prospects.

"So what happens now?"

"Hey, we could practice?" Trevor said, without looking up from his work. His voiced dripped sarcasm.

Seriously? What is this guy's deal? Teddy knew this series would be tougher than the academy, but Greg would have fired anyone who spoke to a driver like that. And Maxim would have made sure he'd never want to show his face again.

Teddy imagined his Russian friend taking a socket wrench to Trevor's hands while giving him a lesson in garage etiquette. "Mechanic . . ." *pound* "respect . . . " *pound* "car." *pound* "Mechanic . . ." *pound* "respect . . ." *pound* "driver." *Pound pound pound.*

He felt a little guilty about the fantasy. But only a little.

"Trev!" Stewart snapped. He tilted his head and nodded it sharply in a way that said, "We talked about this."

Trevor raised his greasy hands in defeat. "Sorry. *Teddy.*"

"Just ignore him. We'll wheel the cars out to the grid in about twenty minutes. Practice starts at nine, so you've got some time to change and explore a bit if you want."

"Where do I—"

Stewart pointed to the back of the bay. Two large tool chests were positioned just far enough from the wall to create a makeshift changing room.

"Oh. Thanks."

I'm in the big leagues now, all right.

Teddy changed into his rash guard and suit, leaving the upper half tied around his waist by the arms. He shoved his gloves into his helmet and headed out the door.

"Here." Stewart stopped him. He was holding another energy drink. "For the road."

Sebring International Raceway was legendary. A road course built on top of a WWII airbase, it had been running continuously since the 1950s. Teddy had read all kinds of crazy things about it. That an alligator had wandered onto the track during a race. That a bunch of cars had snuck into the 12 Hours of Sebring race. He'd driven it many times— virtually, anyway. It was one of his favourite courses in the *GP Pro* series. When he'd heard that this was where the testing would take place, he'd almost wet himself with excitement.

He strolled along pit lane towards Turn 1, ignoring the mechanics and engineers rolling cars into position. He wanted to summon that feeling again. He paused to close his eyes and let the morning sun warm his face. He took long, deep breaths to clear his head.

Forget about Leah. Forget about Allison. Definitely forget about Trevor.

Teddy visualized the course as he'd seen it on TV and in his game. He loved how the straights and corners all had names. There was "Tower Turn," "Collier Bend," and a fiddly double turn called "the Esses." Teddy steered through them all in his mind, as if he were cruising through his own neighbourhood on a lazy summer day. He started to feel calm, centred.

When he opened his eyes again, all the cars were in place. The pits were filling up with drivers and their teams. He spotted Allison and her team up near the front of the lane. He spun on his heel and started walking to the back, where his own stall was.

He made an effort not to look at the other drivers. He was feeling better now and didn't want to give his nerves any excuse to join the party.

Halfway back to his stall, he heard someone behind him shout his name.

So close.

He didn't need to turn around to know who it was. He didn't bother turning around to reply. He didn't even slow down.

"Hello, Alex," he shouted back.

He heard him jogging to catch up. Teddy smiled.

That's right. Chase me.

"What, is that all I get as an old friend?"

"Is that what we are now? Friends?"

LeGuivre came up alongside him and slapped him on the back.

"Hey now. That's all in the past. We both made it. Team Rock Point. Has a nice ring to it."

Teddy stopped and faced the other driver.

His black hair was, as usual, perfectly styled. His olive skin seemed a little darker than Teddy remembered. His grin, on the other hand, was as smug as ever.

"Look, I don't know what you're going on about, but I'm not buying it. So why don't you just go back to your car and try not to crash into anything this time. Sound good?"

"Woah, what's gotten into you, Clark? I don't remember you being this . . . what's the word? *Wild*?"

Despite himself, Teddy laughed.

"Is that it? That's your big move? Seriously, Alex, I'm actually a little disappointed in you. Now, if you'll excuse me."

Teddy marched off feeling a little pumped. Standing up to LeGuivre like that had felt good. Now he was ready to drive.

He'd made it about ten feet before he noticed it. A nagging sensation in the back of his mind. Something didn't feel right. Then he pegged it. It wasn't coming from the back of his mind. It was coming from the back of his shirt. It was bunching between his shoulder blades. He reached back.

You have got to be—

He held a playing card. A joker. "WILD" was written on it in black sharpie.

A burst of laughter sounded from LeGuivre's pit stall.

Oh good. I was worried this day was starting to look up.

Teddy had dreamed about this moment every day for the last five months. At school, at home, at the gym. He'd been itching to sink into a cockpit. To feel enveloped in the fibreglass, hugged by the safety straps, massaged by the engine's vibrations. He'd imagined himself pulling out of pit lane, hitting the accelerator, and coming alive. The world would fall away and he would be thrust into the moment, aware only of the thrilling tension between freedom and control.

In his imagination, though, he didn't stall.

Oh, you have got to be . . .

It was a minor thing, really. He started up again right away. And because his pit box was one of the last in the row, he figured not many people would have seen it. Even so, Teddy felt the gremlin of embarrassment creeping up on him. He hit the gas and peeled out of the pit box.

"Could happen to anyone," said Stewart, over the radio.

Just stay focused.

Teddy followed the line of cars ahead of him. He allowed them to get some distance, to create space for a clean run around the track.

But something was off. This wasn't the welcoming embrace he'd imagined.

I'm rusty, that's all. Just need to shake out the cobwebs.

He reminded himself that he'd only driven this car a couple of times before. And technically speaking, the course was brand new to him.

By the end of the warm-up lap he'd gotten over the incident with LeGuivre, but something still wasn't quite right. When he'd driven the car in the summer, it had felt like twice the machine of anything he'd handled before. It had taken all his strength to control it. This car felt lighter somehow, and more responsive. He kept putting too much into the steering wheel and having to correct.

It wasn't bad exactly. It was just . . . different. Unexpected.

"How's it feeling out there?" Stewart's voice crackled over the radio.

Teddy hit a red button on the steering wheel.

"Yeah. It's just . . ."

"What?"

"Nothing. Gimme a sec."

Did they change something in the cars?

But he knew it wasn't that. Stewart would have told him if they'd made any major adjustments that would affect performance. Besides, it wasn't just how the car handled. It was also him. He felt constricted.

He rolled his shoulders awkwardly.

Did my racing suit shrink?

Then it dawned on him.

He'd been lifting weights for months since the last time he raced. He wasn't adjusting to a new car. He was adjusting to a new body.

Everything snapped into place. He chuckled.

"OK, if you're ready, Teddy, why don't you try picking it up on the next lap?"

"Sounds good."

Teddy settled in. Each lap felt better than the last. He started to pay attention to how the car was handling at different points in the track—how it gripped the corners, how it accelerated on the straights. By the fourth lap, he had enough confidence to spare some of his focus for the display in the centre of his steering wheel. It was a jigsaw puzzle of flashing red numbers. They told him his speed, gear selection, lap time, oil temperature, water temperature, brake bias—way too much for him to take in at once. They quickly blurred together. He blinked a few times.

Just focus on your lap time. That's all that matters.

He knew the record for Sebring's 3.7-mile track was 1:44. And Stewart had said that they were expecting the Formula Firebrands to do around 2:15. Teddy looked at his last lap time: 2:27.

His stomach turned. It was like the energy drink had ignited in his belly. Its fumes scorched the back of his throat.

Calm down. It's just the first day. It's just practice.

But he couldn't calm down. He needed to know.

He pressed the radio button again.

"Hey, Stew, what kind of lap times are people laying down?"

A few seconds passed. Then a few more. Teddy's imagination went to town.

Stewart was trying to figure out how to break the news to him: "Your times are garbage. You're being cut." Stewart had joined forces with Trevor and they'd both walked out in protest. Stewart had passed out from the shock of his tortoise-like performance.

Static replaced silence on the radio.

"Don't worry about it."

Don't worry about it!

"You're doing fine. Come in on the next lap. We'll make some adjustments."

Well, that's just great.

Teddy watched from the cockpit as Trevor and Stewart moved around the car, checking tire pressures and adjusting wing angles. For five minutes they stared at a tablet Stewart was holding. It looked as if they were starting to argue when Stewart seemed to remember Teddy. He guided Trevor to the back of the car, out of view. Teddy felt like a patient being operated on—awake but anesthetized from the neck down.

The day was heating up. Teddy's base layers were already soaked with sweat. Stewart had placed a small fan on the lip of the cockpit when Teddy pulled in. It didn't actually cool things down much, but Teddy felt a bit more comfortable just knowing that air was circulating.

His real problem now was staying alert. The energy drinks' effects were almost spent, and Teddy could feel the crash coming as he sat there idly.

Stewart leaned into the car.

"OK, we want to try a few things on your next run. If you can, pay attention to the slow corners, the Esses especially. We'd really like to hear your feedback."

"You got it."

Teddy forced himself to sound confident, professional. He was determined not to let them know he'd been rattled by the first run—and his lacklustre performance.

"And Teddy? Don't worry about your times right now. We're not trying to win anything today. Our job is just to gather data. Yours is to get a feel for the car. Just tell us anything that comes to mind. Remember, you're the expert here when it comes to driving."

"I'll do my best."

"That's all we ask."

Teddy slapped down his visor. There was no way he could avoid watching his times, but he appreciated Stewart's encouragement. He thought of Greg and Maxim and wondered if he'd ever come to think of Stewart and Trevor as friends in the same way.

Over the next six hours, Teddy was on track four times. During the first two runs, he tried to describe what he was feeling in the car to his crew. But it took every ounce of his concentration just to get the car around the track, and he struggled to find the words.

At lunchtime, his dad took one look at him and suggested he take a nap. Teddy needed no convincing. He retreated to his changing nook in the garage. But the moment he closed his eyes, his mind flashed back to the day before. *Chet.* Just thinking the name made him want to vomit.

By the end of his third run, his brain had turned to pudding. Whenever Stewart asked him a question about the car's grip or suspension, Teddy was hard-pressed to do more than mumble "Uh . . ." over the radio.

He hated that he was dropping the ball. Stewart kept gently reminding him not to be shy, to use the radio, to give them whatever feedback he could. He was letting his engineer down. Stewart didn't actually say anything to give him that impression, but Teddy was sure he could see the man's opinion of him falling as the day passed. He'd notice slight downturns at the edges of his mouth and flashes of doubt in his eyes. On the other hand, by the time they'd called it a day, Trevor was almost perky. It wasn't hard for Teddy to see why—he'd proven the mechanic right.

Back in the garage, Teddy packed up his suit.

Allison stepped inside. "Hey," she said.

"Hey," he replied, without looking up.

Not now. Please. Just go away.

"I've been texting."

"I know."

"I think we should talk."

Teddy jammed his gloves into the bag and wrenched the zipper closed. He glared at her.

"Do you? Do you think we should talk? Because I think you might have missed that train." His voice echoed in the empty bay.

Allison looked stunned, and she shifted her gaze to the floor. She crossed her arms and leaned a shoulder against the side wall.

"Teddy, I don't know what you mean. Is this about Chet? I'm sorry I didn't tell you . . ."

Is this—!

"Of course this is about him! What else would it be about?"

She turned and pressed her back into the wall. "I don't know. You were acting weird even before that. And it's not like . . ."

"It's not like what, Allie?"

Like you should have told me? Like you haven't been lead-ing me on with those Skype calls and gym sessions?

"Nothing. Forget it."

"No, tell me. It's not like what?"

"Can we just drop it?"

Teddy was desperate to make her see his side of things. But how could he explain? He knew she didn't owe him a thing—not in that way. *It's not like I ever said anything.* Still, they were friends, and she'd kept a secret. A big one. And he didn't know why. It was driving him crazy.

"Yeah, Allie. I think we can. I think we should drop eve-rything."

She looked at him. "Teddy, c'mon."

"Just go. Please."

Allison straightened. Behind her, the nose of Teddy's car appeared. Trevor was in the driver's seat steering. Stew-art and a couple of other guys pushed.

"Make way!" yelled Trevor.

"You heard him," said Teddy.

Allison clenched her fists, huffed loudly, and stormed off.

Teddy's legs started to wobble. He leaned against the back wall and slid to the ground.

"Aw, cheer up, Teddy. It wasn't that bad." Trevor smiled smugly. "At least you didn't crash. Am I right?"

Chapter 9

"So, how was Christmas?" Dr. Miller leaned back in his chair, legs crossed, hands folded in his lap.

Teddy glanced around the office. It looked exactly as it had before. Not a thing seemed out of place. There was something rigid, almost militant about it. He felt the need to sit up straight, to answer with "sir," to whip his unruly thoughts and feelings into line. It was a strange contrast to Dr. Miller's pleasant, easygoing tone.

"Good, thanks," said Teddy. "Yours?"

"Ha. Well, I don't get as much holiday as you do, so I worked mostly. But it's nice seeing family, don't you think? Do you guys do it up? All the trimmings?"

"Sure. I mean, we usually do a big dinner together. Mom and Matt came to our place this year."

Dr. Miller smiled. Teddy felt like the man was waiting for more.

"Matt brought his girlfriend, Beth."

"Had you met Beth before?"

"Once or twice. She's nice. An actress or something, I think."

Teddy considered elaborating. He liked Beth well enough. But he'd been seeing a lot less of Matt the last few months, and he couldn't help but think she was a big part of the reason why.

"How exciting."

Exciting? Really?

"And how's training going? I understand you had your first practice during the holidays."

He'd seen this coming. There was no way to avoid it. Wheels locked. Steering gone. Brace for impact.

"I won't lie, it wasn't great."

"No?"

Do I tell him my mechanic is a royal pain? That my results were awful? Should I mention the stuff about Allison? Or that Leah and I had a fight? That she's been trying to get me to talk about what happened for over two weeks? That I've been dodging her because I'm pretty sure she wants to break up?

"Teddy?"

"Huh? Oh, sorry."

"It's OK, I thought I lost you there."

Teddy weighed his options. The truth was that he was dying to talk to someone about all that stuff. His dad knew he'd been upset after Florida, but Teddy had let him think it was because of his performance on the track. Just the thought of explaining the rest of it made him cringe with embarrassment. And he'd been avoiding talking to Richard because of what he'd said to Leah in the gym. He couldn't be sure if she'd told him about it, or whose side he'd be on. So he'd just pushed it all down, letting it simmer. Now that he was forced to think about it, he felt it rising to a boil.

What the heck? He already knows about Graham. No point keeping secrets now.

"I had a rough week. Personally I mean. And the new crew, well, one of them was a real jerk. I was distracted and exhausted and didn't drive all that great."

"Sounds like a tough weekend. Do you mind if I ask about the personal stuff?"

Teddy started talking. And then he couldn't stop. He kept jumping from Leah to Allison to Trevor, even LeGuivre. He knew it probably didn't make sense the way he was telling it, but he had no control. His thoughts were staging a prison break.

When he was done he slumped into the sofa, spent.

"So, yeah," he said. "Not great."

Dr. Miller looked away. He clicked one side of his jaw. His eyes were fixed in a thousand-yard stare.

"Teddy, let me ask you something. Do you think you're special?"

Teddy blinked.

Huh?

"Um . . ."

Dr. Miller returned his gaze to Teddy. "Do you think you're different from other people?"

What is he talking about?

"Not really."

"See, I think you are."

Is this a pep talk? What is going on?

"OK, thanks . . . ?"

"I'm not trying to give you a compliment, Teddy."

Thanks for nothing, then?

"What I mean is that everyone has personal stuff. You, me, your dad—everyone. And we all have to deal with it in one way or another."

"I guess."

"For any athlete, dealing with personal stuff can be the difference between victory and defeat."

No argument here.

"But for people like you, for drivers, it can be the difference between life and death."

Wow. Does he think I don't know this?

"Yeah. I get that."

"Do you, though?"

Dr. Miller was looking at him intently now. Teddy glared back.

Where does this guy get off? He knows very well that I understand the risks.

"Yeah. I do."

"Well tell me, then—how do you deal with it? The personal stuff?"

Teddy had to pause to find the words.

"I put it in a box."

"You compartmentalize."

"Sure."

"And when that doesn't work? When things get to be too much?"

Teddy thought of Maxim and what he'd taught him at the academy.

"I breathe. I focus on breathing."

"That's good. What else?"

This had Teddy stumped.

"I don't know. Nothing."

"Teddy, there are two ways to keep issues like the ones you're experiencing from affecting your driving. The first is to manage them using techniques like breathing exercises and compartmentalization. I can help you with that. And I can show you other strategies to help keep you focused when it counts."

Well, then let's get on with it.

"The second is to deal with the issues directly. Now, it's not my place to help you with that. I'm not a therapist."

Then why bring it up!

"But I need you to recognize that you have to tackle these issues on both fronts. Letting things stew only makes the work we do here harder. And there's more at stake than a victory, or a career."

Teddy crossed his arms and stared out of the window.

So, I've got to help myself, is that it?

"It doesn't seem fair."

Dr. Miller chuckled. "No, Teddy, it isn't. If you want to sit around talking about fairness, take a philosophy class."

Teddy opened the passenger door.

"You wanna drive?" asked his dad.

"No, it's OK."

"How was it today?"

"It was . . . weird. He gave me homework."

"Oh yeah?"

"I'm supposed to pick someone I admire, someone successful, and model their behaviour."

"So you're going into real estate then?" His dad nudged him with an elbow. "Eh? Eh?"

"Hilarious. Actually, I was thinking . . ." Teddy paused.

"You were thinking of Graham."

"Yeah, kinda."

"You could do worse, son. A lot worse."

"But I don't know how. I mean, I don't know where to begin. And he said I should come up with a ritual."

"Like sacrificing goats or something?"

Teddy rolled his eyes."You know what I mean. Something to do before races. To get me in the zone or whatever."

"Doesn't sound too bad for homework."

Yeah. And then there's the whole "fix my personal life" stuff.

"Wait a sec." His dad started rummaging through the arm console.

"Dad, watch the road, jeez."

"Here, put this in," he said, passing Teddy a CD.

"Oh god. Please tell me this isn't one of your business gurus spouting mantras. 'To do good—you have to feel good!'"

"Hey, there's an idea! Let me grab that one."

"Dad!"

"Just put it in."

Teddy complied, and his dad fiddled with the track button.

A two-note guitar riff filled the car. A sustained organ chord punched in.

"I know this."

"Of course you do."

"It's from—"

"Don't tell me." Teddy wracked his brain. "This is going to drive me nuts."

"Give up?"

"Fine."

"It's from *Days of Thunder*. Spencer Davis Group. 'Gimme Some Lovin'.'"

Teddy slapped his knee. "Ah. I had it!"

"'Rubbin' is racin', son. Rubbin' is racin'.'"

"Ha. Not sure the guys at Firebrand would agree."

Teddy pictured himself rubbing his car up against LeGuivre's, trading paint like they do in stock cars.

"You know, this was one of Graham's favourite songs."

Teddy could see why. He could feel the beat resonate deep in his chest. His right foot twitched, searching the footwell for a pedal.

The next practice was in three months. He knew what he had to do. He just had no idea if he could pull it off.

Chapter 10

Sweat dripped from Teddy's forehead. He watched the drops as they fell on the hard black rubber floor, collecting in a puddle that reminded him of motor oil.

He finished his workout, wiped his face quickly with a dank towel, and headed for the exit. The gym was busy. Teddy was eager to escape the clanking weight stacks, simian grunting, and grating mixture of gangster rap and classic rock.

He shoved the towel into the side pocket of his knapsack. The main compartment was bulging with textbooks and binders. His teachers had wasted no time piling on assignments after Christmas vacation. And there was exam prep on top of that. All he wanted to do was grab a snack and plonk down with *GP Pro*. But Laguna Seca would have to wait.

A light snow was falling. Still warm from his workout, Teddy decided to carry his jacket for the short walk home. Steam rose off his back and shoulders, and the flakes turned to beads of water on his arms.

As he crossed the parking lot, Teddy saw Leah and Zana walking towards the school from the direction of the pet shop. They both wore down jackets, gloves, and scarves.

Zana sported a stylish, loose-knit toque. Leah's head was uncovered, her hair frosted with snow.

He halted. He'd done a decent job of avoiding the gang that week. Lunch was always the hardest, since they usually ate together. He would grab a sandwich from the caf and toss out some excuse for leaving, usually saying he needed to study. Then he'd dash for the library, inhaling his food as he went. Leah knew what was going on, of course, and Teddy assumed Richard probably had some idea. Zana too. The others just teased him about how studious he'd become over Christmas. Justin actually seemed a little impressed.

But the girls had spotted him. There was no one else around and no way to change directions without making it obvious.

All right. I guess we're doing this.

Teddy's heart rate jumped, as if his body suddenly realized the workout wasn't over after all.

They intercepted him on the sidewalk.

"Hey guys." He raised his free hand in a feeble wave. His knapsack slid off his shoulder.

"Dude, aren't you freezing?" asked Zana. She gave him a look that made Teddy think she wouldn't be disappointed if he said yes.

"I just came from the gym, so . . . Where are you guys headed?"

"Back to my place," said Leah. Her expression was friendly enough but her tone was cautious.

"We had a shift," said Zana. "But some doofus customer knocked over a shelf and a bunch of the terrariums got smashed. The owner came and told us to go home. I swear he thinks we did it."

"I think he just didn't want us cutting ourselves on the glass," said Leah. "Besides, did *you* want to try catching the tarantula?"

"What, you don't like Fuzzy Legs? I'll take him over those mice we feed to the snakes any day."

The girls continued talking as they walked. Teddy trailed behind them silently. About halfway to his house the cold finally started to nip at his skin, and he paused to put on his jacket. The girls didn't seem to notice, and he had to jog to rejoin them without zipping it up.

They reached an intersection. Each of their homes was in a different direction.

Part of him hoped Zana would change her mind about going to Leah's and head off to her own place. After his session with Dr. Miller, he'd made up his mind to apologize to Leah for everything—for hiding his friendship with Allison, and for reacting the way he had when she confronted him about it. Because of what had happened in Florida, he thought he understood how she must have felt. He'd only been avoiding her to give himself time to gather the nerve, and to figure out what to say.

They stood there awkwardly for a moment. It became clear they were waiting for him to leave.

"Well, OK then. See ya." Teddy turned towards his house.

"Teddy wait," Leah said. She looked at Zana, who shrugged.

"Do you want to come?"

He wasn't sure what to say. The thought of the three of them hanging out at Leah's sounded excruciating.

"Oh, just come," said Zana, apparently finding the whole situation a little ridiculous. "Everyone's going to be there."

Teddy took a second to register this.

"What do you mean?"

"The guys are coming too. We figured if we weren't working we might as well rehearse."

Teddy adjusted the heavy backpack on his shoulder. He scrutinized Leah's expression, looking to see if there was some hidden motivation to her invitation. He gave up.

"Sure."

"Well, then, let's go already. I'm freezing my butt off over here."

As they started towards Leah's house, a thought occurred to Teddy.

"I just realized, I've never heard you guys play."

Leah looked straight ahead.

"Yeah. I know."

Teddy zipped up his jacket.

Richard and Tom arrived shortly after Teddy and the girls. Teddy had seen the inside of Leah's garage only once or twice. It used to be nothing special. Her parents liked to keep things tidy. Rakes, shovels, and gardening implements hung neatly on the walls. Wire shelves held tough plastic bins filled with Christmas lights, Halloween decorations, sports equipment—the usual stuff.

Now, it was transformed. Leah's dad had agreed to keep his truck in the driveway year-round so half of the garage would be empty for the band. A second-hand drum kit and some amplifiers sat on a couple of worn-out rugs, and strings of fairy lights hung from the rafters. Against the side wall, underneath a Canadian flag, sat a beaten-up old sofa—Ben's contribution. He'd rescued it from the side of the road. "Can you believe someone was going to throw away this gem?"

Teddy certainly could believe it. It was the colour of mould and covered in dark stains. He wouldn't have been surprised if Ben had said he'd found it at a murder scene. But it didn't matter. They'd made the space their own, and that gave it a kind of magic. There was even a small bar fridge, fully stocked with sodas and, Teddy noted, energy drinks.

He tossed his coat onto the sofa and sat down while the others warmed up. Ben started rat-tat-tatting on the drums. Richard and Tom noodled around on their guitars while Zana tuned her bass. Leah took a few swigs from her water bottle and sang a few bars of "Hey Jude."

When they finally started playing, Teddy couldn't believe it. *Man, they're pretty good.* Most of their songs were covers. Richard had written a few originals that they were still working on. In between songs they'd give each other notes, poke fun at Tom's absurd attempts to dance while strumming, and just banter good-naturedly. At first they'd seemed keen to get Teddy's opinion on every song. But he never had anything more constructive to offer than "sounds good," and they soon stopped asking.

It was true, though. He enjoyed every song. At the same time, he had this nagging sense that he shouldn't be there. He felt less like he was getting a private concert and more like he was spying on a family dinner.

He watched Richard and Leah especially closely. In every glance, every laugh, every word they exchanged, he looked for some hidden meaning. Jealousy started to bubble up inside him. He forced it back down.

Of course they're acting friendly, he thought. *They're friends for crying out loud. Stop being paranoid.*

It occurred to him that, if there was something going on, they weren't trying very hard to hide it from him. *You think they'd parade themselves around in front of you? Get a grip.* And yet he couldn't shake the feeling that they seemed closer than they'd been before.

Maybe they've always been this close and I just never noticed.

After all, it was the first time he'd ever seen them playing together. Between school and racing, he'd been spending less and less time with the gang.

Stop it. It doesn't matter. Leah isn't the problem here, and neither is Richard.

It was almost six. The others were calling it a day. Teddy knew his dad would be home soon and wonder where he was. But he couldn't leave without talking to Leah. This was his chance to make things right. So he waited.

Richard offered to drive everyone home. "Nah, thanks," said Teddy. "Need to stretch my legs a bit." Ben and Tom bought the excuse without question. Richard and Zana looked at Leah, who nodded. She went to the back and pushed the button to open the door.

Teddy watched the others leave, and he waved as they pulled out of the driveway. The door started to close. He took a deep breath and turned to face Leah.

"Look, I—"

"You're a real jerk. You know that, right?" She stood in front of the drum kit, her arms crossed.

Teddy couldn't have been more stunned if she'd swung a bag of gerbils at his face. The garage door clunked in its tracks behind him. He tried to think of something to say, but there were no words. He opened and closed his mouth like a fish.

"First, you lie to me about this girl you've been having some secret relationship with. Then, when I ask you about it, you deny everything. Then, you disappear off to Florida with her. I barely hear from you for days, weeks even. And now you've been avoiding me at school. Seriously, Teddy, what have I done to deserve any of that?" Leah was trembling.

Shame flooded through him. He wanted to bolt, to burst right through the garage door.

She was right. She'd been nothing but supportive. Supportive of his racing, supportive of him when he'd learned about Graham—she'd always been there for him.

He stared at the floor.

"Nothing," he whispered.

"What?"

"Nothing. You've done nothing."

He raised his head. Her eyes were pink, glistening.

"I'm sorry, Leah. I really am."

He needed to sit down. He moved back to the sofa.

"I shouldn't have . . . I'm sorry." He still couldn't bring himself to say "lied to you."

"I need you to believe me," he said.

"I want to believe you Teddy, but—"

"Please. I understand now how it must have felt."

Leah's eyes narrowed.

"What do you mean 'now'?"

Teddy realized his mistake. *Crap.* He was trapped, caught in a spin. He had no choice but to steer into it.

He explained what had happened in Florida. Leah took it all in calmly. When he was done he felt raw, exposed.

"So you do like her." Her tone was measured, but Teddy could sense the effort behind it.

"I don't know. Maybe. I thought I did."

"And now that you know she has a boyfriend, now that you know how it feels to be lied to, you think you can just apologize and that's it?"

Hearing her say it back to him, he realized how awful it sounded. He wanted to dive between the couch cushions, to be sucked into another dimension. His eyes began to well up.

Leah opened the garage door again.

"I think you should go."

He grabbed his knapsack and rushed out into the snow. It wasn't until he reached the sidewalk that he realized he'd left his coat inside.

He kept walking.

Chapter 11

"Five minutes left, everyone. Five minutes."

The teacher's voice echoed through the cafeteria.

Teddy glanced up from his exam paper. He watched Mr. Larch erase the number 10 from a rolling blackboard at the front of the room and replace it with a 5. He shivered. It looked like some ominous rune, as though the teacher were casting a hex on him and the other hapless students.

It wasn't Teddy's first exam period. He'd been through the ritual twice a year since he started high school, and he'd have one more to endure before the year was out. Normal classes were suspended for the week. A new schedule was posted on the front doors. Any other time, the room was the social hub of the school, buzzing with conversation and laughter. But once they rolled in that blackboard, it felt more like a church during a funeral.

On a good day, Teddy had to write only one exam. On a very good day, it would be late in the morning—late enough for some last-minute cramming, early enough to have the rest of the afternoon to prepare for the next day's trials. Or, more accurately, to work through the morning's trauma with a *GP Pro* marathon.

Teddy scribbled furiously. He still had three questions left to answer.

Prove the identity
$(1 + cos(x) + cos(2x)) / (sin(x) + sin(2x)) = cot(x)$

Solve the trigonometric equation given by
$sin(x) + sin(x/2) = 0$ *for* $0 \le x \le 2\,pi$

If $sin(x) = 2/5$ *and x is an acute angle, find the exact values of*
a) cos(2x)
b) cos(4x)
c) sin(2x)
d) sin(4x)

And of course, he had to obey the holy injunction inscribed at the top of every math exam: *Show* all *your work.*

More than once Teddy had been tempted to staple a picture of himself studying for the exam into his answer booklet. What he was writing on the page was nothing compared to the work he'd put into preparing.

"Pencils down."

Teddy scrambled to jot "= cot(x)."

"Now!"

He dropped the pencil on the table. After gripping it so intensely for two hours, his hand cramped up out of shock, as if someone had just smashed it with a hammer.

He stared at the paper, and its two unanswered questions. He tried to calculate the best possible grade he could get, assuming every other answer was correct. But he was fried.

I can get the cosine of pretty terrible, he concluded.

Teddy followed the mob of students into the hallway. While the others congregated in the atrium outside the cafeteria, eagerly comparing answers, Teddy headed straight for his locker. He grabbed his things and made for the school's side exit, down an empty hallway, past the auditorium and the music room.

He walked home in a daze. He avoided the sidewalks and took a shortcut through a little ravine that ran through the subdivision.

Teddy rarely walked this way. The trail into the ravine was steep and muddy in the spring and fall, icy and treacherous in the winter. He knew some kids went down to the stream at the bottom to smoke cigarettes or drink from bottles they'd managed to sneak out of their parents' liquor cabinets. Thankfully, no one had chosen today to kill any brain cells here. He wasn't in the mood to see anyone.

The one nice thing about exam period was that he had the house to himself. His dad would be at work for several more hours. He grabbed a soda from the fridge and headed down to the basement. He settled in on the couch and checked his phone. No messages. He wasn't surprised. It had been a week since he'd had any contact with Leah. Longer since he'd heard from Allison. And everyone else was studying. He checked it out of habit more than anything else.

His right hand was still aching when he picked up the controller. A few minutes of nimble button-punching and joystick-twirling brought it back to life.

Teddy didn't even bother with Laguna Seca. He needed a few certain wins—for him, nothing was as therapeutic as victory. The game worked its magic for a while, but an hour later he felt restless again. He stopped playing and wandered back upstairs, poked around in the fridge without taking anything, and stared out of the window into the backyard.

He sighed.

I should probably get back to it.

He trudged up the stairs to his bedroom. Textbooks, open binders, and piles of loose papers were strewn over his desk and the surrounding floor.

Yeah . . . no.

He considered texting the guys to see if any of them wanted to head over to Tim Hortons for a study break. But he knew it was impossible. Leah would be with them. They were all studying together. They'd invited him to join the study group, of course, but Teddy had declined. He didn't have to say why. The awkward interactions and loaded glances spoke for themselves.

He flopped onto his bed and promptly fell asleep.

The front door slammed, jolting Teddy awake.

"Ahoy-hoy!"

"Upstairs!"

He heard his dad drop his briefcase and toss his winter armour into the front closet. The warm scent of grease and spices travelled up the stairs and into Teddy's room.

"Soup's on!"

Teddy rushed downstairs and tore open the paper bag. He and his dad spread its contents onto the kitchen counter like kids at Halloween inspecting their haul—hot foil tubs of shawarma, shashlik, hummus, roasted eggplant, garden salad, pita bread, and, of course, French fries.

Teddy scanned the bounty and panicked. He rummaged at the bottom of the bag. It was empty.

"Looking for this?" His dad produced a white plastic bag.

"Don't scare me like that."

Teddy pulled out the pièce de résistance: five plastic cups filled with white goop.

"I got extra," his dad said.

Teddy had already opened one of the cups, torn a strip off the pita bread, dipped it in the fragrant sauce, and shoved it into his mouth.

"Shranks," he said, grabbing another strip.

"So, (A) gross. And (B) how do you eat that stuff? You'll smell like garlic for a week. I hope you aren't planning on kissing anyone anytime soon."

Teddy swallowed and dropped the bread back onto the stack. His stomach clenched. His appetite vanished. He hadn't told his dad about Leah yet.

His dad handed him a plate.

"Here, at least bring it to the table."

Teddy took the plate and set it on the counter. He took a soda from the fridge and sat down at the table.

"Um, I hope you're not expecting me to eat the rest of this? Son?"

Teddy stared at the unopened can in front of him

"Uh-oh. What is it? Exam not go well today? I'm sure it's not as bad as you think. What was it? English? I hated English. All those essays."

"It was trig. That's not it, Dad." Teddy took a breath. The smell of garlic sauce invaded his nostrils.

Oh well. Here goes.

"Leah and I had a fight. About a week ago. I think . . . I think we broke up."

His dad stopped what he was doing and placed his hands on the counter.

"Huh." He paused. "Sorry about the kissing thing." He put some food on Teddy's abandoned plate and took it to the table with his own.

"Do you want to talk about it?"

"Not really," said Teddy.

"OK."

His dad took a bite of food.

And then the story came pouring out, just like it had with Dr. Miller. His dad interrupted him a few times to clarify the details but otherwise sat patiently as Teddy spoke. Their food steamed its way to room temperature.

When he was finished, Teddy looked up at his father. He could see him trying to find the right thing to say. He knew his dad would take his side, but it looked like he was struggling to find an angle. Teddy realized how the whole thing sounded, how he came off—he hadn't even tried to paint himself in a good light.

"Sounds like you've had a rough few weeks."

"Months."

"But your last exam is Friday?"

"Yeah."

"Well, look. I won't pretend to have any advice to give you. I'm sure it's the last thing you want right now anyway."

He wanted to shout, *You're so wrong! Tell me what I should do!*

He said nothing.

"But I have an idea. I was going to do this a little later, when the weather was better, but, heck, why wait?"

Teddy looked at him, confused.

"It's just the thing to cheer you up."

Chapter 12

The tires squealed. The acrid smell of burning rubber wafted through the vents, roughening the smooth scent of freshly polished leather.

"Mind taking it easy there, sport? It's brand new, for crying out loud."

Teddy didn't hear him. He barely even registered his dad's presence. His senses had been hijacked. The engine screamed as he accelerated out of the corners, like a stadium full of hockey fans when the home team scores. Tunnel vision had set in. His eyes fixed on a spot a hundred feet ahead of him, stalking the racing line. His heart seemed to slow its beat, to quiet itself so Teddy could absorb the faint thrum of feedback that had managed to survive the trip through the high-end suspension and power steering. His fingers tingled. They curled tightly around the wheel.

He was home.

It was pure luck, really. The winter had been unusually dry so far. Unseasonably warm days punctuated the crisp cold spells. Even in the city, there was usually snow on the ground by now. So when his dad suggested they make the trip to Motown to visit Greg and show off the new BMW, Teddy had assumed the place would be buried in snow—nestled in for the winter, hibernating. Instead, they found the track clear and empty. It was more than inviting. It was begging for some action.

With each turn, each straightaway, a different memory snapped into Teddy's mind, like pictures in a slide show. The three-car pile-up at the bottom of Turn 2. *Click.* His killer pass between Turns 3 and 4. *Click.* The final stretch, where LeGuivre and Jake Roberts's gruesome contact secured his place in the Formula Firebrand series. The track was speaking to him, reminiscing.

Teddy couldn't remember the last time he'd felt this relaxed, this confident, this in control.

After five laps they came in.

Greg walked into pit lane. He was dressed for weather much colder than the day offered. He wore a puffy blue down jacket with a fur-lined hood, sturdy high-top boots, and a grey wool headband. What caught Teddy's eye were his gloves—worn black leather with a brass-buttoned wrist strap and holes over the knuckles. Not the sort of gloves you wear to keep warm. Driving gloves.

"Sorry to vanish on you like that," Greg said, as Teddy and his dad climbed out of the car. "One of our corporate clients was panicking about his booking."

Teddy had to shield his eyes from the sun glinting off the roof.

"So, how's she handle?" Greg asked.

"Meh. It's all right." Teddy grinned at his dad, who raised an eyebrow.

"I'll have those keys back now, thank you very much."

Greg chuckled. "A little humility, Chex. Goes a long way."

Teddy smiled. "Oh don't worry about that. I'm getting lessons."

"Is that right? The Firebrand boys putting you through your paces?"

"Don't even get me started."

Let's not spoil this moment. Please.

"Well don't think you're getting off that easy. But that can wait. I wouldn't mind taking a spin myself."

"You can get in line," said Teddy's dad. "He hasn't even let me have a run yet."

"Shotgun," shouted Teddy, running around the car to take the front passenger seat.

"Teddy, come on," his dad said sternly. "Greg gets shotgun."

"You're a good man, Steve."

"Teddy should know better." His dad winked. "Age before beauty, right?"

Greg laughed. Teddy opened the door for him with a flourish then hopped into the back seat.

"You might want to sit this one out, Chex." Greg tapped a gloved finger on the window.

Teddy looked across the lawn. A stocky figure stood on the hill next to the squat office building.

"Is that . . . ?" Teddy's eyes widened.

"Called him this morning," Greg said. "Be nice to him, though. He hates coming in on the weekend. Even for you."

Teddy got out of the car and trotted across the mucky yellow grass.

"What's this fuss? You need private lessons now?" Maxim's voice boomed down the hill. He stood with his legs apart and his hands on his hips, a pose somewhere between superhero and scolding gym teacher. He wore faded black jeans and a wrinkled white T-shirt under a thin jacket with the Rock Point Racing Academy logo on it.

Teddy approached him, huffing.

"I think maybe you just need exercise."

"It's good to see you, too." Teddy reached out and hugged the man. Maxim dropped his arms stiffly to his sides.

"Yes, yes. Come. I want to see new car. You tell me how training goes." He slapped Teddy on the back, nearly winding him.

They walked back towards the pits.

"I don't know where to start," said Teddy.

"How about your team. You've met them, yes? Good? Not good?"

Teddy thought about Trevor. He felt his blood start to simmer.

"Not as good as you, let's put it that way."

"Ha! Must be good. Fancy cars. Fancy tools."

"My engineer, Stew, he's all right, I guess."

"Engineer. Very fancy. And mechanic?"

"He's . . ." Teddy searched for a word. He felt like even talking about Trevor would pollute the air. "Challenging."

Maxim nodded. "You think I was challenging, too. In beginning."

Teddy snorted, remembering how Maxim had pushed him in his academy days, forced him to grow as a driver. He was desperate to switch topics, but he hated that Maxim had compared himself to Trevor. The comparison crawled under his skin. He needed to scratch it out.

"No. That was totally different. You were trying to be helpful. This guy's just mean."

Teddy explained his new nickname. To his surprise, Maxim let out a hearty laugh.

"Wild Card. This is good."

Teddy felt a little hurt.

Did he not hear me? The guy's a jerk.

"Thanks, Maxim."

The Russian laughed again. "What? You worry he is not good mechanic?"

Teddy started to get flustered. "No. I mean, I don't know yet. But that's not the point."

"What is point? He is your mechanic. If he is good, you are good."

"But, it's like he doesn't respect me. Even if he is good, how can I trust him? What if he doesn't try? If he thinks I'm a lost cause or whatever." Teddy shrugged.

Maxim stopped and turned. Teddy crossed his arms and stared at the track. The BMW blew past the start-finish line.

"You are wrong, Chex. Many ways wrong."

This is just perfect. That jerk is ruining my day from a thousand miles away.

"You know LeGuivre."

"I've heard of him."

Maxim ignored Teddy's sarcasm. "LeGuivre is good driver, hard driver, rough on cars. Make mechanic's life very difficult."

Teddy couldn't believe what he was hearing. *Oh, so now I'm like freaking Alex! Give me a break.*

"Mechanic's job is to make best car. Give driver best chance. No matter driver. Bad car, bad results—these bad for mechanic, too."

"I *get* that, Maxim."

"You are sure? OK. If you get bad results, do you move to new series? Do you become famous AmRun Pro driver?"

"Of course not."

"Think. I don't give LeGuivre good car. I do not like him. So I give him bad car. Why not? He will bring back bad car either way. Am I still head mechanic next year? Am I any mechanic year after that?"

"But . . ." Teddy felt his indignation start to buckle.

"Even bad driver can get good result in good car. This is good for mechanic. Bad result? Maybe blame on driver. But is risky. Sometimes clear, sometimes not. To give driver best chance—this is best for everyone. This is job."

"That doesn't mean he's not a jerk. It just means he's a self-serving jerk."

"Maybe this. Or maybe he is scared. If you look bad, he looks bad. Scared men can be mean men. But they are scared first, mean second."

Teddy could see what Maxim was trying to tell him. He pictured Trevor as a dorky young boy, nervous about being picked last for dodgeball. It helped.

"All right, fine. I'll buy that. But still. He just gets me so . . ." Teddy grunted.

"That is biggest mistake. Most disappointing. I thought you learned from me already."

"Learned what?"

"You let him in." He tapped a meaty finger on Teddy's head. "Mean people are like, what you call them, *vampir*."

"Vampires?"

"Yes. You invite them, they come in. You don't, they—" Maxim brought his hands up, interlocked his thumbs, and started flapping.

A smile cracked Teddy's face. He laughed.

Still flapping his hands, Maxim started to hop from one foot to the other. His expression remained unchanged, serious. One hundred and eighty pounds of lean Russian muscle with the face of a judge delivering a life sentence—jigging like a cartoon leprechaun.

Teddy lost it.

Once everyone had had a turn taking Teddy's dad's new toy around the track, the four of them left Rock Point in convoy and headed into Morton Falls for lunch. On the way, Teddy described Maxim's performance to his dad. By the time they'd arrived at Ricky's Diner, they were both in stitches.

"What did I miss?" asked Greg, as everyone got out of the cars. He looked at Maxim. The man said nothing but managed to shrug using only his eyebrows.

Takeout from Ricky's had been a ritual part of Teddy's weekends at Rock Point for years. But as they approached the entrance, he realized he'd never actually eaten in the restaurant. He'd barely made it past the front door.

The space was long and narrow, barely ten feet wide, but stretched back at least three times that. Down one side was a bar the length of the whole place. Round, backless stools lined the front. Their padding peeked out of cracks in the dull vinyl covering.

Behind the bar was a counter packed tightly with industrial-sized toasters, soda fountains, and coffee makers. Halfway down, the counter gave way to grimy steel tables, open flame cookers, and glass-front fridges.

Teddy had always thought "greasy spoon" was a charming term of affection. He wondered now whether the term should be added to the food-safety certificate plastered in the front window.

They sat in one of the run-down booths that lined the wall opposite the counter. Teddy and his dad took up one side. Maxim and Greg sat across from them.

Teddy looked at the walls. They displayed a bizarre collection of objects: photographs of the town at various stages in its development; plates commemorating events that happened long before Teddy was born; and an assortment of tchotchkes he imagined could only have been left behind by accident. It was like a flood had come through town and the diner's sticky walls had rescued all the sentimental trinkets washed away from the homes.

Only one item looked like it was supposed to be there: a complete brake pedal assembly mounted next to a photograph of a man wearing a John Deere cap and a welder's jacket. He was posing next to a beaten-up car. Teddy couldn't identify the make of it. The man was giving a grease-stained thumbs-up. His other hand held the very same assembly Teddy was staring at. As Teddy realized this, the man's semi-toothed grin took on a sinister shade. He shuddered as he wondered about the fate of the assembly's former owner.

Burgers and fries were ordered and served. Teddy slathered ketchup onto both.

As they ate, Greg grilled Teddy about the first practice. Whether it was the warm surge of calories, the lingering high from taking the BMW around the track, or the memory of Maxim's imitation of a bat in search of prey, Teddy couldn't say—but he found himself feeling less anxious about how his practice had gone. He happily answered Greg's questions about the facility, the car, the other drivers. Details he hadn't even registered at the time popped into his mind to decorate his replies. He felt as though he were talking about something embarrassing that happened years ago. He felt no shame, no frustration, no regret.

Teddy could see that his audience was charmed. His dad looked more than a little surprised at the sudden shift in Teddy's perspective. Maxim nodded approvingly, though

136 · CHRISTOPHER HINCHCLIFFE

whether he was approving of Teddy's attitude or his own part in bringing it about, Teddy couldn't guess.

Greg slapped the table, rattling the cutlery.

"I gotta say, Chex, I think with the way you're approaching this it's going to be one hell of a season. I couldn't be prouder."

Teddy smiled. His chest swelled with gratitude.

"Thanks, Greg. That means a lot."

"You must be excited to get back down there for round two, eh?"

"Honestly I haven't thought about it much. I was pretty focused on exams the last couple weeks. And it's not until March, so I've got some time."

Greg's expression suddenly changed. He looked confused. Worried, even. He wasn't looking at Teddy.

"Everything all right, Steve?"

Teddy turned to his dad. The colour had drained from his face. He plonked his elbows on the table and dropped his head into his hands.

"Dad?"

Teddy's heart sank into his stomach.

"Oh, Teddy. I'm so sorry."

"Dad, what?"

"There was a message for you on the home phone the other day. I deleted it after I listened and . . . I was going to tell you but you were having a rough week and . . . I guess it just slipped my mind."

Teddy's mind raced. A thousand disastrous scenarios ran through his mind. He fought to hold on to the calm, mature version of himself he'd been a few minutes ago.

"It's OK, Dad. You're telling me now. What is it?"

"Dan called. Dan Williamson. From the series?"

"Yes, Dad, I know who Dan is. What did he say?"

"There was a mix-up or something with the scheduling. They double-booked the track in March. They needed to move the second practice to the twenty-eighth."

"Of February?"

"No, January."

"But that's next weekend," said Greg.

Teddy glanced up at the brake vandal. There wasn't a doubt in his mind. That menacing grin was aimed squarely at him.

Chapter 13

The tired springs creaked in protest as Teddy dropped his backpack onto the motel bed. He unzipped it. A clump of rumpled clothes sprung out and landed on the floor.

"Bah."

He hunched over and gathered them up, scrambling to find something decent to wear to Firebrand Headquarters. He didn't have much to choose from. A couple of wrinkled T-shirts, some underwear, a pair of jeans. He'd had to force them all into his bag on top of his laptop, textbooks, and binders.

I should just go in my race suit.

His dad rummaged frantically through his own bag on the next bed.

"I don't understand how bad weather in Chicago makes a direct flight to Florida late," he snapped.

"Yeah, well, I don't see why we have to go to this thing tonight at all. Can't I just skip it?"

"I don't think that's wise. This is only the second practice, and the series clearly wants to show its 'dedication to driver development.'"

Teddy snorted, recognizing the line from a brochure.

You'd think with all the fuss they're making they might have sent some branded shirts with all the other material.

"Besides," his dad said, sitting on his bed with his back to Teddy. He swapped his loafers for some dressier Oxfords. "It's not like . . ." He paused.

Ah, there it is, Teddy thought, spotting the shirt he'd been looking for. He threw it on and tried to iron it out a bit by pressing it against his body. He glanced in his dad's direction. "It's not like I made a great first impression?"

"That's not what I was going to say."

"It's OK. Seriously. I'm over that. All in the rearview. Just gotta get through tonight. Tomorrow's another day, right?"

"That's the spirit. There."

His dad stood up and turned around. He looked Teddy up and down.

"You absolutely cannot wear that."

They entered the shop. The enormous overhead lights were brighter than Teddy remembered. He felt exposed. He pulled at the white golf shirt his dad had given him. It was at least two sizes too big and made Teddy feel even smaller beneath the lofty ceilings.

In the centre of the floor were two tables draped in black and red tablecloths. They were covered with platters of food, small paper plates, plastic cups, and bottles of wine. A cooler sitting open on the floor next to the tables was heaped full of ice and cans.

Teddy recognized many of the people milling around the tables—other drivers, Firebrand employees.

No crew, he noted. *Well, that's something anyway. A Trevor-free evening.*

The others were folks he'd never met, but he knew who they were—representatives and executives from the various companies that were contributing to the series. Teddy suspected this event wasn't about the drivers at all, despite Firebrand's big talk. It was about the money.

Dan greeted them as they approached. Two heavyset, middle-aged men in smart blazers were with him.

Here we go.

"And here's one of our youngest drivers. Let me introduce Teddy Clark and his father, Steve. They hail from Toronto."

What is this, Star Trek? *Pretty sure I've never done any "hailing."*

"It's a pleasure to meet you," Teddy said, smiling widely.

"I'm Chip Weston," said one of the men, grabbing Teddy's hand. "And this is Jack Harbourn."

"Chip and Jack are with Sparco," said Dan.

"I love your suits," Teddy said.

Chip frowned, looked down, and fiddled with his lapel. "What? Oh, you meant our race . . . Ha! Nice one, Teddy! This boy's a quick one, isn't he, Jack? Better watch out for him, Dan."

Everyone laughed along with Chip.

Teddy's face was already getting sore. Dan and his dad gave him looks that said, "Keep it up."

Dan excused himself and the Sparco men and told Teddy and his dad to help themselves to refreshments. After three more encounters like the one they'd just had, they finally reached the table. By the time Teddy had managed to crack a soda, his throat was so dry he had to chug it. He felt the carbonation in his belly begin to plot its escape immediately.

"You're doing great, sport." His dad patted him on the shoulder.

He tingled with pride. A faint current of electricity emanated from his shoulder and into his chest. "I had a good teacher." His father was the businessman, the schmoozer. It was like a new connection had formed between them.

"Hi, Teddy, Mr. Clark."

Teddy turned quickly. His dad's hand fell away.

"Allie—"

He belched.

Teddy slapped his hands over his mouth. His cheeks burned.

Allison, her uncle Jim, and Chet stared at him. Allison looked stunned and a little embarrassed. Chet and Jim looked more amused than anything.

That's right. You cover that mouth. That's how gas works. Idiot.

"Excuse me," he said.

"Ah, ha, well," said his dad. "It's nice to see everyone again."

"This is quite the place," offered Jim. "I didn't get a chance to check it out last time. Must cost a fortune to cool."

While his dad and Jim talked about the latest developments in HVAC technology, Teddy shrank backwards towards the table and turned away.

Pull it together, pull it together, pull it together.

He felt a tap on his shoulder. He took a careful breath and turned around.

"Are you feeling OK?" asked Allison.

"I'm fine. I just . . . how are you?"

"Dude, that was impressive."

Chet loomed over Teddy. His light brown hair was dishevelled in a way that screamed "I'm too cool to care how I look." A fine stubble coated his cheeks and accentuated his jawline.

Teddy wanted to punch him.

"So, are you ready for tomorrow?" Allison's tone was friendly but measured, distant.

All Teddy's confidence, all his resolve to patch things up with Allison—gone. AWOL. He realized he'd have to fake it.

Just picture Chip and Jack, he told himself. *Schmooze.*

"I'm actually really looking forward to it," he said. "I think I learned a lot last time." Big smile.

Green flag. Clean start.

Allison looked relieved. Her face brightened.

"That's great. Isn't it crazy that we're driving at Sebring?"

"Right? It's a bit unreal."

First turn. No incidents.

"And isn't it wild how it's just like *GT*—"

"—*Pro*. I know! I couldn't believe how accurate it was."

They smiled and shook their heads.

Back straight. No traffic.

"Babe." Chet placed a hand on Allison's shoulder. He'd apparently lost interest in the conversation.

Car in front. Obstacle.

"You think they have any beer in there?" Chet started eyeing the cooler at the end of the table.

An opening!

Teddy jumped in. "I think I saw some, yeah."

"Sweet." Chet ambled off.

Pass.

"Chet's more into football," said Allison shyly.

"Seems like a great guy." Teddy smirked.

Easy. Don't push your luck.

Allison scrunched her nose and punched Teddy in the arm.

He started to relax. "How's your team?"

"They're good. Really intense, though. My engineer, Rob, is total dork, but in a cute way, you know?"

"Better not say that too loudly," Teddy said, glancing over his shoulder towards Chet.

"Stop it."

Teddy noticed Chip filling a plate at the table. "Wait," he said to Allison. "Hang on."

He stepped over to Chip and leaned in, whispering something. Chip's face lit up, and he strode over to Chet, who had just opened a can of beer and was taking a long sip worthy of a Budweiser commercial.

Allison grabbed Teddy's arm.

"What did you say to him?"

"Nothing. I just gave him the impression that Chet was extremely curious about how they made our suits fireproof."

"I'm going to kill you. Like, actually kill you."

"Gotta catch me first." Teddy winked.

Allison pursed her lips and inhaled sharply through her nose.

"Excuse me guys," Dan said, walking up to them. With him was a good-looking man, older than the drivers but younger than everyone else. Close behind them was LeGuivre.

"I want you to meet someone. This is Nick Scott, our head of marketing. And of course you know Alex."

They exchanged pleasantries with Nick and restrained nods with LeGuivre.

"So these are our Canadian shootout winners," said Nick. "I hear it was quite a race."

"Oh, it was a battle, all right." Dan pointed towards the loft above the offices. "We're still scraping the wall paint off Alex's car. You and Jake really did a number on those machines. But it worked well for you, eh, Teddy?"

Dan said this in a good-natured way, but Teddy could tell from the way LeGuivre's eyes twitched that he took it personally.

In fact, LeGuivre didn't seem like himself at all. His usual vapour of cockiness and hair product was absent. Not a whiff. Instead, he seemed on edge. He glanced around the room constantly as though looking for an exit.

"And it's great to have another female driver in the mix. I guess Kayla's got some competition," Nick said to Allison.

Allison smiled sweetly. "She sure does," she said. "Just like the rest of them."

Teddy forced down a snicker. Nick appeared unfazed. If anything, he looked intrigued by Allison. His gaze lingered on her a moment. Teddy narrowed an eye.

"Well, look, I don't want to occupy your whole evening. I'll be working with all the drivers during the season. Media training, that sort of thing. But I was thinking about doing something special with just the three of you, and I wanted to put some faces to names. See what I was working with."

Well, that doesn't sound creepy at all.

The men left. LeGuivre hung back.

"Guys, hey."

"Uh, can we *help* you with something?" said Teddy.

LeGuivre looked over his shoulder and then leaned in close.

"Did you guys hear anything?"

"What?" asked Allison. "Alex, are you OK? You're act-ing weird." At first she'd seemed no more interested in talking to LeGuivre than Teddy had. Now she looked curious.

"C'mon. Did you hear anything? About me? About anything?"

Now even Teddy was interested. LeGuivre was talking rapidly, almost breathlessly. But he wasn't about to let LeGuivre think he actually cared.

He decided to play with him instead.

Teddy darted his gaze left and right, mimicking LeGuivre, and leaned in too.

"Is this about"—he paused, savouring the suspense— "*the Illuminati*?"

Out of the corner of his eye Teddy saw Allison stifle a laugh.

"What?" said LeGuivre. His face tightened. "Oh. Very funny, Clark. Wouldn't surprise me, though. They look like they belong in a cult. Robes and chanting. The whole bit."

"You mean the twins?" Allison said, without whispering.

"Shh! They'll hear you. Freaks are probably watching us right now."

LeGuivre started to bend sideways, slowly, as if trying to make it look natural. Teddy realized he was checking under the table behind him.

"Alex, you're losing it, man."

And it's awesome.

"Look, all I'm saying is, if you hear anything—" He stopped short. Something to his left had caught his eye. He took off in the opposite direction, weaving through the groups of chatting people.

Allison and Teddy turned to where he'd been looking.

At the far end of the table stood Kyle and Kayla, side by side, staring back at them.

"Sweet cheesus." Allison jerked behind Teddy and grabbed both his shoulders. He felt her breath on his neck. Her unfamiliar perfume seeped into him. His heart started to race.

Woah. Woahwoahwoahwoahwoah.

"Easy, I need those to drive with," he said, shrugging her off.

Kayla took a sip from a bottle of water and then passed it to Kyle, who took a sip as well. Neither of them broke eye contact with Teddy and Allison.

Teddy smiled and held up a hand.

"Did they see me jump?"

"Oh, no. It was very subtle."

Allison poked him in the ribs.

"Hey!" a voice called from behind them.

They spun around. Chet was striding their way.

Teddy froze. His brain kicked into overdrive, trying to conjure up an explanation for why he and Allison had been pressed up against each other.

It's not what it looks like!

She grabbed me!

It was the Illuminati!

Chet stopped in front of them.

Allison tried to speak. "Chet, we—"

He raised a hand. "Hold on. Before you say anything, I need to ask you something."

Would I prefer you break my nose or my ribs?

"Who *is* that guy?" Chet pointed a thumb in the direction of Chip. "Dude's, like, seriously into race suits."

Chapter 14

Teddy removed the balaclava and gloves from his helmet and then placed all three items on the retaining wall in a neat row. Balaclava, helmet, gloves. He zipped up his suit and then picked them up again, one at a time. He put on each piece thoughtfully, pausing for a second to consider its appearance and its function.

It had been Dr. Miller's idea. "A lot of athletes create rituals around their equipment," he'd said. Teddy felt a little silly doing it at first.

Oh, balaclava! How you shield my face from fire. Om . . .

But when he came to the gloves, something sparked inside him. They weren't the ones he'd raced with at the shootout. They weren't Graham's gloves. These were almost brand new, with barely a trace of grease or grime. The fresh padding made them feel thicker, while the synthetic leather made them lighter. Their scent was a weak, chemical impersonation of the oily musk trapped in the frame above his bed at home. In fact, they had only one thing in common with the gloves he'd worn that summer. They were red. That was why he'd chosen them. It dawned on him that without even knowing it, he'd already created his own ritual.

Feeling pumped, Teddy hopped over the retaining wall and slipped into his car.

The plan today was simple. Drive a few laps, take notes on the car's performance, come in for adjustments. Wash, rinse, repeat. Same as the first practice.

The sun was peeking over the grandstands as Trevor secured Teddy's safety belts.

It's going to be a good day.

On the first session out, Teddy enjoyed himself so much he had a hard time finding things to report to his crew. Stewart had said they'd learned quite a bit from the data collected at the first practice. Back in the garage, he'd suggested a few things to Teddy about how to time his gear changes at various points on the track to optimize his power. Teddy had paid close attention, wanting to internalize those suggestions before he got in the car.

But by the time he'd reached the second corner, he'd forgotten them. The drive consumed him. He found his rhythm almost immediately and had no intention of letting it go, whatever Stewart squawked over the radio.

The cars were spaced out, so the track seemed deserted. He felt as if he'd arrived at the beach before anyone else. Empty sand, ocean breeze, friendly sun, powerful waves.

When Teddy pulled into the pits, Stewart gestured for him to lift his visor. Trevor stood near the nose with his hands on his hips. Neither seemed impressed.

Teddy was still glowing inside, but he felt a little guilty, too. He'd indulged. Now he'd have to buckle down.

"Having fun out there?" Stewart asked.

Teddy felt himself blush but didn't look away—he knew the helmet would hide it.

"A bit, yeah."

"Good. Now remember what I said back in the garage? About the changes in 3, 5, and 7?"

Stewart's tone was patient but Teddy could sense disappointment.

"Got it."

"Now, mechanically, how'd it feel? Anything jump out at you?"

Teddy hesitated. He didn't really have anything to say, but he wasn't keen to give Trevor any ammunition.

"Could use with less downforce, maybe. I felt pretty sluggish on the straights."

It was the first thing that came to mind and not remotely true. But it seemed to satisfy Trevor, who set about adjusting the angle of the rear wing.

I guess we'll just call this an experiment.

He set out for a second run.

The first turn was smooth enough. He was still getting up to speed. Between Turn 1 and Turn 3 the course ran basically in a straight line. What they called Turn 2 was more of a course correction than anything else. With the reduced downforce, Teddy rocketed through it.

Then came the Esses—two almost-ninety-degree left-hand corners with a wiggle between them.

Teddy miscalculated how much he'd need to slow coming into Turn 3. Without the extra downforce pushing the car into the asphalt, it was like hitting a patch of ice.

He recovered going into Turn 4, which was barely a kink in the road, but only by reducing his speed to what felt like a crawl. At this pace, the next two turns were easy to manage, but he knew it had cost him time.

Having learned his lesson in the Esses, he began decelerating early into the hairpin, Turn 7, the sharpest corner on the track.

"OK," said Stewart, over the radio.

Teddy was puzzled.

What's OK?

Until now, he'd been sure they thought he was playing it too safe.

I guess I hit the gear changes he wanted?

He inched around almost 180 degrees, before accelerating again into the long stretch and soft bends of Turns 8 and 9.

Still anxious about the time he'd lost in the Esses and Turn 7, Teddy pushed the car harder into Turn 10 than he should have. He pulled right and almost lost the back end.

He took a breath and pictured the track in his mind.

You'll make it up on the last two straights, he told himself.

He curled through Turns 11 and 12 and made his way carefully around the next hard corner, Turn 13.

Now he had a long clear shot to the gentle Turn 14.

Teddy gunned it. He couldn't believe what a difference there was from the first session. He was soaring.

He used the slight bump of Turn 15 to prepare for the next right angle at Turn 16. After the sustained speed of the straightaway, this section felt glacially slow.

The feeling was short-lived. The back straight was even longer than the one he'd just crossed. Seconds were just lying on the track waiting to be picked up, like tokens in a video game.

He didn't want to get cocky, not with only one turn left in the lap. He knew he'd have another chance to push harder on the next go around.

He steered through the final turn, which brought him a full 180 degrees and back onto the front straight.

As he passed pit lane and crossed the start-finish line he heard Stewart over the radio.

"That was good. How's it feeling?"

"Great. A little loose in the turns. But the straights feel better."

"To be expected. Keep it up."

With each lap Teddy honed his handling through the turns, exploring the limits of the car with its trimmed-up rear wing.

After ten laps he came in. He was confident that Stewart and Trevor would be in better spirits now.

The engineer crouched next to the cockpit and rested an arm on the side.

"OK, that was all right," he said. "An improvement for sure." Stewart's tone was reserved, cautious.

Teddy was confused.

C'mon. That was better than "all right." Right?

"Yeah, it felt pretty good. It took a bit to figure out the corners, but the car loved those straights."

Stewart looked over his shoulder at Trevor, who rolled his eyes. The mechanic started to move around the car, checking tire pressures.

Something's wrong.

"What's up? Wasn't that better? It felt better."

"Oh, for sure it was better," Stewart said. "But . . ."

"But?"

"Well, even in the straights, you're still a bit off the pace. Compared to the other drivers, I mean."

What? This made no sense to Teddy. *How could I be off the pace? It felt so much better than the first run. Sure, the turns were choppy at first, but by the end I was definitely hitting my marks.*

"OK. So what can we change? I don't think I can handle any less downforce."

Stewart's lips tightened. He bobbed his head slowly, rhythmically.

"Yup. I don't know what to tell you. I'm not sure there's anything more we can do with the car."

So you're saying it's me. Great.

"There must be something. What about Trevor? What does he think?"

Trevor was kneeling by the front left tire. His head turned when Teddy said his name. He raised an eyebrow and stood up slowly.

"You want to know what I think?"

Stewart winced and leaned his head back, as if he were holding a lit roman candle.

Teddy looked desperately into his mechanic's eyes.

Please.

"I think Teddy's right," Trevor said.

Stewart cocked his head. The bomb was a dud.

"I noticed some heat coming off the front left here. Could be the brake pad is rubbing."

Yes! That must be it. The brake pad. Check the brake pad!

Stewart straightened up.

"Huh. Well, OK. Let's check the brakes then."

"You got it, boss."

Trevor's eyes fixed on Teddy.

Teddy nodded.

Thank you.

Teddy jogged back to the garage feeling energized. During the third run, he'd gotten the hang of handling the car through the turns with the new setup, and Trevor had fixed the problem with the brakes. The result was, in Stewart's words, "a qualified success." Teddy's times weren't the fastest of the morning, but they were hardly the slowest. Even Trevor seemed, if not impressed, at least a little less grumpy.

Now Teddy was ravenous. He dropped his helmet off in the bay and headed to a large semi-permanent tent erected in the paddock. Because of the last-minute change to the schedule, the series had sprung for a hospitality area for all the teams.

His dad was waiting for him when he arrived. "Quite a spread they've laid out."

Against the back wall, shiny metal warmers with roll-top lids lined two folding tables. Chicken, beef, pasta, roasted potatoes, grilled veggies, salads—it was a proper buffet.

Despite feeling famished, Teddy was careful not to pile his plate too high. He was convinced he could improve his times in the afternoon sessions and didn't want his brain fogged up by a food coma.

While Teddy ate, his dad talked. "Of course, when I saw your times after the second session, I just knew there had to be something wrong with the car." He shovelled a forkful of stewed beef into his mouth. "Just knew it."

"Uh-huh," Teddy said, carefully slicing a piece of chicken. He was only half-listening. The rush was starting to ebb. His mind had wandered back to the night before. He was still trying to piece together what exactly had happened. It seemed that things with Allison were on an even keel—for now. *But what was up with Alex? What was he going on about with the twins?*

He looked around the tent. LeGuivre was sitting by himself at a table off in a corner. A plate of food steamed in front of him, untouched. Dark bags hung under his eyes.

Man, he looks rough.

Teddy searched for the twins but didn't see them. *Probably roasting a baby in their garage.*

Allison was sitting at the opposite end of the room with Chet and her uncle. Chet was making animated gestures with his hands while the others laughed.

Teddy felt his stomach tighten.

Is this what it's going to be like from now on?

Teddy was going through his new ritual. The first group of cars was already out on the track. He'd just pulled on his gloves when Allison walked up to him.

He quickly removed his helmet and balaclava, almost dropping them in the process.

"I hear you did all right this morning," she said.

He blushed.

"It was OK. I hear you crushed it, though." *Great. Now I sound like Dad.* "Top time. Good for you."

"I had a good setup."

A car buzzed down the front straight.

Why does this feel so awkward?

Before the reception, he'd just wanted things to go back to normal with them. He'd hated the silence of the past weeks. Nursing his anger and his sense of betrayal had only made him miserable. And for a few minutes the night before, everything had felt right again. Better than normal, even. Normal was joking over Skype. That moment in the shop had been *real*—as real as her hands clutching his shoulders, as her breath on his neck, as the warmth of her body next to his. Not just real but natural.

Now it felt like they'd crossed a line. Teddy sensed Allison felt it too. She wouldn't meet his eyes and dragged a foot in little circles on the tarmac.

This is stupid, he thought. *This is absolutely ridiculous.*

"So . . ." They spoke in unison and laughed.

"Are we cool?" she asked.

"Yeah, we're cool."

She lunged forward, pulling him into a hug. "You're such a dork."

"And you're a—" He stopped. Halfway between his pit stall and hers, Chet was watching them. The expression on his face filled Teddy's veins with ice.

He pushed Allison away.

"Hey, what—?"

A flashy orange-and-white pickup truck blew past them down pit lane. The lights on top of its cab were flashing. A white medical van followed close behind.

Teddy and Allison turned to Stewart, who was standing by Teddy's car. His head was cocked to one side, his hand pressed against his headset.

"Stew?" Teddy said.

His engineer raised a finger.

Teddy and Allison exchanged looks.

"Sorry, guys. Looks like you might not make it out this afternoon after all. There's been an incident on 13. Pretty bad by the sounds of it. Cleanup's gonna take a while."

"Who was it? Are they OK?" asked Allison.

"The 2 and 10 cars. Who's that?"

"That's Kyle Tusk and—"

"Alex."

Chapter 15

"Do you know why I asked you to come in today?"

The guidance councillor sat with her hands folded in front of her on the desk. Cream-coloured folders spilled out of a wire tray by her elbow. The bookshelf behind her contained more picture frames than books. A dog wearing a paper-cone birthday hat. Two cats displaying aggressive indifference to a ball of yarn. A fat middle-aged man wearing a camouflage vest standing in a boat and proudly dangling a greenish spotted fish.

What is that? A trout? Maybe a bass?

"Teddy?" She blinked. Her eyes looked enormous behind her pink square-framed glasses.

"Sorry, Mrs. Reynolds. I'm not sure, actually."

"Well." She took a folder from the pile. "I have your midterm reports here."

Ah. Right. Should have seen this coming.

"Your first-term exam results were satisfactory, but your teachers tell me you've been slipping a bit this term. They say you seem distracted. Would you say you've been distracted, Teddy?"

On a scale of 9 to 10? Hmm, let me think . . .

Over a month had passed since the last practice. From what Teddy and Allison could gather, LeGuivre's car had malfunctioned and lost power. Kyle caught up with him and then—*wham*. He slammed LeGuivre into the wall. LeGuivre suffered a mild concussion and a sprained wrist. Kyle emerged unscathed but apparently couldn't explain how he'd managed to hit a car travelling sixty miles an hour.

Once the officials cancelled the rest of the practice, everyone had pretty much packed up and left. There hadn't been another opportunity for Teddy to speak to Allison alone. In a way, he'd been relieved. They'd smoothed things over, but only on the surface. Nothing had been dealt with. Nothing had been solved. At least for him. His feelings hadn't changed because they'd swapped a few jokes. He'd only hidden them, shoved them in a closet like he did with his clothes when his dad told him to clean his room. It wasn't enough. He needed to kill them, to cram them into box and bury it deep, and then pray they would suffocate in silence.

When Teddy returned from Florida, he'd resolved to do whatever it took to make things right with Leah. He knew he couldn't explain his behaviour, not entirely, not without making things worse. But he had to try. She'd put up with more than her fair share of crap from him, and he felt horrible about it.

At first, she'd put him off. "I'm just not ready," she'd said. They avoided each other at school as much as they could, but things soon got awkward. She finally agreed to meet him at Tim Hortons. Teddy had prepared an elaborate apology, but he never made it past "I'm sorry."

"Oh, I don't doubt it," she said. "I'm sure you're sorry about a lot right now." She glowered at him across the table. Teddy fought the urge to look away. "But that's not enough. Not even close. You need to *do* something, Teddy. You need to change something."

He felt himself crumbling in his chair. *What? Anything. Tell me!*

Her expression softened. "Look," she said. "I want this to work. I really do. But I need to know that you're in it. That you're here, with *me*."

"I am here," he said meekly. "I'm here right now."

"You know what I mean. You're always so wrapped up in your own stuff. Your racing, your training, your . . ." She paused and glanced out of the window. Her back stiffened. "Your other friends."

He swallowed a lump of guilt. "I get it."

"Maybe. But I need to see it." She looked back at him. "I'm not asking for a lot, you know."

"I know."

"I shouldn't even have to say this."

Leah was right, and Teddy knew it. At the end of the day, all she wanted was for him to be honest with her, and to feel like he supported her as much as she had supported him.

She just wants a normal relationship. For me to act like, you know, what do you call it? Oh yeah. A boyfriend.

Over the next few weeks he spent as much time as he could with her. He'd join the gang after school and watch them rehearse. On the weekends, they'd go to the movies or

Demetres or just hang out at one of their houses. He never mentioned racing unless someone else brought it up.

Leah even started going to the gym with him. She'd hop on the treadmill while Teddy went through his routine.

This surprised him. "I didn't know you liked to run," he'd said, the first time she came.

"I used to do cross-country in middle school. I haven't really run in years, but it's good for my singing—improves lung capacity."

Her explanation was believable enough and Teddy enjoyed the company. He liked the idea that they were, in a way, working together towards their own goals. At the same time, he couldn't shake the feeling that there was more to it. Like she was keeping an eye on him. Like every hour they spent together was an hour he wasn't talking to Allison.

Stop it. Boyfriend. Not suspicious maniac. Boyfriend.

Leah hadn't asked him *not* to talk to Allison. Teddy was immensely relieved that she hadn't. If she had, he probably would have agreed—really, he would have agreed to anything. At the same time, he knew it was a promise he couldn't keep. For one thing, the season would be starting soon, and there was no way to avoid running into Allison at the track. More than that, though, he didn't *want* to avoid her. He was still determined to snuff out his feelings for her, and he knew that it would be easier if they didn't talk between race weekends. But he was also thrilled that they were back on speaking terms. Shutting her out again would have killed him.

Instead, he'd decided to stop answering Allison's texts at school, and only talked to her when Leah was too busy to hang out in the evening. At first it seemed like a fair compromise. Slowly, it started to feel a bit sneaky. Now, even Skype's sound effects seemed to be scolding him. *Bleep-bloop. Ted-dy*. Frowny-face emoji.

Teddy didn't want to discuss any of this with Mrs. Reynolds. So far, the only "guidance" she'd ever offered him was in the tenth grade, when she suggested he stop thinking about racing as a career.

"What about following in your mother's footsteps?" she'd said. "You could be a surgeon? Or, I don't know, a pediatrician? I'll bet you're good with kids."

Teddy blinked. *Good with kids? Based on what, exactly?* He'd wondered if she had some sort of quota she had to fill each year.

From: District Board of Education
To: Guidance Councillors, District-Wide

We're running low on chiropractors, aviation engineers, and pediatricians. Please advise accordingly.

p.s. Kindly remind students that "YouTube celebrity" is not a real career.

Mrs. Reynolds cleared her throat. Teddy realized she was waiting for him to say something.

"I guess I've been focusing on training. The racing season starts soon."

"Yes, I'd heard you were still doing your racing thing."

I'm sorry—"racing thing"? Oh, it's on.

"It's a pretty big deal, actually. If I do well this year I have a shot at a ride on a professional team."

Mrs. Reynolds smiled. It was a sweet, ferociously patronizing smile.

"Of course, Teddy, of course. It's wonderful to have dreams. But it's also important to keep a foot on the ground. You know, in the real world."

Teddy gripped the arms of his chair.

"I don't think you understand, Mrs. Reynolds."

"Oh, I do, Teddy, I do. You can't imagine how many bright and talented young people like yourself have sat in that chair, full of hope and promise and ambition. Every one of them deserved to reach the top of . . . whatever it is they wanted to be at the top of. Some of them make it, and I'm extremely proud when they do. But—and it's important to face facts here—most of them don't."

Teddy's knees started to shake. He placed his hands on them and squeezed. Hard.

"Maybe they just needed better guidance."

Mrs. Reynolds closed the folder.

"Teddy, the last thing I want to do is to discourage you from pursuing your passion, but you must be sensible. *If* racing doesn't work out for you, what then?"

I could always bully kids from behind a desk for a living.

She continued. "I think you should know that your father contacted me."

Teddy froze.

News to me. Why is this news to me?

"Apparently you'll be away quite a bit in the coming months."

Teddy thawed.

Oh, that.

"Well, we race on weekends. But I'll need to travel on Fridays."

"I understand. I hope *you* understand that you'll be expected to keep on top of your work. You'll have to borrow notes from friends for any classes you miss. And I'm afraid we can't grant any extensions for assignments."

Teddy couldn't take any more. "No, Mrs. Reynolds. I wouldn't dream of asking. Can I go now?"

The room was shrinking around him. The air felt humid, dank, oppressive—like he was stuck inside a Ziplock bag, a forgotten sandwich mouldering in the back of a locker.

Mrs. Reynolds flopped her hands on the desk.

"Well, I guess so. But Teddy, do think about what I said."

"You bet."

He snatched his backpack from the floor and opened the office door. The air in the hallway felt as pure as a mountaintop. He inhaled deeply and then turned.

"Hey, Mrs. Reynolds. You going to the game this Friday? Against Maplewood?"

The councillor looked stunned.

"Well . . . I . . . yes. I am."

"Gotta support our boys, right? Go Devils."

Teddy slammed the door behind him.

Chapter 16

The room buzzed with nervous chatter. The static charge of anticipation hung heavy around the drivers.

It was race day.

Mike banged a travel mug on the side of a gleaming white trailer. Dan stood beside him, holding a clipboard.

"Good morning, everyone," Mike growled. "Welcome to Lime Rock."

The drivers applauded politely. They were seated around half a dozen circular tables draped in black table-cloths. A dozen more tables sat empty behind them.

The Firebrand mobile hospitality suite. Teddy had never seen anything like it—at least not from the inside. In essence, it was just a tent. But to call it "a tent" would be like calling Toronto's Casa Loma "a house." Its PVC roof was supported by at least eight poles of varying heights, giving it a big-top feel. The walls weren't even tent walls at all but instead were made of metal and tinted glass. The floor was a checkerboard of black-and-white interlocking tiles that smelled of fresh rubber. Trendy light fixtures hung from the steel cables that connected the poles, and they were powered by cords wrapped in meticulous spirals.

The suite's entrance was a proper double-door made of glass and brushed aluminum. The door was built into a large white hollow cube that extended out from the front of the tent. The wall opposite the entrance was the side of a trailer—the one Mike had banged his mug against. Narrow tables holding the remains of an elaborate breakfast buffet were placed next to it. Several flat-screen TVs had been mounted on the trailer. One of these was running a flashy Firebrand promo video on a loop. Another displayed a timing board with all the drivers' names listed. A third showed a live image of the front straightaway from a camera positioned somewhere above pit road.

Teddy had been the last to arrive. Since Allison's table was full up, he'd grabbed a seat at a table off to the side with a couple of drivers he hadn't met before. They introduced themselves—Pete Hardwick and Simon Wrigley. Teddy couldn't remember much of what he'd read about Pete. He was from Wyoming or Wisconsin—something with a *W*. But Teddy had been eager to meet Simon. At sixteen years old, Simon was the only driver in the series younger than Teddy. If he was intimidated by the others he didn't show it. Teddy found him friendly, polite, and cool as an Iced Capp.

I should get lessons from this kid.

Mike and Dan went over the schedule and the rules. Every event in the season involved two races, one on Saturday and one on Sunday. Each race day would start with a forty-minute open practice followed by a twenty-minute qualifying session. The length of the race depended on the length of the track. The race had to be at least thirty-seven-

and-a-half miles, but it couldn't last longer than thirty minutes. At Lime Rock, that meant twenty-five laps.

As the men spoke, Teddy tried to get Allison's attention. He couldn't tell if she was ignoring him or just engrossed in Mike's refresher course on practice session etiquette. Apparently the incident in Florida had rattled a few of the series officials. But she kept her eyes firmly forward.

LeGuivre sat at the other side of the room, so Teddy couldn't get a good look at him. Even though the accident had happened months ago, he was secretly hoping LeGuivre was still wearing a cast or, at the very least, sporting a black eye or something.

When the meeting broke up he made a move towards Allison. She darted for the exit.

What the . . . ? There's no way she didn't see me. And if she didn't, why wouldn't she look for me?

He considered jogging after her. But he knew that if something *was* wrong, she probably wouldn't want to talk about it with everyone else around. Instead, he walked slowly towards the entrance, wondering if he should be worried.

Stewart unbuckled the restraints, and Teddy lifted himself out of the car. He was still getting used to the HANS device and needed help removing it before he could unstrap his helmet. It was a funny-looking thing, sort of like a headrest that sat on his shoulders. All the drivers had to wear them to protect themselves from whiplash in an accident.

His engineer undid the clips that connected his helmet to the device and then walked away. Teddy removed the rest and placed everything on the pit wall in a row.

"Teddy, come have a look at this when you're ready." Stewart stood at the back of the pit stall, where a laptop sat open on top of a tool chest.

Something in Stewart's tone made Teddy feel rushed. He wasn't sure why. Qualifying was over and they had an hour before the race started. In fact, Stewart's mood had been a bit funny all morning. He wasn't being rude exactly, but he seemed less approachable, and all his comments were abrupt. It was unsettling. He was usually patient and encouraging.

I guess this is "down to business" Stew.

Even Trevor's attitude seemed muted. Teddy couldn't tell if he'd won any points with his mechanic by deferring to him at the last practice day. If Trevor still thought of him as an unlucky "wild card," he wasn't letting on. He seemed to be concerned only with the car. He took whatever feedback Teddy offered without comment and then set right to work.

Teddy thought about what Maxim had said to him back at Rock Point. He reminded himself that his crew was there to win. That was their job.

It's my job, too.

They had their work cut out for them. Teddy had qualified P10—tenth out of eighteen cars. Starting in the middle was almost as bad as starting in the back. There was plenty of distance to make up if he wanted to podium, and he'd be stuck in traffic right from the start, fighting a battle on all sides.

They studied the results of all the cars on Stewart's laptop. The good news was that Teddy seemed to be a shade quicker than the drivers who'd qualified immediately behind him. That meant he'd have a chance to pull away from them early. The bad news was that he was two seconds off the fastest car—LeGuivre's.

I guess even the twins can't slow him down.

Looking at the list, he realized that LeGuivre would have his hands full from the get-go. Kyle and Kayla had qualified in P2 and P3.

Allison was starting in P7.

He frowned. *But she did so well at Sebring.*

He glanced up from the screen to see if he could spot her, but her pit stall was empty.

Must be with her crew somewhere.

He turned his attention back to the computer. The display had changed. Stewart was now showing him graphs that detailed the car's performance at various points around the track. Teddy nodded as his engineer spoke. He tried his hardest to translate what he was hearing into his experience of moving twelve hundred pounds of metal around a course at a hundred miles an hour.

When Teddy first started racing, he'd learned about things like "heel-toe" shifting and "the racing line." Years of practice had turned these and a dozen other technical ideas into instincts. He no longer thought about driving the car—he just drove it. Now Stewart was asking him to turn things around, to take what he did naturally and put it into words. Teddy thought about his mom's spaghetti. To him, it was something you appreciated as a single thing, a delicious tangled heap. It was like Stewart was asking him to evaluate each strand of pasta.

Ugh. This is worse than trig.

The sun dipped behind the sky's only cloud as the field of cars swept around the final corner and took formation. Teddy's heart rate spiked as he watched the frontrunners pass the raised wooden hut at the start-finish line.

"Green, green, green," Stewart's voice crackled over the radio.

Teddy hit the accelerator, keeping a close eye on the cars around him. The pack moved cleanly under the footbridge that arched over the track at Turn 1. One by one they fell into line, snaking around the first half of the course. Teddy held his position.

During practice, Teddy had thought about how much the track reminded him of his home track, in Motown. Lime Rock was small but old. Tucked within the rolling woods of upper Connecticut, the track had no grandstands to speak of. Its loyal local fans were happy to pitch up on the grass. The natural elevation provided all the views they could want.

Even though Lime Rock had no sharp turns, Teddy had learned it was difficult to maintain speed here for very long. The straights were relatively short—the course was mostly a series of wide bends. With the downforce his car could generate, these bends should have been easy work. But while the turns were soft, they were bunched fairly close together in the first half of the course.

"The breakaway point is just after Turn 4," Stewart had explained. "There's a slight downwards slope that you can use to grab enough speed to overtake someone—if you time it right."

If he missed a gear change, or failed to accelerate early enough out of the corner, gravity would soon turn against him. And it would slam the door in his face as he entered the chicane at Turn 5. Only once he'd broken free on the other side could Teddy really gain any steam. Two short straights, the second one downhill, and he'd be back where he started.

For the first few laps Teddy focused on nothing but holding the racing line and keeping his spot in the order. Stewart had been right—the cars behind him weren't putting up much of a fight. But he wasn't going to give them an opportunity, either.

By Lap 10, he'd started to relax into the rhythm of the course, letting the racing line pull him along. His radio had been silent since the green flag dropped. He decided this was a good sign.

Then again, it's not like I need them to tell me if I'm messing up. I've got eight guys behind me who'd happily take that job.

By Lap 20, he was keeping pace with the car in front of him. Only a couple of car-lengths separated them. Too much to attempt to pass but enough to make Teddy feel like he was applying pressure.

They dove under the footbridge into Turn 1. The car ahead started to pull away.

Crap! I braked too early.

Then the other car went wide through the turn, clipping the far curb.

No! He braked too late!

Teddy was on top of him. The next two bends were too close to give Teddy a chance to pass, but he was on him now. His window was coming.

They rounded Turn 4.

Teddy planted his foot.

He moved to the outside line.

Stewart's voice popped into his head. He thought it was the radio.

"Just hold the line a second longer than he does."

Teddy froze.

The window slammed shut.

Chapter 17

Teddy strode towards the paddock. Off to his right, a small crowd had started to gather for the podium ceremony. He considered changing course. He hated the thought of watching LeGuivre climb to the top tier and receive his trophy. But he was a little curious to see what Kyle and Kayla would look like with LeGuivre standing between them.

Maybe like sharks circling the prow of a sinking ship, he thought. *With LeGuivre grasping the railing.*

Not much had been said when he pulled into the pits after the race. There was nothing obviously wrong with the car to report to Stewart and Trevor. He'd held his starting position until the end and earned a respectable top-ten finish. But Teddy couldn't resist the urge to apologize for missing his chance to pass.

"There's always tomorrow," Stewart said, without much feeling.

"For sure," Teddy replied, before making a swift exit.

Can't do much worse, anyway.

Tenth position was awarded a single championship point. Anything below that got nothing.

What's that they say about a journey of a thousand miles?

178 · CHRISTOPHER HINCHCLIFFE

He put thoughts of the championship out of his mind. It was only the first race, after all. He was much more interested in finding Allison and asking her why she'd been avoiding him all weekend.

Teddy walked past his own trailer and headed straight for hers. The crews were still bringing the cars up from the pits, so the covered workspace next to the trailer was empty.

Teddy banged on a door in the trailer's side wall.

Maybe she came back first, he thought.

No response.

He sat down on a plastic step stool beneath the door and waited.

A few minutes later, Allison's crew wheeled her car into the workspace.

Teddy jumped up.

"Uh, hi," he said. "You guys seen Allison?"

The men looked at each other for a second before the one steering the car answered. "She left for the day."

What? Already? How is that even possible?

Teddy scrutinized the faces staring back at him.

Something's not right. They're lying to me. I can feel it.

"OK, thanks," he said. He cast a final glance at the trailer door before heading back to his own trailer.

"That'll be twenty-two even," said the cab driver.

Teddy pulled a wad of bills from his pocket. The money felt strange. It was soft, flimsy, worn-out. And it was drab. The colour of pea soup. He had to study each bill to figure out how much it was worth. He'd never realized how much he took the bright colours of Canadian money for granted.

And what's with one-dollar bills? Barely fifty bucks in my hand and I feel like a gangster.

He paid the driver and opened the door.

"Good luck tomorrow, bud."

"Thanks."

It was only late afternoon, but even with the drapes open the motel room felt like a cave. Teddy dropped his racing bag on the floor, kicked off his shoes, and flopped onto the bed.

His backpack, stuffed with homework, sat against the wall opposite him. He felt like it was staring at him.

He took out his phone. Missed calls from Leah and his dad. He flipped off the silence function.

The room felt empty. Teddy could count on one hand the number of times he'd been without his dad on a race weekend. He'd never been out of the country on his own before.

"I'm really sorry, sport, but I have two closings and an open house and no one who can cover," he'd said, before Teddy left.

Teddy had brushed it off. "No problem. I'll be so busy anyway. Don't even worry about it."

"Oh, I'm not. I'll start worrying in July, when you turn eighteen and won't need my permission to go gallivanting around the world."

"I promise to keep my gallivanting to a minimum."

Teddy had just dialled his dad when a text came in.

It was Allison.

His heart rate jumped. He scrambled to cancel the call to his dad before it connected.

"Hey."

"Hey."

A few seconds passed.

Should I say something first? No—she initiated. Wait.

A little bubble appeared on the screen. She was typing.

"Top ten today. Good job."

Hey, thanks! Oh, and what the heck is going on with you?

"Thanks. You too. P6. Not bad."

"Yeah, PH messed up on 18. Easy pass."

PH?

Teddy realized she must mean Pete Hardwick, the guy he'd met that morning at the drivers' meeting.

"Cool."

A minute passed.

This is stupid.

"Is everything else OK?" he wrote.

The stillness in the room was maddening. Teddy got up and started to pace.

"Sort of. Not really."

Care to elaborate?

"I need to tell you something, but I can't do it yet."

Oh, for crying out . . .

"Allie, what is going on?"

"I'll tell you tomorrow, OK? I just wanted to say I'm sorry for blanking you today."

Ugh.

"K. Find me in the paddock in the AM."

"No. After the race."

Is she serious?

"Fine. Whatever."

Guilt jabbed him in the ribs. For all he knew, her house had burned down, or her dog had died.

Stop acting like she broke your favourite Tonka truck.

He stared at the screen, half-expecting her to call him out.

Another five minutes passed.

Guess she's done.

His phone dinged.

"Good luck tomorrow," she said.

He punched in a hasty "Thanks you too" and tossed his phone on the bed.

He kept pacing, shaking his arms as he walked. He felt as if he'd just downed a triple espresso.

On his third lap of the room, he stubbed his toe on his backpack.

"For the love of—" He glared at the bag. "What are you looking at?"

Chapter 18

When Teddy arrived at the track on Sunday morning, Trevor and Stewart were already hard at work on the car. Yesterday their detached, business-like manner had thrown him off. Today, he welcomed it. He had zero idea what Allison planned to tell him. But he couldn't spend all day wondering and worrying about it. He even avoided the Firebrand hospitality suite, just to be safe. Instead of fuelling up on eggs, bacon, toast, and pastries, he opted for a couple of granola bars and a bottle of orange juice he'd snagged from the motel's vending machine.

He jumped up into the trailer and closed the door behind him.

The trailer was, in its own way, just as impressive as the hospitality suite. A mobile garage that held not only the car but also spare parts and tires and all the tools a mechanic could want. Many of its treasures were now set up on the tarmac outside, beneath a canopy that rolled out from the trailer's side wall. So Teddy had plenty of space to change into his race suit.

As he stuffed his jeans into his bag, he felt them vibrate. He grabbed his phone from the pocket. His dad had sent him a message with an audio file attached.

"For inspiration," it said. "Good luck today."

Teddy half-smiled. Not sure what would happen when he pressed Play, Teddy searched for earbuds. He rummaged through the drawers beneath the narrow workbench that ran along the inside wall and found a pair attached to a walkie-talkie.

He plugged them into his phone and hit Play.

The pulsing bass line was unmistakable. Spencer Davis Group. "Gimme Some Lovin'." Graham's song.

Almost immediately, his heart took up the rhythm.

All right, he thought. *Let's go racing.*

The tune stuck with him all morning. It had burrowed into his head, migrated down his spine, and made a home for itself in his chest. It infused him with a boldness that pushed him through practice and qualifying, that prodded him to test the car's limits at every turn.

When he returned to the pits after qualifying, Stewart and Trevor were left scratching their heads. He'd shaved half a second off his best time from the day before—no small feat on a track that took under a minute to complete. And good enough to let him start the race in P8.

Teddy smiled to himself while his engineer and mechanic debated whether his performance was due to the subtle changes they'd made to his tire pressure or wing angles. But he knew the truth, even if they weren't able, or willing, to recognize it. He thought about saying, "Guys, maybe I just *drove better*."

Nah. Let them have this one. It doesn't mean much yet anyway. Not until the checkers drop.

They were still on the parade lap, but Teddy could already feel the car in P9 sniffing for an advantage. Simon Wrigley. Teddy was glad he'd finally get to see Simon in action. But the young driver seemed a little too eager to prove himself.

He shook his head. *Aren't we all?*

Simon would have the inside line in the first turn.

OK. No room for error.

The field formed up, gathering speed down the final bend. The green flag dropped.

Teddy gazed down the front straight. The leaders, LeGuivre, Kyle, Kayla, and Allison, entered Turn 1. LeGuivre and Kyle disappeared round the bend. Allison held tight to the outside line but Kayla went wide. She seemed to be trying to shove Allison out of the turn and onto the runoff zone—a short bit of track extending directly out from the front straightaway.

Allison was having none of it. She pushed right back, shoving the nose of her car deeper into the turn than she had any right to. Kayla didn't budge. She held the inside.

They made contact.

Teddy cringed and almost jerked his own steering wheel.

So it's going to be that kind of day. All right, then.

Kayla's car jumped as her front right tire crossed the inside curb. Allison backed off but only a little.

With the outside of the turn wide open, the next three cars in line whipped passed them.

Teddy now found himself directly behind Allison—and directly beside Simon, who had pulled up next to him while he was distracted.

Teddy held fast through the long right-hand turn. Simon started to inch ahead, but Teddy retook his lead as they moved left into Turn 3. Simon stole the advantage again in Turn 4.

OK, that's enough.

Teddy was barely through the turn when he accelerated. The ground sloped downward. It was like gravity had given him a little extra horsepower—just enough to pull in front of Simon and hold his position.

Allison and Kayla did a similar dance right in front of him. There was barely a foot between them as they entered the chicane.

To get in front of Simon, Teddy had kept his foot on the gas until the last possible second. Now he had to brake hard if he wanted to avoid slamming into the back of Allison.

The four of them crawled uphill through the chicane like boxcars. Then, one by one, as gravity released its grip on them, they sprung onto the back straightaway like pinballs.

Since Kayla was first to exit, it seemed as if she were pulling away. Teddy knew it was only an illusion. Assuming the cars were evenly matched, they'd bunch up again at the next corner. He checked his mirrors to see if Simon would try to take advantage of the draft and make a move. But there was nowhere for him to go—Teddy was too close to Allison. So Simon stayed hitched to the back of Teddy's car.

The pack stayed tight as it rounded the final turn and made the downhill sprint to the start-finish line. Only then could Teddy see what was going on up front. LeGuivre and Kyle had pulled ahead of the others but were locked to each other.

He started to feel dizzy and realized he'd been holding his breath for the whole lap. He exhaled.

OK. Only twenty-four more laps to go. No sweat.

Each lap passed in the same way. Teddy would defend as Simon poked his nose at the slightest opening in the first few turns. Then Teddy would try to create some distance on the downhill stretch between Turns 4 and 5. By the time Teddy was through the chicane, Simon was right back on him.

Man, why can't I shake this kid?

Allison followed Kayla relentlessly but never attacked. She just stayed glued to her tail wing—waiting for what? Teddy couldn't decide.

Then something occurred to him. Kayla was holding them up. For some reason, she was braking earlier than she needed to, causing a chain reaction. When she braked, Allison braked. And when Allison braked, he had to brake. That's why Simon kept catching him going into Turn 5. When Kayla braked early, Teddy lost whatever ground he'd managed to steal from Simon on the downhill stretch.

Why won't Allie take her? He prayed that she would make a move soon. Anything to shake them out of the pattern.

By Lap 15 it was clear that he'd have to do the shaking. He stomped on the gas on the way out of Turn 4. When Allison started to brake, he pushed on, leaning his car towards the inside line. He had no hope of passing—not here. But he hoped Allison would get the message.

There's more road here, Allie! Use it!

The next time around, he prepared to repeat the manoeuvre. This time, Allison beat him to it. She launched out of Turn 4 and immediately moved to Kayla's inside. She brought her front left tire alongside Kayla's rear right.

Come on! Come ON!

They sped towards the chicane.

Uh-oh—she's not going to make it.

Kayla braked first. With Teddy on her tail, Allison pushed a second longer than she should have. Her front tire struck Kayla's back, which sent Kayla off to the left, over the outside curb. Allison yanked the other way and braked. The momentum took her onto the grass on the inside.

Teddy didn't think. He slowed just enough to avoid hitting Allison and then steered smoothly around her.

Holy freaking . . . what the!

He frantically checked his mirror as he exited the chicane and headed onto the back straight.

His heart sank.

Simon was behind him, followed by Kayla and Allison.

He pounded his wheel in frustration.

She's going to kill me.

Teddy knew he had little chance of catching up to the top five in the remaining laps. *At least without anyone in front of me I can keep Simon at bay.* He settled in and tried to focus on the upside.

P6—that'll make Stew and Trev happy.

Once Stewart—and even Trevor—had slapped his back and offered congratulations, Teddy hurried back to the paddock. He was more than ready to finally hear what Allison had to say.

After what had happened on the track, though, he wasn't sure if she'd be any mood to talk to him.

He hadn't done anything wrong. Not exactly. He'd raced his race. *She has to understand that,* he thought. But he also knew that a bad race, however well fought, could put any driver in a funk. He couldn't just rush over to her trailer and demand she explain why she'd been acting so weird. *No, I'll act normally.* He decided to go back to his trailer, change his clothes, and get ready to leave. *I'll let her come to me.*

His plan made it as far as the paddock's entrance.

Nick Scott, Firebrand's head of marketing, was waiting for him.

"Teddy," Nick called out, as Teddy approached.

Teddy took a quick look around to see if he could conjure up an excuse to wave Nick off and move in another direction.

It was too late. Nick was walking towards him.

He wasn't alone. With him was a young woman with platinum blonde hair tied into a bun. Her complexion was fair, dappled with freckles. She looked familiar, but Teddy couldn't place from where.

His mind changed gears and started working on excuses to cut the interaction short.

"This is Teddy Clark," Nick said to the woman. "He's our wild-card entry from Canada."

Teddy stiffened.

Don't correct him. It's not worth it.

"Teddy, this is Claudia Smith, one of the track reporters for the series. She writes for *Road & Race*."

Ah—that's it.

"It's really great to meet you." Teddy smiled and shook her hand. He tried to pass off his eagerness to leave as enthusiasm to be there.

"I was hoping I could snag you for a few minutes to talk about the weekend?"

Teddy had his line ready: *Oh, I'd absolutely love to, but I really have to run. I'm so sorry.* But a glance from Nick made it clear that refusing her wasn't an option. He remembered what he'd told them during their media-engagement seminar on the first practice weekend. *"What you do on the track is only half the job."*

I see. This is a test.

"Sure thing," he said. "Fire away."

The interview was mercifully short, the questions predictable. Teddy had seen so many post-race interviews on TV growing up, he barely even had to think about his answers. "The car was great." "My crew is amazing." "A little excitement on the start." "I got really lucky on 16." "I can't thank Firebrand enough for this opportunity."

Teddy could see Nick checking off a list in his mind as he spoke. When they were finished, the man gave him a subtle thumbs-up.

That wasn't so bad, he thought, as he walked away. *It was actually kind of fun.*

Part of him wished he'd lingered a little longer. He found himself thinking of a dozen things he could have added—little details about his pass, a joke or two.

Teddy was so distracted by these reflections that he didn't notice Allison, sitting on the stool by his trailer, until he stepped under the canopy.

Her arms rested on her knees. Her hands were interlocked. She was trembling. Her eyes were pink but dry.

Is she upset about the race? About whatever she wants to tell me? Both? Neither?

He moved a little closer.

"Kayla's something else, eh?"

"Can we not talk about the race right now?"

OK, she's mad. Proceed with caution.

She looked at the ground.

"I'm going to tell you something, but I need you to promise not to freak out." Her knees started to bob.

Because that's something I can definitely promise.

"Sure . . ."

She took a deep breath and went still. She looked Teddy in the eye.

"Chet knows."

Teddy frowned, puzzled.

"Knows what?"

"Everything. He knows everything."

Chapter 19

"You've got to be kidding me." Leah pulled her legs onto the sofa and crossed them. She grabbed her ankles and leaned forward, eyes wide. "How did he find out about Graham?"

Teddy sank further into the cushions and folded his arms. He stared at the drum kit. The sunlight entering through the garage door's narrow windows landed on the band's equipment in dusty golden swathes chopped up by shadow.

"He hacked her computer," he said.

"He's a *hacker*?"

"Well, not actually hacked. I guess he knew her password or something. Anyway, it was all there. All our texts. All our emails. Everything."

Almost everything. Thank god Skype doesn't save video chats. Does it?

"What a creep. What was he looking for?"

"I don't even think he knew."

Teddy remembered the expression on Chet's face after the second practice. He knew exactly what Chet had been looking for. Not that he could tell Leah. After everything that had happened between them, telling her this much had been hard enough. But he'd promised her he'd try to be more open, and this felt like a step in the right direction.

"But he didn't, like, find anything, right?"

"Other than that I'm the son of a famous AmRun driver who died seventeen years ago? Nah. Not much."

Leah blushed and looked into her lap.

"You know what I mean."

Easy killer. She's being ridiculously cool about this.

Teddy reached out and placed a hand on hers.

"I'm sorry. No. There was nothing for him to find. We were just friends. We *are* just friends."

"So why is he so angry?"

Why were you?

The answer seemed obvious. Teddy was surprised Leah couldn't see it. He needed to choose his words carefully.

"I think he was surprised when he saw us together in Florida. I don't think he knew that we had, you know, history or whatever."

They sat in silence for a moment. Teddy watched the motes of dust in the air drift between light and darkness.

"There's something I still don't get."

Teddy wriggled in the sofa. He knew what was coming.

Leah spoke softly. "Why did you tell her about Graham in the first place? I mean, you've worked so hard to keep it a secret from everyone else."

Teddy felt a stab of guilt. He could see from Leah's expression what she was really worried about. *She's wondering what it means that I told Allison about my birth parents. Whether we're actually closer than I've been letting her think.*

But the truth was far more complicated, and it was tearing him up inside.

He hadn't told Allison anything. She'd figured it out for herself. It was Allison who revealed the whole story to Teddy. Even his parents didn't know that Allison was in the car that killed his birth mother.

The silence grew. Teddy kept his eyes on his hands, which were locked together on his lap.

Teddy wanted to tell Leah everything. She deserved to know everything. He knew that. And he'd already learned the cost of hiding things from her. He figured she could handle the truth, and that it might even help her to see better why Allison was so important to him, as a friend.

But to admit to having another secret, especially one involving Allison—it would destroy everything he'd done to patch things up over the last few months.

With no time left to weigh his options, Teddy finally made his decision.

"Actually, I didn't tell her. She figured it out for herself."

"Really?" Leah seemed as much stunned as relieved. "How the heck did she do that?"

"It wasn't that hard really, once she started looking. The racing community isn't all that big when you get down to it."

Leah nodded.

"I guess." She paused. "But why did she start looking?"

Moment of truth.

"She . . . was doing a project on Graham. For school."

He could feel the colour drain from his face. A vortex formed in his gut, an icy whirlpool that sucked up all his organs. Only a cold void was left inside him.

Leah laughed. "Wow," she said, shaking her head. "What are the odds?"

"Yeah." He shivered. "What are the odds?"

There was a loud knock. The garage's side door swung open. Richard, Tom, Ben, and Zana entered, nattering about something.

Leah hopped off the sofa.

"Oops!" said Tom, covering his eyes. "I hope we're not interrupting anything."

"Wait, wait." Ben ran over to the drum kit and, using his fingers, banged out a feeble rim shot.

The others groaned.

"Since you're there, why don't you give us a drumroll?" said Zana.

"A drumroll? What for?" asked Leah.

"Didn't you guys check your mail? The first acceptance letters arrived today."

"Rejection letters in Ben's case," said Tom.

Ben took the cushion off the stool behind the kit and threw it at Tom.

"I can't believe I forgot," said Leah. She turned to Teddy. "You should run home and check. Then come back and we can open them together."

She looked so excited, so happy. He thought about how different this moment would have been if he'd told her the truth.

"OK, sure."

Standing, Teddy heaved his backpack off the floor and onto his shoulder.

"Hurry back," Leah called, as Teddy walked out the door.

Well, that's it. I can never tell her the truth now.

He clutched himself as he walked. A wave of nausea moved in to fill the vacuum his lie had created.

The problem wasn't whether or not he could continue keeping the truth from Leah. The problem was that she might find out anyway. They'd been interrupted before he could tell her the worst part. If Teddy didn't stay away from Allison, Chet was going to tell everyone his secret.

Chapter 20

The letters had indeed arrived. Teddy thought his parents had taken the news reasonably well.

"A conditional acceptance is still an acceptance," his dad had said. "You'll just have to knuckle down during final exams."

His mother had stopped short of suggesting that he pull out of the series, but only just.

"Just remember what we agreed, Teddy, and prioritize accordingly. Have you considered going to the guidance councillor for advice?"

Teddy had shot down that idea immediately.

Have you considered burning your tongue on the stove?

"What about tutoring?"

Hey, how about boot camp?

"I don't need help," he'd explained. "I need time. Tutoring would just be one more thing to do."

"Maybe. But at least it would force you to stay on top of your homework."

He didn't have the strength to argue with her. "I'll think about it."

"Just don't think too long."

A ten-hour drive to Road America should just about do it, he'd thought. The next race was that weekend.

No way was he going to see a tutor. Not a chance. *If I can't get the grades I need for college, then I'd just better make sure I drive well enough to keep racing.*

He spent most of the trip to Elkhart Lake, Wisconsin, trying to convince his dad that everything was fine, that he didn't need extra help at school—and that he wasn't interested in talking about it anymore. By the time they arrived, Teddy had only persuaded him of the last. That was good enough for him.

They checked into their motel and walked to a road-house across the street for dinner.

"It's amazing how hungry sitting all day can make you," his dad said, carving off a thick chunk of his steak. "I can't believe tomorrow you'll be racing Road America." He smiled dreamily and shook his head. "That's something else."

Teddy dunked a potato wedge in the pool of ketchup on his plate and chomped down on it. "I know. And the best part is, it's one of my best tracks."

"What do you mean?"

"In *GP Pro*. The game."

His dad snorted. "Oh yeah. Right."

"Seriously, it's really accurate."

"Well then why did we bother with the trip? Coulda stayed home and saved on gas."

They plowed through their food, telling jokes and talking about racing. It felt almost as good as that first morning at Sebring. The stress, the anxiety, the doubts—everything that had been twisting him into knots for the last few months faded into the background, left in the pits.

Teddy felt himself melt into a contented drowsiness.

This!

The thought repeated itself over and over, like a favourite song on a loop.

Just . . . this!

Teddy arrived at the drivers' meeting feeling refreshed and alert. He walked to the table where Allison was sitting.

His heart sank.

She looked awful. Her skin was like newsprint, with two inky smudges beneath her eyes. Her dirty-blonde hair hung loosely around her face, looking more dirty than blonde. It was oily and matted, as if it had already spent thirty laps inside a helmet.

She tried to wave him off with her eyebrows and little flick of her head.

Teddy ignored it and took the seat next to her. She adjusted her chair, angling her body away from him.

The other drivers at the table fiddled with their phones, oblivious to the silent drama going on beside them.

When the meeting began, Teddy bumped his knee against hers under the table. Allison turned her head just enough for him to see her squint disapprovingly.

"You OK?" he mouthed silently.

She looked back to the front of the room.

Teddy slouched in his chair and crossed his arms. *All right. If that's how she wants to play this.*

The meeting finished and everyone got up to leave. Allison tugged at the back of Teddy's shirt as she stood. He walked slowly and Allison followed, letting the others pass them on their way out of the tent. Just inside the entrance they stopped.

"Can I turn around?" Teddy whispered, half-jokingly.

"Don't be a jerk," she said. "Anyway, are you nuts? What do you think you're doing?"

Teddy faced her. "What? I wanted to talk to you. You look . . . I was worried."

"I'm not the one you should be worried about."

His mind snapped to attention. "Why, is Chet here?"

"No. But that's not the point. We need to be careful. If it got back to him—"

"Who's gonna tell him? Seriously."

"I *am* being serious, Teddy. If Chet finds out I was talking to you—"

"This is insane. Not calling or texting is one thing. But it's not like we can ignore each other at every race."

"Well we have to try. At least until I can figure out something else. I'm trying to protect *you*, you know."

Her words felt like a slap in the face. His cheeks reddened with shame. Allison looked so tired, so worried—and it was all for him. All to keep his secret from getting out.

He placed his hands on her shoulders. "You're right. I'm sorry."

Allison's eyes widened and she pulled away sharply.

"What?"

He heard the glass door open behind him. He spun around.

Kyle and Kayla entered the suite. "Hi guys," said Kyle.

"Hi," Allison and Teddy said together.

The twins smiled warmly.

"We just wanted to grab a couple bottles of apple juice before practice," said Kyle.

"We don't have any at our trailer," Kayla explained.

"Don't you just love apple juice?" said Kyle. He didn't wait for a reply. The twins walked right past them and headed towards the refreshments table.

Well, that was . . . what the heck was that?

"I guess you guys are running a pretty low wing angle this weekend, eh?"

Arms folded, Teddy's dad leaned over Trevor's shoulder. The mechanic stayed focused on the table in front of him, pretending to work on a spare part.

"That's the plan," Trevor said. His tone was strained, almost curt.

Teddy listened to the conversation from the pit wall as he laid out his gear. He smirked. His dad had been amiably grilling the man all morning, asking him about setups and gearing and tire pressures and whatever else occurred to him. Why he'd chosen to play twenty questions with the mechanic, Teddy couldn't understand. It must have been obvious to his dad that Stewart would have been happier to chat with him than Trevor. *Maybe he sees Trev as a challenge—a nut to crack.*

"Strangers are just friends you haven't made yet," he always said.

You'll need a sledgehammer for that one, Teddy thought. Not that he minded. He cheered a little inside as the mechanic's face grew increasingly crimson. He knew his dad could handle Trevor, even if the man was having trouble handling himself.

In fact, his dad had a point. Teddy knew that on a track like Road America, you did want to run a low angle. It was just over four miles of almost nonstop straightaways spread over 640 acres. Half of the turns were little more than kinks in the road. There were only a few real turns, and Teddy had already picked his favourite. Turn 12 wasn't especially exciting or technical. He just liked the name: Canada Corner.

In the practice and qualifying sessions that morning, Teddy had experienced speed like he'd never imagined. Screaming up the Road America Straight, on the front side of the course, was like flying a jet. A four-thousand-foot uphill strip. Gas pedal pinned to the floor. G-force plastering his heart, lungs, and guts against his spine. Each second an eternity more exhilarating than the last.

It was pure motion.

After the practice, Teddy had insisted they reduce the downforce, even though Trevor and Stewart were concerned about sacrificing control in the hard corners that bookended the straightaways. "Look, I can handle it, OK?" Teddy assured them. He had no idea if he could. But his run-in with Allison had dimmed the glow of the previous evening. He hoped that faking a little confidence might fire it back up.

It had worked. It had taken everything he had to keep the car on the track through the turns, but he'd been rewarded on the straights. He would start the race in P3—right behind the twins and ahead of LeGuivre.

Allison was having a rough day. She'd only squeaked into the top ten. Teddy couldn't help feeling at least partly responsible. They'd barely spoken since the last race, so he had no idea what she was going through at home. But it was a safe bet that Chet was making her life miserable. And it seemed that the twins had thrown her for a loop when they walked in on their conversation. But as much as he wanted to, he couldn't help her. All he could do was stay away. He pushed it down as deep as he could and tried to focus on the race.

I can't solve this now. Gotta compartmentalize. Right, Doc?

The cars completed their parade lap and formed up. Cruising onto the front straight, Teddy accelerated. The sense of freedom he'd felt earlier was nowhere to be found. He felt only the weight of the cars behind him, like a great wave eager to smash him on the rocks.

The green flag dropped. *Oh god, I hope this works.* The cars sped along the remaining stretch of the straight. LeGuivre pulled up along his left-hand side, while the car in P5 snuck around to his right in an attempt to steal the inside. He couldn't pull away—he was trapped.

Teddy braked hard. He needed to shave off as much speed as possible if he had any chance of holding his line through the first turn. He watched as the car on his right held on a fraction of a second longer and pulled ahead.

There's no way he can make that, he thought—he hoped.

But it did. The car hugged the inside curb, stealing the racing line from Teddy, who was now stuck taking a slow course through the middle of the turn.

While he was cursing the car that had taken him on the inside, he failed to notice LeGuivre attacking him on the outside until he'd sailed past him as well.

No, no, no!

Teddy stayed boxed in the middle of the track as the next car in line pushed up on his right. Again, the inside line was Teddy's to lose. And again, he lost it.

In two turns he'd lost three positions. He punched his steering wheel.

Stay cool—you'll get them back on the straights.

He finally took the proper racing line on his way towards Turn 5. He pushed the car in front of him through the almost nonexistent Turn 4 without lifting his foot off the gas at all.

But he lost ground again as he crawled through the next pair of right angle corners. He sensed the pressure mounting once more as the line of cars behind him inched closer.

I just need to hold them until 10, he thought. *Then I can really open up.*

He swung around the wide arc of Turn 9, the Carousel, and prepared to floor it.

The back straight opened up before him, interrupted by only a small kink at Turn 11. He slammed his foot on the gas.

It was like the cars in front of him hit their brakes all at once. They grew bigger with each passing second.

This is what I'm talking about!

Adrenaline surged through him. He took a deep breath. He couldn't believe how quickly he was gaining ground. As he positioned himself for a pass halfway down the straight, he realized that his sudden advantage wasn't due to his car or his abilities—a yellow flag had dropped. Everyone was slowing down. No passing was allowed.

Teddy cursed in his helmet.

He watched for wrecks as the line of cars worked its way back to the start of the course. Nothing.

Just my luck.

If the incident had occurred in front of him, he might have grabbed a spot or two for free. Instead, he'd have to dig in where he was, in P6, wait for the track to clear, and prepare for another restart.

Unfortunately, the laps under yellow still counted. The clock continued to run. He could feel his chances to retake his position fall away like sand through an hourglass.

Despite his disappointment, when he finally reached the crash site, Teddy heaved a sigh of relief. Neither of the two cars involved belonged to Allison.

Teddy steeled himself for the restart. Again, the cars behind him got the edge on the first two turns, and he lost another two spots.

Oh, come on! Give me a freaking break! Teddy struggled to keep his cool. The car fought him through the turns. He attacked the straights viciously, almost recklessly. Lap after lap, he'd recover ground only to lose it again on the few turns where the missing downforce compelled him to decelerate earlier than the cars around him. Just holding on to his position was exhausting.

When the checkered flag dropped, he fought back a scream.

Chapter 21

Trees and fields. Fields and trees. They passed like images in a zoetrope. Teddy watched sombrely.

The weekend had ended in disaster.

After the first race, Teddy had returned to the pits with his tail between his legs. His dad wore an expression of disappointment mixed with sympathy. Stewart seemed merely disappointed. Trevor looked disgusted. The mechanic said nothing, but Teddy could tell what he was thinking. "How'd that setup work out for you, champ?"

Teddy tried to make the best of it, to chalk it up as a learning experience. He acknowledged his mistake and let his team change the car back to the original setup for the second race.

It hadn't mattered. He'd qualified sixth but never made it past the first turn. The car in seventh made a reckless dive for the inside line, clipped Teddy's back tire, and sent him careening off the track. The damage to the car was minor but enough to take him out of the race. He'd been forced to watch the rest of it from the pits.

The drive home was quiet. After a few failed attempts to lift Teddy's spirits, his dad took the hint and turned to the radio for company instead.

They arrived home Monday evening. Teddy dropped his bags on his bedroom floor and sat at his desk. He hadn't opened his backpack all weekend. He could feel the mounds of homework it contained waiting for him patiently, like a malevolent spirit lurking in the shadows.

His phone dinged. It was Richard.

Teddy smiled. *He must have finally got himself a new phone.*

"Hey man, how'd the wknd go?"

"Could have been better."

"Sorry to hear it. U didn't miss much at school. Lol"

"Lol"

Teddy heard his dad call up from the kitchen. He walked over to the door.

"Yeah?" Teddy yelled.

"I'm thinking we should order in tonight. Nothing in the fridge. Any requests?"

Teddy's phone dinged again.

"Wanna hit the plex tn? New Bond is out."

"Teddy? Hello?" his dad shouted.

Teddy glanced at his backpack. His stomach turned.

"I think I might catch a movie with Richard, actually. So don't worry about me."

"Oh," said his dad. A moment passed. "OK then."

Teddy texted Richard. "I'm in."

What Richard—and only Richard—called "the plex" was more than just a movie theatre. It was an entertainment compound. It had themed restaurants (New York–style

Italian dive, 1950s diner, Australian barbecue), pubs, an indoor glow-in-the-dark mini-golf course, and a laser tag facility. All clustered next to a sprawling parking lot just off the highway. The theatre itself had twenty screens, spread out over three wings. It was designed with a spaceship theme—pinpoint LED lights scattered across blue-black ceilings and industrial tubing painted in a shimmering metallic grey running in all directions. Flashy arcade games filled little alcoves throughout the building.

Dinner consisted of nacho chips heaped with salsa and a warm orange-yellow goo that everyone happily pretended was cheese. Richard also went for the optional jalapeño slices.

"Gotta get my veggies in," he said, as they strolled down the corridor.

"You need all the help you can get," said Teddy. "Clearly your brain is vitamin deficient. I mean, Timothy Dalton? Seriously? Connery, I can understand. But Dalton?"

"Whatever, Brosnan boy." Richard placed a dripping chip into his mouth.

"I'm sorry? What was that? *GoldenEye* is a classic? I couldn't agree more."

After the movie they went to Demetres for waffles and ice cream.

A cute girl about their age arrived with their order. She gave Richard a shy smile. He grinned back at her and shifted a lock of hair behind his ear. He held her gaze for a second before turning his attention to the dessert.

"Delicious," he said.

Teddy raised an eyebrow. Richard wasn't like Tom—he didn't chase every girl he saw. He didn't need to. He had that sort of laid-back slacker vibe that girls seemed to like. But he rarely did anything about it. Seeing him flirt with the waitress made Teddy uneasy. They'd been friends forever, but he couldn't stop himself from wondering if Richard ever looked at Leah that way.

The bell rang, and Teddy started packing his bag.

"Teddy, a word please."

He gave Richard a look that said, "Kill me now," before glancing up at his teacher.

"Yes, Mrs. Gottlieb?"

"Do you have something for me?"

He swallowed nervously.

"I'm sorry, Mrs. Gottlieb, I didn't have a chance to finish it."

The teacher removed her glasses and squinted.

"You've already had an extra day. Everyone else managed to get their essays in yesterday."

Everyone else wasn't making cross-border road trips to go racing.

"I know, I'm sorry. I'll have it tomorrow. I promise."

"Teddy, I'm trying to be accommodating, but you need to keep up your end."

Accommodating. Right.

He looked at her blankly.

"Well, how did you do?" she asked.

Teddy was stunned. She'd never shown any interest in his racing before.

"Um, well, I . . . not great. I mean, I qualified well in the first race but—"

She cut him off. "I'm sorry to hear that. But you know what they say about trying to talk while you're chewing."

Huh?

"It's rude?"

She put her glasses back on and turned towards her desk.

"If you try to do both at once, you'll end up doing neither very well."

And there it is.

"Right."

"Tomorrow, Teddy."

He stormed out of the classroom. Richard was waiting for him in the hallway. Leah jogged up to them.

"Hey! Tom, Ben, and Zana are skipping fourth period. Wanna come to Subway with us?"

"Sounds delicious," said Richard. "I'll drive."

Teddy cringed. He desperately wanted to go, but he'd exaggerated slightly when he told Mrs. Gottlieb he hadn't finished his essay. He hadn't even started it.

"Actually, I think I'd better hit the library."

Leah put a hand on his shoulder. Her mouth fell into an almost cartoonish frown.

"Oh, no. Please come. You can study after school. Come over to my place. I'll help." Her lips reversed course, and her teeth joined the battle.

Teddy's heart fluttered.

"Well, I guess—"

"How's that gonna work?" asked Richard. "We're rehearsing, aren't we? I mean, the show's on Friday."

"Ugh, right." Leah shook her head. "Sorry, Teddy. Well, you should definitely get your work done then. You're still coming right?"

"Uh . . ."

Oh crap. The talent show. He'd completely forgotten.

"You promised you'd come." Leah's expression shifted again. The sweetness of her tone was cut with a hint of something scolding, even threatening.

"Yeah, of course," Teddy said. "Obviously."

"Great. Well go get your work done so you won't have any excuses."

She kissed him on the cheek then took off down the hallway with Richard. Teddy watched them go. His chest tightened.

He trudged straight to the library, skipping the cafeteria altogether.

Teddy waited in line for tickets.

His neck and back ached. Over the last few days, he'd spent every hour he wasn't in class in the library, or hunched over his desk at home. But the aches were nothing compared to the relief he felt. It wasn't because it was the weekend, or because he'd managed to catch up on the work he'd missed. Tonight was the school's talent show. The night the gang had been working towards for months. After this, he figured, they'd take a break. No more rehearsals after school. No more talking about lyrics and chord changes at lunch. He was relieved because after tonight, things might go back to normal. Or as close to normal as they had been back in the fall.

He looked around at the other people in line. The girls from the hockey team. Some kids from last year's drama class. The guy who always wore chunky Doc Martins and a black trench coat, even in the summer. It occurred to him that he didn't really know any of them beyond their names. His friends were all backstage.

"Hey, no cutting," a short freckly girl behind him huffed.

"Relax, I was here before. I just went to the bathroom," said Justin, sidling up to Teddy.

Teddy had no idea where Justin had come from, but he was fairly certain it wasn't the bathroom. And he was entirely certain Justin hadn't been in line with him before.

"I'm back," he announced, winking at Teddy.

Teddy felt both surprised and grateful to have company.

"Oh good." Teddy grinned. "I was about to send out a search party." He leaned in and lowered his voice. "I thought you couldn't make it."

"You think I'd miss a chance to see Ben choke in public?"

Teddy rolled his eyes. *Poor Ben.*

The line advanced.

Two tenth graders manned the ticket table. They looked harried, busily shuffling money into a silver box and tidying up the stack of tickets next to it.

"That'll be five dollars each ple—" The girl looked up. "Oh, Teddy, right?"

Teddy furrowed his brow. "Uh, yeah. I'm sorry, I've forgotten your name."

"Oh, it's Candice. Don't worry, there's no reason you should know me."

OK, but how do you know me?

"Here," said Candice, passing him an envelope. "One of the performers left this for you. Leah? Your girlfriend?" She blushed as Teddy took the envelope. Inside was a ticket with a little heart drawn on it.

"Lucky man," said Justin. "How do I get me one of those?"

"What, a girlfriend?"

Justin smacked the back of Teddy's head.

"You could pay me five dollars," said Candice.

The boys looked at her for a second. She blinked. Then they burst out laughing.

"What?" she asked, a concerned look on her face.

Justin handed her the money and helped himself to a ticket.

They were still giggling when they took seats near the back of the auditorium. The windowless walls muffled the sounds of the crowd outside but amplified the chatter of the people around them. Translucent paper of various colours covered the lights, giving the room a vaguely smoky atmosphere.

Then the lights dimmed and a spotlight appeared on the stage. The emcee walked up to the centre microphone. He wore torn blue jeans and a T-shirt meant to look like a tuxedo. Teddy recognized him from trigonometry class. Roger Epsom.

He and Justin snickered.

"Are you guys ready to rock?"

The crowd cheered.

"Is he for real?" said Justin.

A woman in front of them turned around and *shh*'d.

"Sorry!" Teddy raised his hands apologetically.

Roger continued. "We have a great lineup for you tonight. But first, a round of applause for our judges!" He made an elaborate gesture towards the front row. The spotlight swung over and landed on three teachers holding clipboards. They turned and waved awkwardly at the audience. "These fine people will be deciding the winner of tonight's . . ." Roger clasped the mic with both hands and dropped his voice into a raspy bass. "Talent Showdown!"

More cheers rose from the crowd.

"Does he know this isn't a wrestling match?" asked Justin.

"The victors will not only live on forever in glory, they will also be invited to play at the most prestigious, the most exclusive, the most anticipated event of the year . . ."

Wait, what?

". . . the Senior. Spring. Formal!" Roger held the last word for an obnoxiously long time. The crowd, dutifully, went wild.

Teddy's spine snapped to attention. "Did you know about this?" he asked Justin.

"I knew Roger was a little nuts. I had no idea he was raving mad."

"No, I mean about the formal."

"Sure. Why? Didn't you?"

Teddy racked his brain. Had Leah mentioned it? He couldn't remember. A sinking feeling washed over him.

Oh, man. What if they win? They'll be holed up in that garage another month.

"You OK?"

"Yeah, fine."

One by one the bands performed their sets. Most of them played covers. One group of kids from the symphonic band had formed a chamber orchestra, and they played a weird fusion of classical and pop songs. Another girl alternated between singing and playing the trumpet. And (of course) there was an a cappella group called The Prime Minstrels. Justin gagged audibly when they introduced themselves. Teddy didn't think they were half-bad, but he wondered if they'd be better if they spent a little more time practicing their songs and a little less time practicing their choreography.

Meh. I could dance better. The thought surprised him. *Where did that come from?*

Then Ben took his place behind the drums. Leah and Zana stood in front of him to the right, Richard to the left. Teddy and Justin cheered and whooped.

Tom stepped up to the front of the stage. He stood silently for a moment, holding the microphone with one hand, head hanging, eyes closed. The crowd went silent.

Then Tom raised his head. "We are . . ." He paused. "Trending Fury!"

Before the crowd could react, Ben raised his drumsticks and counted them in with animalistic flair.

They launched into their first number. Teddy hummed along. He knew the songs only because he'd heard them in Leah's garage. Unlike the other cover bands, Richard had chosen songs by lesser-known, indie artists: The Emersons, Ainslie Woods, The Oof-Mas.

Justin leaned in. "Did you know they were this good?"

Teddy smiled. "Kinda, yeah."

"Huh." Justin looked a little disappointed.

Teddy watched Leah sway to the beat as she sang.

She really is good, he thought. His skin started to tingle with pride.

They all looked like they were having a blast. Ben wore a manic grin as he looked back and forth between the drums and the audience. Tom couldn't stop wiggling his hips. Richard seemed the most focused, his eyes fixed on his hands as his head bobbed lazily. When Leah started the next chorus, Richard looked up at her. And she looked back, smiling.

Teddy's heart froze.

Was that? Did they? No. No way.

Chapter 22

Teddy's head was buzzing. His knees bounced rapidly. His body pulsed back and forth in the seat. The belt dug into his neck each time, imprinting a raw red line. He moved as if he thought his momentum could push the car to move faster. But nothing he did made a difference. He wasn't in control.

"Almost there," his dad said, keeping his eyes on the road.

Teddy didn't need to be told. He could see for himself. Their destination loomed in front of them like a monument. An eighth wonder of the world. Thick girders rose from the ground like steel monoliths. These were connected at the top by the lip of a great wall of metal slats that cascaded down and inwards, away from the road. It was like a stepped pyramid flipped on its point—a pyramid without corners. An elliptical rampart of metal and concrete that stretched for a mile before curving back on itself.

They'd travelled only half of the massive building's length when Teddy's dad turned the car towards it. The road dipped sharply, leading them under an archway and through a dim tunnel supported by rows of cement columns. As they crested the slope on the other side, a white building appeared in front of them atop a grassy mound. It was plain-looking but solid. A two-storey box with tall narrow windows spaced evenly across its face. A row of flagpoles stood guard in front. A different flag flew from each pole. Red, yellow, white, black, checkered—the language of the race track.

Teddy's eyes widened.

He and his dad said nothing. The hum of the engine filled the car.

Teddy read the bold black words fixed on the building's façade. They were too simple, he thought. Too prosaic. They couldn't begin to capture the history, the tradition. This was St. Peter's Cathedral. This was Mecca. The Temple Mount and Bodh Gaya. The spiritual home of every driver.

INDIANAPOLIS MOTOR SPEEDWAY
RACING CAPITAL OF THE WORLD

His dad broke the silence. "I hope we'll have time to check out the Hall of Fame."

Teddy made a sound that was more like a purr than a word.

They followed the signs to the paddock. Several helpers in bright yellow shirts waved them along. Teddy shivered a little when he stepped out of the car. It was early morning still. The sun had yet to break its second dawn over the track's high walls.

"I'm gonna wander around a bit. See you after the meeting?"

"No prob," said Teddy.

Stewart and Trevor were already at their posts when he reached the trailer—Trevor hunched over the car, Stewart transfixed by a laptop perched on a tool chest. They didn't notice him until he spoke.

"Morning." His voice cracked. He hadn't felt this nervous since his first day at Rock Point.

The others looked up.

"You're here early," Trevor said.

"Wasn't sure what traffic would be like," Teddy replied.

"Well it's good you came now," Stewart said. "Give it another hour and Georgetown Road will be a parking lot."

Teddy knew the crowd wasn't coming for him or the other Firebrand drivers. They were coming for the big show—the AmRun Pro American Grand Prix. Every track he'd raced on this season was used by the pro series. But today he'd be sharing the track with legends. In a few hours his tires would be laying down rubber that the pros would later use for grip. By tomorrow, he'd be driving on a racing line carved by his heroes.

Teddy felt dizzy, nauseated. He stepped forward and placed a hand on the wall for support.

"There's juice and granola bars inside if you don't feel like going to hospitality," said Stewart.

"Thanks," said Teddy. "Do you guys need me for anything before the drivers' meeting?"

Stewart looked at him and smiled. "I think we've got it covered. You just focus on getting your head on straight."

Teddy floated through the morning in a daze. The drivers' meeting, the prequalifying briefing with his team, even conversations with his dad—everything seemed to happen at a distance, like watching TV with the sound down low. It wasn't an unpleasant sensation, but as qualifying approached he started to worry that he wasn't going to be able to focus.

I'll take the long way to the pits, he thought. *Maybe the walk will clear my head.*

First he headed for the garage area, a block of four long concrete buildings. Inside the bays, the pro teams were busy attending to the cars. Outside, fans were gathered in little clusters. Some snapped pictures. Others wandered the rows, clutching programs, hats, T-shirts, and felt-tipped markers, hoping for a chance encounter with a driver who'd be willing to give them an autograph. Teddy smiled, remembering how he used to camp out for hours at the paddock in Toronto every year.

He made his way towards the Pagoda Plaza, a loose grouping of pavilions that served cold drinks, greasy food, and merchandise of every conceivable variety. He turned and looked up. Six tiers of glass, steel, and concrete towered over him, each level a bit smaller than the one below. The Pagoda. The speedway's inner temple. The keep inside the castle walls. From there, VIP guests, reporters and television commentators, and even the president of the speedway himself would be watching the day's events. Banners hung on the wall of the building's base level, each one displaying an AmRun Pro driver. Some had their arms crossed and wore grim, determined looks. Others stood with their hands on their hips and had wide smiles that would have made them seem approachable if they weren't fifty feet tall.

Teddy started to feel dizzy again. *This isn't working*, he thought.

He turned his face to the ground and hurried towards pit lane, his helmet swinging by his side.

It took another hour for Teddy to feel like himself again—right about the time he got out of the car. As he stepped onto the tarmac, his qualifying run already felt like a distant memory. He wished it would fade away altogether.

He'd started shaking the moment he entered the pits. Waves of nausea had washed over him as Stewart strapped him into the car. By the time he was hitting his first fast lap, all he could think was: *Don't puke. Don't puke.* Still, it could have been worse. The races that weekend were on the in-field road course—not the historic oval. If he'd had to deal with the g-forces of nonstop straightaways and left-hand turns for half an hour straight, it would have been barf city. And that's assuming he didn't just stuff it in the wall. It felt like a miracle he'd managed to qualify where he did, in P10.

Stewart and Trevor started grilling him before he'd removed his helmet. He'd been mostly silent on the radio during the session, and they were eager to identify any adjustments they could make before the race.

But Teddy couldn't take it. He threw up his hands and walked away. He knew it was a childish thing to do, but it felt easier than admitting the truth—he had nothing. The whole run had been a blur. He wasn't even sure how he'd kept the car on the track. There was no way he could make any suggestions to improve it. It was like his instincts had taken over the driving the moment his foot hit the gas pedal. His mind had been a spectator. Barely even that. He'd never experienced anything like it.

It was just too embarrassing to put into words.

Teddy caught a glimpse of the confused look on his dad's face as he scooted past him and left the pits. He needed to cool off before he could talk about what had happened. His first thought was to go to Allison's trailer. She'd qualified behind him, in P14.

Maybe we can just sit and stew silently together, he thought.

But he scrapped the idea immediately. Chet had flown in with her for the weekend. He'd have to give her a wide berth.

Instead, he dashed into his trailer, swapped his helmet and gloves for his wallet, and made his way to the Pagoda Plaza.

No one will think to look for me there, he thought. And now that his nausea had passed, he was famished.

It was still a little before noon, so the plaza was busy but not packed. Teddy sat down at an empty table near the merchandise tent. He worked away at his lunch almost mechanically, alternating between mouthfuls of soggy French fries and long swigs of soda. He watched the people milling around, buying snacks or shopping for T-shirts and knick-knacks. He thought about all the races he'd been to growing up. Seeing the cars up close or catching a glimpse of a driver whizzing by on a golf cart had filled him with pure excitement. The drivers never seemed exactly real. Whenever he got to meet one, it was like meeting a character from a movie—not the actor but the actual character. Like seeing James Bond killing time until the next supervillain threatened to blow up London. Or Wonder Woman telling fans the story about the last time she'd saved the world. He hadn't realized then that they weren't just drivers, they were also people. People whose lives were probably as messed up as his felt.

Teddy was finishing up his lunch when he noticed a young boy tugging at his father's shirt and pointing in his direction. It took him a second to realize the boy was pointing at him.

Duh. I'm still wearing my race suit.

He recognized the look on the boy's face. He was screwing up the courage to come over to him.

He doesn't see me *though*, Teddy thought. *Just the suit. The circus. I'm nobody. Just another clown.*

He gathered the remains of his lunch, tossed them in a trash bin, and walked briskly back to the trailer. He found the car sitting on the pad. His team wasn't there.

He was alone.

Chapter 23

"He's coming up on your left." Stewart's voice was steady, but Teddy could sense his engineer's frustration. He was about to lose his second spot and they were barely two laps into the race.

Teddy took a breath. *It's still early*, he thought. *There's time to make it back.*

He whipped past the Pagoda. He knew that whoever was inside was probably enjoying a buffet lunch or the open bar. Not watching the junior-level race below them. Still, he felt scrutinized, as if the building itself were watching him, judging him.

Teddy forced the thought from his mind, gritted his teeth, and focused on the approaching turn. He prepared to brake.

The car that had just passed him was already pulling away. He had a clean entrance to the corner. It was hardly a comfort. He'd have to work hard to close the distance again before he could reclaim the spot. But he was convinced that it was just nerves slowing him down. He took the opportunity to try to find his rhythm without the pressure of being head-to-head with another driver.

Teddy pulled his car to the right, off the main oval and onto the infield track. The second turn, a hard left, came almost immediately. There was no space to build up speed. He could feel the car in front of him gaining distance. It was visceral, painful—like having a nail pulled slowly from his finger.

He steered back to the right around Turns 3 and 4. He knew his line wasn't clean, but he was anxious to get through the kink in the track formed by Turns 5 and 6 and onto the back straightaway, where he could finally put his foot down again. Two car-lengths now separated Teddy from the driver ahead of him, but the gap had stopped growing.

Well, that's something, at least.

They manoeuvred through the kink and entered the back straightaway.

Dammit!

The car in front had started to pull away again.

"Careful," said Stewart. "It looks like you braked early entering 5, there."

Teddy clenched his jaw. "Thanks."

Between practice and qualifying, he'd spent an hour on the track already that day. But it felt as if he were driving it for the first time. He struggled to hit his marks and stick to the line. As the car in front of him gained more and more ground he took a moment to check his rearview. The car behind him was a ways back. Teddy breathed a sigh of relief.

At least I'm not being pushed along.

He wondered how Allison was making out.

For the next twenty minutes Teddy continued to fight. By the time he managed to find and hold the line, the car ahead of him had gathered a commanding lead. The cars behind him had disappeared altogether. When he crossed the finish line, there wasn't another car in sight.

After the race, Stewart tried to console him. "Any day you walk away from the track is a good day. And any day you don't put it in the wall is a great day for us."

Teddy forced a smile. "Thanks. I'll see you tomorrow."

Allison intercepted him and his dad on their way back to the trailer.

"Hey guys, wait up!"

Teddy froze and quickly scanned the area. Allison made a subtle "all clear" gesture.

"Not a great day for anyone, eh, Miss Reading?"

"Oh, I don't know about that," she said. "Alex and the twins seem to be having a good weekend so far."

"They do have a knack for finding their way to the podium, don't they?"

Teddy shot his dad a look.

"Well, why don't you guys compare notes," his dad said, reading the expression on Teddy's face. "I'll see you back at the trailer, sport."

When Teddy was sure his dad was out of earshot, he turned to Allison.

"Are you crazy?"

"It's OK," she said. "Chet's waiting for me back at the hospitality suite. I told him I had a media thing to do."

"Yeah, well, here." Teddy ducked behind a nearby vendor's stall and indicated for her to follow.

"Your dad's right," she said. "Crappy day."

Feeling more comfortable now that they had some cover, Teddy relaxed a little. "You can say that again. You didn't make it out of P14, eh?"

"Honestly, I've been a wreck all weekend," she said. "My team thinks we got the tire pressures wrong, but I know my head just wasn't there. This whole Chet thing . . ."

"Tell me about it. So what's the big emergency?"

Allison faltered. "I don't know. I just . . . I just wanted to see you."

Teddy felt a rush of warmth. He'd been eager to see her, too. But he was also annoyed that she'd taken the risk.

"We need to be more careful," he said.

They stood silently for a moment, watching the people strolling around the stalls.

Then Allison sighed. "Teddy, do you think that maybe it would be better if you just told everyone yourself? Or, like, just accept that the truth will come out? Take away Chet's power over you? Over us?"

"You're kidding me, right?" *I'm still trying to figure all this out for myself.*

"I'm not. I mean, at this point, wouldn't it just be better to have it out there? Wouldn't you rather not have it hanging over your head?"

"That's not the point, Allie, and you know it. It's my secret to share, no one else's."

"OK, but then why not share it? I get that it's not what you want right now, but you can't keep this a secret forever."

I can try. "Why not? It's not like anyone is looking into Graham's accident or what happened to his son. It was years ago. You're probably the only other person who would care anyway—and you already know."

"Well then?"

Teddy didn't know how to explain it to her. More than that, he didn't want to try. He didn't want to put his fears into words. He grew angry with Allison for making him try.

"Maybe you haven't noticed, but I'm not exactly having a great season here," he said.

"Teddy the season's not even half over. And what difference does that make anyway?"

"It makes all the difference. Think about what would happen if word got out. Everyone would start comparing me to Graham. I'm barely holding on as it is."

"Maybe, maybe not. But did you stop to consider that keeping it a secret isn't doing you any favours either? Especially now that it might come out anyway. Wouldn't it be better just to have it off your mind?"

Teddy looked away. He watched the stands on the far side of the track start to fill up for the big race.

"Look, I'm scared, all right? Is that what you want to hear? I'm terrified that I'll screw up. That I'll . . ." He began to choke up. "That I'll let them down."

She stepped closer and hugged him from behind. Teddy felt her warmth on his back. He inhaled the scent of grease and sweat wafting up from her suit.

"I understand, Teddy. But you're not alone. Just remember that, OK?"

Teddy turned to face her. His eyes glistened.

"OK," he said. "Thanks."

"Don't mention it." She kissed him on the cheek. He felt his whole body swell. "Dork."

Teddy was still buzzing as he walked back to his trailer. Allison had given him a head start so they wouldn't be seen walking together. Three men stood near the entrance to the paddock talking. Teddy recognized the owner and head strategist for one of the big AmRun teams. The third man was Trevor.

Trevor stopped talking as Teddy approached and pretended not to see him as he passed.

Well, that was weird, he thought.

When he arrived at the trailer he found his dad chatting with Stewart about the day.

"What do you think, sport? Stew was just suggesting they might try playing with the wing angles tomorrow."

"Sure, whatever you think," he said, heading for the trailer door. He stepped inside and paused. "Maybe the tire pressures, too."

Teddy laid out his gear on the retaining wall. He'd forgotten to perform the ritual the day before. He tried to convince himself that this was the real reason for his disappointing performance. The ritual had done the trick in the morning practice session. His times had been much better than they'd been the previous day, and he hadn't even been pushing the car as hard as he thought he could.

Feeling optimistic, he donned his balaclava, helmet, and gloves and jumped into the car.

Stewart leaned in. "We've made a few adjustments, but it's basically the same setup as this morning. So just keep doing what you were doing. Plus, you know, a bit more. If you can." He winked at Teddy and hopped back over the pit wall.

Teddy liked this Stewart better than the one he'd been working with for the last couple of months. He seemed to be enjoying himself for the first time since they met.

The warm-up laps were smooth and quick. His first two fast laps were lightning. *I'll put down a third for good measure*, he thought. As his times popped up on the steering wheel's display, his confidence soared. They were among the best times anyone had set all weekend. When the session ended Teddy popped out of the car and perched himself on the retaining wall to watch the rest of the session. He tried not to get too excited. Not yet. LeGuivre and the twins still had to do their qualifying runs, and they would certainly put whatever they'd learned the day before into their setups today. But as the session went on and the times came in, Teddy almost bounced on the spot. Only one driver qualified in front of him—Allison.

The excitement was almost more than he could bear. Before Stewart could even finish saying "P2!" Teddy was already hugging him. Even Trevor seemed pleased, though there was a strange look in his eye that Teddy couldn't read. *Maybe he's regretting doubting me*, he thought.

Teddy's dad stepped up and pulled him in.

"What? Too good for the pole?" he joked.

"Thought I should leave something for the race," said Teddy. "Wouldn't be much of a show if I won from the front."

"Go grab a snack and rest a bit," Stewart said. "We need you fresh and ready."

"Oh, I'll be ready."

Teddy bolted back to the trailer. Once the door was closed behind him he clenched his fists and screamed. He paced the narrow space inside, punching the air. He couldn't believe it. He was going to start on the front row at the Indianapolis Motor Speedway. Whatever happened during the race, no one could take that away from him.

OK, gotta stay calm. This isn't over yet. It hasn't even started.

Teddy dug into his jeans for his phone and started texting the news to everyone he could think of. His mom. Matt. Leah and the gang. Soon, "Congrats" texts started to come in. Teddy replied to each of them. He offered little details about the run, and swapped jokes with Matt and the guys. "I'm so proud of you," his mom wrote. "I knew you could do it," said Leah.

"I haven't done it yet," he replied. "But it's a start!"

Teddy was startled by a bang on the wall.

"Teddy?"

He put down his phone and opened the door.

His dad was holding a bagel wrapped in a napkin. "Here," he said, offering it up. "Rescued this from hospitality. It's not Tim Hortons, but it might do the trick."

"Thanks." Teddy took the bagel and devoured it. The look on his dad's face fell somewhere between amusement and disgust. He handed Teddy a bottle of orange juice.

"Here," he said. "In case you find time between bites."

Teddy replied with a tight-lipped grin. A large chunk of bagel dangling from the side of his mouth lost its grip and made its acquaintance with asphalt.

"Be ready in twenty, OK?"

Teddy nodded and retreated into the trailer. He polished off the juice in two long swigs then dragged his gear bag into the middle of the floor and shaped it into a pillow. He popped in his earbuds, laid down on the floor, and closed his eyes. The music started to pulse through his body. A simple guitar riff. Then an organ.

Teddy's feet twitched.

Left, right. Left, right. Like a pair of skiers carving figure eights into fresh powder, Teddy and Allison wove a braid over the racing line. The rhythmic movement around the track warmed Teddy's tires and centred his mind. He melted into the car. Its vibrations became his heartbeat. The steering wheel and pedals became extensions of his body. It felt nothing like it had the day before—this was how driving was *supposed* to feel.

He revved the engine once and his heart rate spiked. A few more times and it settled into an upbeat tempo: one that would carry him through the race.

They turned the final corner and accelerated down the front straightaway. Teddy knew the other drivers were positioning themselves behind him, but his eyes were fixed on the tower. The marshal leaned over its railing, the green flag suspended over his head.

Three, two . . .

"Green, green, green!" Stewart called over the radio.

Teddy hammered his foot down. Within a second he was side by side with Allison. He glanced to his right, hoping to catch her eye. But she was focused straight ahead on the first turn.

Teddy smiled. *OK, I guess we're racing.*

Allison took full advantage of the inside line going into Turn 1. Teddy slotted in behind her. He checked his mirror. LeGuivre was right behind him. Though he couldn't see them, he knew the twins would be pushing LeGuivre hard. Teddy followed Allison closely around the first half of the course, waiting to see if a yellow flag would drop. Had any of the other drivers gotten tangled up at the start? he wondered. By the time he'd reached the back straightaway, the battle was on.

Teddy shadowed Allison through every corner. Each time they entered a straightaway, she'd gain a few feet on him only to lose them as they approached the next turn. LeGuivre stayed glued to Teddy's back end. The nose of his car popped out at every opportunity, sniffing for an opening. Teddy shut him down each time. Whenever LeGuivre moved off the line, Teddy peeked in his mirror to check on the twins. And every time there was Kayla. It was like her whole car was glaring right back at him.

Looks like no one's going down easy today.

Lap after lap, Teddy could feel the pressure building behind him. He had no choice but to push forward. Part of him wished his car was just a little faster, that the battle for first would come down to machinery rather than driving. But by the halfway point it was clear that the cars were too evenly matched. He'd have to wait for Allison to make a mistake, or try to force her to make one. He didn't love the idea, but he hadn't come this far to hold back.

Teddy was halfway down the back straight and LeGuivre was deep in his draft. His spine tingled.

He's gonna go for it.

LeGuivre shot out to the right. They were only a few hundred feet from the left-handed Turn 7. Teddy knew LeGuivre would be hard-pressed to execute a clean outside pass before the corner. But he also knew that LeGuivre didn't always drive clean. His opponent creeped forward, clawing away Teddy's lead on him foot by foot.

Stay cool, Teddy thought, exhaling. *He'll never make it around me before the turn.*

Of course, Teddy knew he didn't have to. All LeGuivre had to do was stay beside him through Turn 7—the right-hand bend of Turn 8 would give him the advantage of the line.

Teddy's only option was to aim for the corner and hope LeGuivre braked first. Tunnel vision set in. Everything around the track faded to white. The world in front of him seemed to stretch. Each foot became a mile. Every second felt like a minute.

They reached the deceleration point. Time to slow. But LeGuivre held firm. For as long as he could, Teddy fought his body's instinct to brake and downshift. Finally, his sense of self-preservation proved stronger. They entered the turn side by side. Teddy had one last chance to save his position. He slammed the gas pedal down a hair sooner than he normally would have, trying to beat LeGuivre out of the corner. The sudden acceleration midturn caused the back end of his car to slip just a little—not enough for him to lose control but enough to clip the side of LeGuivre's car and send the other driver a message: *Not this time.*

LeGuivre jerked away when they touched, and the right side of his car rumbled off the track. This slowed him enough for Teddy to take back the line going into Turn 8. The next time Teddy checked his mirrors, all he saw was Kayla's car bearing down on him.

Awesome! LeGuivre's her problem now, he thought. His relief disintegrated immediately. *And Kayla's my problem.*

He'd never been head-to-head with one of the twins before. His desire to get around Allison suddenly became urgent. Teddy felt as if he were driving for his life.

For the next ten laps Kayla's pursuit was patient but relentless. He quickly learned that her style wasn't like LeGuivre's. She didn't poke or prod. She settled herself into his draft and let him pull her along. Though he was in front her, he couldn't help feeling as though she was in control.

Well, this is new.

He shifted his focus to Allison. As they crossed the front straightaway on the second-to-last lap, he sensed that his car had more to give. Whether it was the pull of her draft or something else he couldn't say. But he was positive he wouldn't need to wait for Allison to slip up to make his move. He started to pull out from behind her.

What the heck!

Teddy felt a sharp bump from behind. He checked his mirror. Kayla had chosen the same moment to make her move. His rear tire had rubbed up against Kayla's front.

Teddy recovered his focus and advanced on Allison. The three of them sped towards the first turn in a diagonal line, like migrating geese.

Allison held her line all the way to the first turn.

I won't get past her. Not this time. He tucked back in behind her and checked on Kayla. She'd moved so far to the outside that she'd left a perfect opening for LeGuivre, just as LeGuivre had done for her a few laps before. Teddy knew LeGuivre wouldn't miss the opportunity. When Kayla tried to fall back in line behind Teddy, her spot was already gone.

Teddy resumed his attack on Allison. He was running out of time. But with LeGuivre back on his tail, his focus was split. He had to keep adjusting his line to defend against him as he probed for a chance to take Allison.

Less than half a lap to go. Only one shot left.

242 · CHRISTOPHER HINCHCLIFFE

Teddy dug into Allison on the final corner. Any closer and his front wing would scoop up the back of her machine like a spatula. Before he'd even straightened his car he slipped out from behind her. With every second he gained another inch. He looked up.

Just two more seconds!

The marshal dropped the checkered flag.

Chapter 24

His team's excitement was clear even before he'd pulled into the pit box and turned off the engine. It wasn't the victory Teddy had hoped for, but a podium finish was nothing to sneeze at.

Stewart's hands were shaking as he helped Teddy out of the restraints. Before he knew it, Teddy found himself pressed against the engineer's chest, caught in a hug that threatened to crush his ribs. He'd been free less than a second, barely enough time to catch his breath, before he was trapped again.

"That was incredible!" his dad said.

Teddy was overwhelmed. With every beat, his heart pushed a fresh surge of warmth and adrenaline through him. His eyes began to well up as he pulled away and looked his dad in the eye.

"One hell of a show."

"Thanks, Dad," he said, beaming. "Glad you enjoyed it."

Everyone around him was chatting and laughing and slapping him on the back. Even Trevor had forgotten he was supposed to be terse and sullen. *Oh, we're best buds now, are we?*

"Teddy!"

It took him a moment to realize someone was calling his name. He looked up. Allison was jogging towards him.

Without thinking, he brushed past the others to meet her.

All he could see was her smile. It had taken over her whole face, her whole body. It was like she was running just to catch up with it. He noticed that she had a crooked tooth, just behind her left canine. He fixated on it. He found it so charming it was almost painful. And then it vanished. A bundle of sweaty hair obscured his vision as she pulled him into a hug.

"We did it!" she said.

"You did it. I just watched from behind."

"Stop it. You drove the hell out of that race."

"Just following your lead."

She pulled back, still beaming.

That tooth. Why have I never noticed that tooth before?

"What?" she asked.

"It's nothing," he said. "It's just . . ."

He didn't think. He just leaned in and kissed her.

A voice inside him screamed *Stop! No!* but he barely noticed it. And when Allison kissed him back, it disappeared entirely.

When they separated, she was smiling and her cheeks were flushed. He looked into her eyes.

Did she? Did we? Was that . . . ?

Her expression darkened. Her smile died. The pink in her cheeks retreated. Her eyes widened, as if Teddy had transformed into a monster. He could tell she wasn't looking at him. Or, at least, she wasn't seeing him. She was see-ing someone else. She was seeing . . . *him.*

Teddy knew who Allison was seeing in her mind's eye. He could see him, too. In fact, Teddy could see him staring at them from the other end of pit lane.

"Chet," she whispered.

"Chet," he said.

Is he going to come over? Is he going to clobber me? Is this how I die?

It occurred to him that he was probably safe from a di-rect assault. After all, they were surrounded by people. People who were staring at them.

Teddy looked around at their faces. Some looked puz-zled. Others looked amused. His dad looked shocked. But they all looked.

Teddy's ears started to ring.

What have we done? What have I done?

His legs turned to cement. Everything looked brighter, washed out. He felt the need to squint, to cover his eyes. Teddy looked back at Chet. He was gone.

"He saw?" Allison asked.

Teddy nodded.

"I should go."

He nodded again.

She took a step back. "Teddy—"

"Just go," he said. She lingered. "It's OK."

This is not OK. This is NOT OK.

Allison turned and trotted out of the pits. All eyes watched her go then turned back to Teddy. His cheeks burned. One by one the spectators seemed to lose interest. But Teddy remained frozen.

He felt a hand touch his shoulder.

"You all right there, sport?"

"What have I done?"

"Nothing to be too embarrassed about, son. I promise you that. Though you might have an awkward conversation or two in your future."

Oh crap. Leah!

"You don't understand."

"Heat of the moment. Could happen to anyone. We can forget all about it if you want. You know, if it didn't mean any—"

"No, Dad, you don't understand. Chet knows."

"Well, yeah. It looks like he had a pretty good view."

Teddy raised his voice. "No, Dad. He knows about Graham!"

His dad pulled back and looked around. No one was paying attention to them anymore, but Teddy could see that his outburst had caught his dad off guard.

He grabbed Teddy's arm and started to lead him away from the pits.

"Maybe we should talk about this back at the trailer?"

Teddy's feet reluctantly allowed him a few steps before they stopped him again. He moved his dad's hand from his arm.

"No," he said. "I'm not going to the trailer."

"Well, um, I don't think here's a great place to—"

"I have to go to the podium, Dad. I finished on the podium. So that's where I'm going."

My life might be about to implode, but I'm going to stand on that damn box first.

"Right. Of course."

Teddy headed towards the Pagoda, his dad at his side.

As they approached the podium, someone from the series pointed Teddy to a staircase behind the stage and ushered his dad under a red velvet rope that cordoned off the area in front of it. Teddy climbed the stairs. Allison and LeGuivre were already standing on the platform at the top.

"What's with you two?" said LeGuivre. "You should be taking this all in, Clark. Might be the only time you get to see this view.

"Shut up, Alex!" Teddy and Allison snapped in unison.

LeGuivre was about to speak when the announcer called his name. He looked at them a second longer, huffed, and walked out onto the stage.

Teddy looked into Allison's eyes. He knew exactly what she was thinking. He was thinking the same thing.

This changes everything.

Chapter 25

Teddy felt a sharp elbow in his ribs.

"Dude," said Richard. "Lunch. Subway. Let's go."

Teddy blinked. The period had ended. Everyone was getting up to leave. The last thing he remembered was sitting down.

"I hate to say it, man, but you're looking grizzly. You feeling all right?"

Teddy shrugged. "I haven't been sleeping well."

He was fried. It had been almost a week since the US GP—since the kiss. He hadn't heard a word from Allison. Every night when Teddy closed his eyes, his mind played him a marathon of disaster-movie scenarios. An asteroid headed towards Earth. A massive solar flare. A supervolcano under Yellowstone National Park. Nothing could stop it. A lone scientist knew it was coming and had to decide: would he tell anyone? Teddy knew the comparisons were ridiculous. It's not like anyone else was standing on the brink of catastrophe. When it struck—and he felt certain it would—only his world would be devastated. Everyone else would pretty much carry on as normal.

Almost everyone.

Since it was Friday, the gang had decided to make a run to Subway during fourth period. This meant that Ben, Zana, and Tom had to skip class.

"But it's only English lit., so, whatever," Zana said, on the way to Richard's car. "Mrs. Ryerson has been making us read *The Merchant of Venice* out loud all week. I swear. I'd rather cut off a pound of *my* flesh than sit through another hour of that gong show."

"I won't stand for such a slight on my noble kinsman!" Tom said, puffing out his chest. "To be or—"

Zana shoved a hand in his face. "I'm gonna stop you right there, Shakespeare," she said. "That's *Hamlet*, and you damn well know it."

"Fine, fine," he replied. "As you like"—he paused—"it."

This earned him a slap upside the head.

The six of them crammed into Richard's car. Zana took shotgun. Ben had to lie down on Tom's, Leah's, and Teddy's laps.

"Keep your head down," warned Richard. "Mr. Greyson almost saw you last time."

They all kept their eyes straight ahead as they drove past the vice principal, who stood at the edge of the school property, monitoring the smokers in the Pit.

Once they were in the clear, the others resumed their banter. Teddy was in no mood to join in, but he couldn't seem to tune them out either. He knew that it wasn't their fault, that they couldn't know what he was dealing with. But he was dealing with it all the same, and the lame jokes and mindless gossip were starting to get on his nerves.

"Six-inch tuna on white please," Teddy said to the chirpy "sandwich artist." "No toppings." It was a reflex, that order. The same thing he got every time. He wasn't even hungry.

Leah bumped her shoulder against him. "Plain Jane." She smiled.

Teddy tried to smile back but could only twitch his cheeks.

Richard hadn't been the first to ask Teddy how he was feeling. "You look like a wreck," Leah had said to him on Monday. "I must have picked up a bug or something on the plane," he'd said.

What's one more lie at this point?

She'd seemed satisfied with this explanation. It was the first thing he'd thought of, but it had turned out to be a stroke of genius. It made it easy for him to keep his distance—"I don't want to get you sick"—and to avoid late-night phone calls—"I should probably turn in early."

They squeezed into a booth by the window. Teddy was pressed up against the glass. He felt trapped, imprisoned. He squirmed and looked out at the parking lot, trying to imagine the smell of fresh air.

"Shove over. My butt's hanging off the bench," said Ben.

"Closest it's been to 'off the bench' all year," quipped Tom.

Teddy was pushed harder into the window. He could feel the air in his lungs getting compressed, the pressure building.

The conversation turned to the band's upcoming performance at the spring formal. They'd dominated the talent show a couple of weeks earlier, and Teddy felt like since then, they hadn't talked about anything else.

"Will we still have to dress up?" asked Ben.

"Yeah, Ben. You'll need to send your formal jersey to the cleaners," said Zana.

Teddy started to feel warm, claustrophobic.

"Just leave that phone book you sit on at home," said Tom. "Then no one will be able to see you behind the drum kit and it won't matter."

The others started to laugh.

Teddy burst.

"Why don't you guys ever leave him alone? He hasn't done anything wrong! Not to any of you!"

Everyone went silent and looked at Teddy.

"Uh, thanks, man," said Ben. He looked confused but grateful.

"Teddy?" Leah squeezed his arm.

Teddy shook off her hand. "I need to go. I need to get out of here."

Leah and Ben shuffled off the bench.

"Let's get some air," she said.

"No. I'm going home."

"You want a ride, or . . . ?" Richard said.

"I'll walk." Teddy got out of the booth and went to the door. "Thanks."

As he crossed the parking lot, he glanced over his shoulder. The others were staring at him through the window. Richard said something to Leah, who shook her head.

That's right. Teddy's lost it. Take a good look.

Teddy was surprised to see his dad's car in the driveway when he got home.

"Teddy?" his dad called from the kitchen.

He didn't reply. He walked into the kitchen and sat down at the table. Stacks of manila folders formed a little fortress around his dad's laptop.

His dad looked at his watch then at Teddy. "Playing hooky, are we?"

"Free period," he said, staring into his lap. "What's your excuse?"

"The grim reaper of the living, my boy. The tax man cometh."

Teddy nodded. His dad gave him a concerned look, but didn't press him. They'd had the whole trip home from Indianapolis to discuss what had happened. What might still happen. At first his dad had gone nuclear—he'd offered to have a "friendly chat" with Chet. He'd even suggested that legal action wouldn't be out of the question if Chet followed through on his threat. Teddy had talked him down. He didn't pretend to know what to do, but getting his dad involved would be like driving a fuel truck into a forest fire. They'd agreed to adopt a sit-and-wait policy.

Teddy pulled out his phone. He'd had it on silent for class and hadn't checked it in over an hour.

One text was from Leah, asking if he wanted to talk later.

The other was from Allison. It was three words long.

"He did it."

Teddy's heart stopped. He felt the blood drain from his face. His hands started to tremble. He had to put the phone on the table.

"What's wrong?" his dad asked.

"It's happened."

They sat silently, staring at the table. Teddy's mind, which had been swirling all week, was blank, stalled on the grid.

His dad broke the silence.

"How?"

Teddy hadn't even thought to ask.

He grabbed his phone. Typing out the word acted like a spark. It jump-started his brain. All the scenarios and questions and worries and fears came roaring back.

He could see Allison was typing something. The wait was agonizing.

"Twitter."

He opened the app and clicked on his notifications. Chet had tagged Teddy in a post. Two photographs placed side by side. The first was the same photograph Teddy had studied a hundred times, the one in the *Road & Race* magazine he kept in his closet. Graham Thompson posing in his race suit next to his car. The second was Teddy's profile picture for the Firebrand series' website. The caption read: "Family resemblance?" It was followed by the Twitter handles of half a dozen Firebrand drivers—including LeGuivre. The post was still fresh. No likes or retweets yet. But Teddy knew it was only a matter of time.

He passed the phone to his dad.

His dad read the post, returned the phone, and leaned back in his chair.

"What should I do?" Teddy asked.

His dad looked out the window. He chewed his lower lip, an unconscious habit he had that Teddy had seen a thousand times before. He was thinking.

"The reality is, sport, that this doesn't mean anything. Not yet."

Teddy was stunned.

How can he say that?

"You're going to have to walk me through that one, Dad. As soon as someone like LeGuivre retweets it, it'll get noticed by every racing blog and magazine out there."

His dad crossed his arms. "Right. The blogs you probably can't do anything about. But no serious magazine is going to spread a rumour like that. Not without verification."

"Well don't you think they'll try to get verification? 'Legendary driver's long-lost son found at the bottom of the Formula Firebrand barrel'—how could they pass that up?"

His dad frowned but ignored Teddy's "headline." "Well, that's the thing, isn't it? How are they going to verify it?"

"I don't know, records or something? There must have been paperwork."

"Those records aren't just open to everyone. Sure, *you* could write the ministry and request them, but Joe Blow reporter? Not a chance."

Teddy massaged his face.

"That can't be right. Allison figured it out. And all she did was talk to a few guys in Edmonton and find a picture of me online. I mean look!" He thrust the phone in his dad's face. "Anyone can see it!"

His dad calmly moved Teddy's hand onto the table.

"I'm not saying you can kill the rumour, son. But Allison didn't *know* anything. Not until you confirmed it."

Teddy wouldn't have believed it was possible, but this news made him feel even worse. He now understood what his dad was trying to say. Unless he confirmed the story himself, no one could prove a thing.

It was all on him.

Teddy thought back to his conversation with Allison behind the vendor's stall. She'd suggested that he just break the news first, take away Chet's power. But the power that Chet had over him wasn't what they'd thought it was. Teddy knew Chet could make his life miserable. He could spread all the rumours he wanted. But that made him no different from anyone else—no different from LeGuivre or any other bully. What Teddy had feared all this time was the truth.

But it was *his* truth, no one else's. It was his burden, yes. But it was also his power.

"So the question is, what do *you* want to do?"

Chapter 26

Teddy tugged at the collar of his sweat-soaked dress shirt. He crossed his legs under his desk. He double-checked that his phone was on silent. He undid his top button. He did it back up. He turned off his phone. He uncrossed his legs.

Why am I even wearing a dress shirt? It's not like they're taking a picture.

"It'll make you feel confident, more professional," his dad had said.

Confident professionals must feel like uncomfortable dorks.

"How's it going in there? Anything yet?" His dad used a stage whisper to talk through Teddy's bedroom door.

"No," Teddy whispered back mockingly.

He checked the time. Five after three.

So they're a few minutes late. No big deal. No. Big. Deal. Breathe.

A dialogue box popped up on his computer screen. *Bleep-bloop.*

"Good luck," Teddy heard through the door.

"Shh!"

He took a final deep breath and accepted the call.

Nick Scott's face appeared, his Cheshire-Cat grin and shimmering purple shirt in high definition.

Teddy felt a surge of jealousy. *What's that*—three *buttons undone? That's allowed?*

"Teddy Clark, man of the hour," he said. "Or should I say, Theodore Thompson?" He winked.

You absolutely should not.

"Hi, Nick, good to see you again." Teddy smiled and plunged his hands between his knees to hide his clenching fists. "And Teddy Clark is fine, thank you."

Jerk.

"Wait one, Teddy. I'm just plugging in Claudia. Claud? You there?"

The screen split, and the young track reporter's face appeared.

"Yeah, I'm here. Hi, Teddy."

"Hi."

"I'm sure Nick has already explained, but this is just a friendly chat about everything that's been going on the last couple of weeks. It's a little different from our track interviews, but don't worry. We don't have to talk about anything you don't want to. OK?"

"Yup. Sounds good."

Nick gave him a thumbs-up.

Claudia asked a few easy questions about his career and what it was like growing up outside Toronto. Teddy knew that she was just trying to warm him up, but he appreciated it. After a few minutes, he stopped having to wipe his brow with his shirt sleeve every thirty seconds. She paused to make some notes before moving on to his family. She asked about his parents and Matt. "Is the whole family into racing?" "Are you and Matt competitive?" "How does your mom feel about you driving for a living?"

Teddy's answers came smoothly.

Then Claudia paused again. Teddy could see the gears in her mind shifting.

"OK, now let's talk about this rumour that surfaced on Twitter a couple of weeks ago. It's been making the rounds online but you haven't responded. I think it's fair to say that a lot of people want to know if it's true."

Teddy heard the bedroom door creak open.

Christmas on a cracker, Dad.

"I want to be clear about one thing," Teddy began. "My dad is Steve Clark and my mom is Cynthia Clark."

Claudia and Nick leaned away from their cameras. Looks of confusion and concern washed over their faces.

"So you're denying the rumours that you're actually the son of AmRun Pro driver Graham Thompson and Susan Thompson?"

Moment of truth.

"No. I'm not denying it. Graham and Susan Thompson were my birth parents. I've been told they were really great people. Graham was an awesome driver and one of my heroes growing up. But they died when I was a baby. I never knew them. To me, my parents are the people who raised me. That should be enough for everyone."

The others leaned in again.

"Of course," said Claudia. "I understand. But you can understand why others would be interested to know the whole story."

"Sure, I get why they're interested. What I don't get is why they think it's any of their business." Teddy did his best not to sound hostile, to sound as though this was a genuine point of curiosity for him. But he could tell he'd put Claudia on the defensive. Nick's face tightened in restrained frustration.

"OK, Teddy. Fair enough. But then I've gotta ask, why would you agree to an interview like this?"

Teddy had been grappling with this question since seeing Chet's tweet. He was convinced it wouldn't just blow over. He had a hunch that Chet wouldn't let it go, that he'd keep pushing until Teddy had no choice but to respond. Part of him just wanted to get it over with. But that wasn't the real reason. He'd come to see that Allison was right. Keeping his secret wasn't doing him any good.

It doesn't matter what anyone else knows, he thought. *I'm always going to compare myself to Graham. Hiding only makes things worse. I have to stand in Graham's shadow before I can step out of it.*

That Graham and Susan were his birth parents was only half the truth, though. If he was going to set the record straight, he needed to make sure people knew the whole story. He needed to hammer home the point he'd begun with.

"Why? Because if people are curious about who my parents are, they need to know that they are Steve and Cynthia Clark. And I owe them everything."

And that's *the truth.*

Teddy hid in his trailer. It was the first race weekend since Chet's tweet and his interview with *Road & Race*, and he couldn't walk twenty feet without someone asking him about Graham.

He started to think doing the interview hadn't been such a hot idea. *Great, here I am hiding again. It's like they didn't even listen to what I said!*

The trailer wasn't exactly private. Between track sessions Stewart and Trevor would pop in to grab snacks or tools. But they'd learned to recognize when Teddy was trying to get some space and wouldn't talk to him unless it was racing related. They'd even worked out a signal: earbuds in meant "do not disturb."

Today, Teddy didn't have that luxury.

"So do you spend a lot of time in here?" asked Leah.

They sat on the floor with their backs against the cupboards, shoulder to shoulder, arms wrapped around their knees.

"Not a lot. I usually just use it to change or grab a nap or something before a race."

"It's cool. Like a submarine galley or something."

Teddy looked around. He'd never thought of it before, but her comparison was a good one. He imagined himself beneath two hundred feet of water, the weight of it trying to crush him from all sides.

"Yeah, I guess it is."

Leah had insisted on coming to this race. She hadn't come to any of the others because flights were expensive, and she always had band rehearsals or family commitments on the weekends. But Mid-Ohio was close enough to drive to, and after everything that had happened, he knew she wanted to be there to support him.

If she knew the truth she might not be so enthusiastic.

He still hadn't told her about what had happened with Allison. Things felt tense enough around the track because of the Graham business. But at least twenty people had seen them kiss. He was sure it had gotten around by now. No one had said anything yet, but it was just a matter of time. *One run-in with LeGuivre and . . .* He didn't even want to think about it.

There was still half an hour before qualifying. Leah was doing her best to keep the conversation going. She commented on how interesting practice had been and asked him questions about the car and the rules of the race—things that he was pretty sure she really didn't care about. He replied without much enthusiasm. He was touched but knew he didn't deserve any of it—her support, her politeness. If anything, her words stung, like a swarm of mosquitoes nibbling at his conscience.

He tried to change the subject. "Everyone seemed to really enjoy you guys at formal." It was the first thing he'd thought of.

"Yeah, it's been great! Did I tell you? We even got another gig."

"Oh yeah?"

"You know Dr. Wilmoe?"

"Dr. Bear? Sure."

Dr. Wilmoe was the gym teacher at their school. There was a rumour that he had a PhD in philosophy or law or something but had decided to teach gym so he could spend the summers surfing. He was the sweetest teacher at the school—a real teddy bear.

"Well, remember how he chaperoned the formal? Apparently he plays in a band, too. Mostly folk stuff, Bob Dylan covers, things like that. Anyway, he came up to Richard the other day and said he could get us in at a bar his band plays in downtown. Isn't that wild?"

Teddy stiffened at the mention of Richard. He regretted starting this conversation.

"A bar? Are you guys even allowed to play in a bar?"

"It's not like we'll be drinking."

"I know but, like, will they let you in?"

Leah shrugged. "I guess so. I mean, why would Dr. Wilmoe suggest it if he didn't think they would?"

There was a knock at the door. It opened before Teddy could reply.

"Y'all set in there, Teddy?" Stewart called from outside. "We're heading down now."

Teddy looked at Leah, who squeezed his knee and smiled.

"Can I watch from the pits?"

"Not much to see from there," he said. Disappointment flashed across her face. "But yeah, why not? You can keep Dad company."

On the way down to the track, Teddy made sure that he and Leah stayed close to Stewart, Trevor, and his dad. He felt safer travelling in a pack. Still, he couldn't help but notice the glances from the other teams as they entered the pits.

Eyes forward. Just make it to the car.

To save time, Teddy decided to skip his dressing ritual. But before he could throw his helmet over his balaclava, Leah hopped up next to him and kissed him on the nose. "Good luck," she said. "Be safe."

Teddy could feel his face turn red. He stepped back and almost tripped over the pit wall.

"Thanks, you too."

"You too"? Seriously?

Teddy jumped into the car and fastened his belts. By the time Stewart came to help him there was nothing left to do but tighten them.

"Feeling a little eager today are we?"

Teddy gave his engineer a sideways glance and slapped his visor down.

Just let me get out there.

The track at Mid-Ohio was a peculiar shape. It had two back-to-back straightaways separated by a short U-turn that stuck out from the rest of the course like a handle. Most of the turns were less than ninety degrees. Teddy knew that, like him, most of the drivers would be running without much rear wing. Everyone would be sacrificing grip for speed.

During the morning practice, Teddy had spent as much time focusing on clearing his head as he had on learning the track and getting a feel for the car's setup. But the moment he'd stepped out of the car, everything had come flooding back.

Behind the wheel again, he tried to push everything out once more. He focused on the whine of the engine as the car accelerated down the straightaways. He wanted to feel every tremor in the frame, every bump in the pavement. He gripped the steering wheel tightly, to better sense every twitch of feedback. He took long, deep breaths. His balaclava was infused with the dank scent of dry sweat and residue from his exhalations during practice. Combined with the fumes of gasoline and melting rubber, the smell was far from pleasant. But he took it in greedily, let it settle in his mind.

His first fast lap was barely good enough to earn him a spot in the top ten. His second was slower still. Had they trimmed the car out too much? he wondered. Taken away too much downforce? It was fast and smooth on the straightaways, but he struggled with it in the turns more than he had in practice. The second he released the gas to enter a corner, he could feel the car losing its grip, and keeping it on the line was a battle.

He debated whether to say something to Stewart about altering the car's setup. *No*, he thought. *I can't give up any of my speed on the straightaways. Not if I'm going to have a chance.*

He took his last fast lap. Again the car fought him at every turn, and he fought right back. He pushed it as hard as he dared, knowing that a single slip-up could destroy his time.

"Great lap," said Stewart over the radio, as Teddy barrelled across the start-finish line. "Should be good enough for top five."

Teddy heaved a sigh of relief and began his cool-down lap.

Back in the pits, Stewart confirmed that he would start in P5. It was good news, but Teddy felt spent. He wanted nothing more than to run back to the trailer and be alone.

"How about we head over to hospitality for some lunch?" his dad suggested. "Leah hasn't seen the spread yet, has she?"

"Sounds good to me," she said.

"Well . . ."

"Don't worry, sport. We'll get you back to the trailer in plenty of time to get ready for the race. You really should eat something now."

Teddy shifted his weight. "OK, sure."

The hospitality suite was buzzing. Waiting for his turn at the buffet table, Teddy felt exposed. He tried to keep his eyes fixed on Leah, who was chatting with his dad just ahead of him in line. But he couldn't help glancing over his shoulder every few seconds to see if anyone was looking at him.

"Let's grab a seat next to Alex," said his dad, gesturing to a table near the back. LeGuivre was sitting with his father and two men Teddy didn't recognize. "That's René LeGuivre," he said to Leah. "The Dragon of AmRun Pro. A legend."

"LeGuivre?" she said, turning to Teddy. "As in . . ."

Teddy clenched his jaw and nodded. Leah knew all about LeGuivre and the grief he'd given Teddy at the academy. His dad knew, too, but it always seemed to slip his mind when an opportunity to rub shoulders with René popped up.

"I think I'd rather sit closer to the entrance," she said. "It's warm in here. There's more fresh air by the door."

Teddy thanked her with a look.

"You heard the lady," said Teddy's dad, barely able to keep the disappointment out of his voice.

They had just started to eat when Allison entered the suite. Only Teddy saw her come in. The others faced away from the entrance. His back stiffened. At first she stopped, as though about to change directions. Their eyes met. He tried not to change his expression, and when Allison caught sight of Leah she quickly resumed her course to the buffet table.

Leah glanced at him and then over her shoulder. She started to say something but turned back to her food.

Well this is going pretty much perfectly.

A few minutes later, Nick walked in with Dan Williamson by his side. Teddy tried to shrink down in his seat, to hide his face behind his dad's head.

It didn't work. Scanning the room, Nick spotted him and then tapped Dan's shoulder. The two of them strode over.

"Well, if it isn't the man of the hour," said Nick. "How are you gentlemen?" Teddy thought of Raymond at the car dealership. "And lady," he added, noticing Leah.

Teddy's dad stood up and shook hands with the men.

"Have you two met Teddy's girlfriend, Leah?"

Nick looked intrigued. "Teddy's girlfriend you say?" His eyes flickered and his head twitched as if he were still scanning the room somehow through the back of his skull. Teddy could almost see the man tag Allison in his mind.

Teddy clenched his fists.

"I was just telling Dan how I still wanted to get you, Alex, and Allison into a room together for a little group photo op. Cars and Canucks, that sort of thing. Although maybe we should do something with just you and Alex."

Teddy cleared his throat. "Why us?"

Nick chuckled. "Oh you know. The sons of legends. Something like that. No offence, Steve." He patted Teddy's dad on the shoulder.

"None taken, Nick. I think it's a grand idea."

"Well we'll let you guys eat. Good luck today, Teddy."

Teddy's dad sat back down as the men walked away. "That guy's a piece of work—am I right?"

You have no idea.

The whole warm-up lap, the phrase echoed in Teddy's head. "Sons of legends." He saw the faces of everyone who'd approached him that day. "Heard about Graham. What's that like?" "Cool news, Teddy! We'll see you on top of the podium in no time."

He rounded the final turn. Green flag. He pounded the accelerator. Time slowed. The g-forces piled on. He felt the cars behind bearing down on him. *Simon?* The cars in front blocked him. *Allison?* Panic seized his chest.

He was trapped.

He couldn't breathe.

His heart pulsed like a strobe light.

He looked ahead.

The U-turn. Need to slow. We all need to slow.

His muscles clenched.

His gaze darted back and forth—road, mirrors, road, mirrors.

I need to slow. I can't slow. Slow! No!

Chapter 27

Beep. Beep. Beep.

Teddy felt the electric chirp deep in his chest. A throbbing pain with its own soundtrack. A torturous alarm clock inside his body.

What is that? Why is it hurting me?

He tried to move his arm. To find the source of the pain. To hit the snooze button. His limb screamed in protest.

OK, don't panic. Wait. I can't see anything. Panic! Panic!

Other aches started to crowd their way into his consciousness. From his wrists to his shoulders, his hips to his collarbone—everything shouted for his attention.

Quiet! Why can't I see!

"Teddy, can you hear me?"

Yes! I can hear you. Why can't I see you!

"Can you open your eyes, Teddy?"

Open my . . . ?

Teddy lifted his eyelids.

Well, at least that didn't hurt.

Everything was blurry. He blinked a few times. The room started to come into focus. A tile ceiling. Fluorescent lights. A woman's face. Brown skin, dark eyes, soft features. A flashlight.

Teddy blinked again and winced. His neck muscles joined the chorus of agony.

For the love of . . .

"Teddy, can you try to look straight up?"

Can you stop shining that thing in my face?

Grudgingly he complied.

"Good."

A finger.

"Now can you follow my finger?"

Left. Right. Up. Down.

Can I sleep now? This minor exertion had devoured every ounce of energy he had.

"That's good, Teddy. Very good."

Teddy tried to speak, but his throat was so dry and his face so sore that he managed little more than a wheeze.

"It's OK, Teddy. You don't need to say anything. Here."

The woman moved to the side of his bed. He wasn't willing to turn his head to see what she was doing, but it didn't take long for him to figure it out. A warm, soothing sensation seeped from his belly and oozed into every nook of his body.

"That should help with the pain," she said. "I'll be right back."

Teddy felt genuinely sad to see her go. *She seems nice*, he thought. *Mom has a coat like that.* His mind soaked in a peaceful narcotic bath. The aches were still there, but they didn't feel like his aches. They were detached, just bobbing on the surface like rubber ducks.

The woman came back. Someone was with her.

"Teddy, can you hear me?"

Oh, hey Dad! What are you doing here? Do you know Doctor . . . uh . . . Doctor Nice Lady?

"He's not talking?"

It's fine, Dad. Really. Everyone just needs to chill out . . .

"It's nothing to worry about. I've just given him something."

. . . to take a nap. We all just need to take . . .

Teddy woke in a sweat. The pain was back. It was weaker now, and duller. But it was everywhere. The room was dark. He tried to remember where he was. Slowly, painfully, he sat up.

This is a hospital bed. I'm in the hospital. Why am I in the hospital?

He noticed a figure in the corner, a man asleep in a chair, a jacket draped over his torso.

The man snored. Teddy recognized the sound instantly.

Dad's here. OK. Should I wake him? I should wake him. No, I shouldn't.

His head began to swim. He lay back down and fell asleep.

The next time he woke up, the room was light.

I'm in the hospital.

He sat up gingerly. The chair in the corner was empty. He concentrated, gathering his thoughts.

I'm in the hospital. I must have been in an accident. I'm in one piece, so that's good. Everything hurts. That's probably good too. At least I can still feel things. I can probably drive again. How soon, though?

He looked down and yelped. His right arm was in a cast. It started below his elbow and ended at his fingers.

He sucked in panicked breaths.

OK. OK. Breathe.

It wasn't working. His heart raced. Tears pooled in the corners of his eyes. Soon little streams were running down his cheeks.

The door opened and his dad entered holding a little plastic bag and a paper coffee cup.

"Well! Morning, son." He froze then ditched the bag and cup on a table by the door and rushed to the bed. "Hey, hey," he said, in a soothing tone. He perched awkwardly on the edge of the mattress, his arms searching for a way to hold Teddy without hurting him. He rested a hand on Teddy's thigh.

"Dad," Teddy gasped. "Dad, my hand. My *hand*!"

"I know, son, I know. It's OK. It'll be fine."

Teddy could've spat the words back in his face.

Fine! Are you freaking kidding me? Fine?

Despite the anger and frustration quaking inside Teddy, his dad's presence focused his attention. The pain was consumed by his burning desire to know.

"What happened? How bad is it? When can I *drive* again?"

"Easy, son. Easy. What's the last thing you remember?"

Teddy probed his mind. From behind the delirious dreams and panicked midnight awakenings, a fuzzy image started to emerge.

"I was in the car. Sitting in the pits. The first race at Mid-Ohio was about to start." His head started to throb. He forced himself deeper. But there was nothing. Only blackness.

"I reckon that's a good sign," his dad said. "You haven't forgotten much. There was an accident on the first lap. Going into Turn 2. You hit the wall pretty hard."

Questions erupted from his brain like ants from an anthill. *Was anyone else hurt? Who caused the accident? How long have I been here?* He stomped them down. They could wait.

"And my hand?"

"It's not as bad as it looks. It's fractured in two places."

It was like the air had been sucked out of the room. His chest quaked again.

His dad squeezed his thigh. "The doctor said they were clean breaks. Easy to set. Shouldn't take more than a few weeks to heal."

"A few?"

"Well, six for the cast to come off."

"Six weeks? That's . . ." Teddy choked on the words.

"I know, Teddy. Most of the season."

The room spun. His stomach imploded.

"Why don't I go find Doctor Liddar? She can probably explain things better."

Teddy didn't respond. He stared at his arm.

She can't explain this away.

The story had come together. He was in a hospital in Columbus. Most of his injuries were superficial. He'd bruised his ribs and shoulders and had a decent case of whiplash. Dr. Liddar wanted to keep him in the hospital for a few days so she could monitor him "for any internal injuries that might not have appeared right away." Teddy sensed she wasn't being entirely truthful. Each day she would give his body only a quick exam, pushing and prodding at his abdomen. She spent far more time asking him questions to test his memory, or checking his reflexes and the response of his pupils.

They're worried about brain damage, he realized. *Well, the joke's on them. You've gotta have something wrong in your head to get into a race car in the first place.*

She told him his eagerness to get back in the car was a good sign. He laughed.

When the initial shock wore off, Teddy pumped his dad for more information. The field had stayed close together around Turn 1. They'd hit full speed on their way towards Turn 2. Teddy had had the outside line, with Allison on the inside and Simon behind him. Simon had pulled to the outside of Teddy and was gaining ground. According to his dad, what happened next was a little unclear.

"Everyone agrees that Simon had no business trying to get around you on the outside like that. Not there."

But Teddy could read between the lines of the story. He'd failed to slow down enough to enter the turn safely.

When he did turn, he lost control. The back end of his car slipped out and clipped the front of Simon's. Teddy spun 180 degrees, careened off the track, and slammed sideways into the barrier. Simon followed Teddy off the track and sandwiched him into the wall. His dad was careful to make it sound as if Simon's recklessness and inexperience had caused the accident.

Teddy was positive that there was more to it than that.

His memory of the race was still shrouded in fog, but some things had started to emerge. Not really images but feelings. The pressure he'd been feeling that weekend. The fear of screwing up. *"The sons of legends."*

To top it all off, Trevor had quit the team.

"It seems he'd been talking to some sports-car team in Europe," his dad said.

Well, that figures. He remembered seeing Trevor talking to those men at the track in Indianapolis. He'd thought it looked suspicious. Now he knew why.

"So he won't be there for the end of the season?"

"I guess not. Caught everyone a bit off guard. I gather they're scrambling a bit to find a replacement."

"I'm surprised they let him go. Didn't he have a contract or something?"

His dad shrugged. "Search me."

A Trevor-free race. At least that's something to look forward to.

By the third day in hospital, Teddy was feeling more or less like himself again. He knew the pain was probably subsiding, but since they kept reducing the strength of his medication he didn't notice a difference. Everything still hurt. But his mind was clearer and he no longer had an incessant urge to nap.

Wakefulness had its downsides. The hours passed slowly, like the steady drip of saline into his IV. His dad was doing his best to work in the hospital room. He popped in and out to make calls or fetch coffee and snacks from the cafeteria. Teddy spent most of the day staring at the tiny TV mounted on the wall. He kept the sound low enough not to disturb his dad but loud enough to give the impression that he was watching it. He wasn't. As the medication stupor wore off, thoughts clamoured in his brain. Teddy spent most of his time trying to sort them out.

The season was lost. That much he knew for sure. Before the crash, he'd still had a shot—a long one—at placing well in the championship. Now, even if he recovered in record time, he'd miss the next six races, on top of the two he'd lost the weekend of the crash. There was just no coming back from that. And with the series lost, so was his career. He felt certain of it. Waves of nausea took hold of him every time he remembered this.

On top of everything was the guilt. It wasn't just that he'd slipped up. Even in the best conditions drivers made mistakes. Those were merely frustrating. He was already getting used to dealing with that sort of thing. But this was different. Teddy remembered the weekend at the cottage when he'd almost rolled the Big Red. He'd lost control because he'd given it up. He'd taken an unnecessary risk just to show off to his friends. Everything that had led to the crash—to sitting in that hospital bed, to the ruin of his driving career—was a result of *his* choices. *He* had decided to reveal the truth about Graham. *He* had kissed Allison. *He* had lied to Leah. So many lies. All the pressure, all the anxiety, all the distraction. He had no one and nothing to blame but himself. The realization was more painful than any of his injuries. It tore at his insides, like a demon trying to claw its way out of his gut.

Sometimes, he'd hear supportive voices in his head as he fought back tears: Allison's, reminding him that holding in his secret had been just as distracting, that he would feel the weight of Graham's legacy whether or not anyone else knew about it. His parents', assuring him that they'd love him no matter what, that they were proud of everything he'd done to get this far. Leah's, encouraging him to see that there was more to life than racing, if only he would take the time to realize it.

But none of it consoled him. Instead, it made him feel as if he were trapped under a heavy blanket that weighed on every bruise, every cut. He'd not only let himself down—he'd made life hell for everyone who loved and supported him. His parents were worried sick about his safety and his future. When he'd kissed Allison in front of everyone, he'd dropped a bomb into her relationship with Chet. And Leah. *Have I done anything but jerk her around for the last six months?* He thought about when they were raking leaves at the cottage. How certain he'd felt about her in that moment. She didn't deserve any of what he'd done. And she didn't even know the worst of it.

It was too much. It was all too much. The secrets. The lies. He felt himself accelerating towards the obvious conclusion. When he'd kissed Allison, he'd revealed his feelings for her. When he'd acknowledged that Graham was his birth father, he'd taken his first real step towards coming to terms with it. There was only one thing left to do. He had to tell Leah the truth. And he knew that would be the end for them.

A hollow blackness consumed him. *It's all been for nothing.*

Teddy gripped his chest. He felt as if his heart were being squeezed in a vice. He could manage only short, trembling breaths. His eyes welled up with tears.

Just then his mother stormed in. She held a clipboard. A frazzled-looking man in blue scrubs followed her.

"I'm sorry, ma'am, but only the doctors can handle the charts."

"I am a doctor," she snapped, without slowing. She didn't stop until she was leaning over Teddy. She squeezed his hand and kissed his forehead. "Darling, how are you feeling?" Before he could reply, she straightened and examined the pages on the clipboard. Then she gasped and looked at the drip bag attached to Teddy's IV. "Is that all they're giving you? Oh, you must be in so much pain!" She turned to the nurse. "Saline only? Is there a Demerol ration? What kind of place is this?"

Stunned, he backed out of the room. "I'll get the . . . I'll be right . . ."

The door closed behind him.

"Hi, Mom." Teddy's voice quivered.

"Cynth, take a breath," said his dad. "He's fine."

She shot him an impatient look and then seemed to catch herself. Huffing, she turned back to Teddy.

"Are you, dear? Are you fine?" She hugged him. "I'm so sorry I couldn't make it sooner. But, work, I . . ." She squeezed harder.

"Easy, Cynth, he's bruised all over."

"I'm good, Mom, really. Dad's been taking good care of me." His words came in clipped, breathless bursts.

And then the tears broke free.

His dad lunged to the side of the bed opposite his mom. They both tried awkwardly to cradle him while gushing soothing assurances.

He wanted to explain everything. It wasn't his injuries. At least, it wasn't only his injuries. He'd forgotten how to speak. His tears had turned the pages of his mind's dictionary into grey pulpy mush. Only two words remained.

"I'm . . . sorry."

Chapter 28

Teddy was released from hospital the next day, Friday. His mother insisted on driving him home. He didn't mind. He was even kind of looking forward to it. Because of her job, she usually couldn't come to races farther away than Motown. And even though he visited her often in the city, it wasn't the same as taking a road trip together.

Teddy loved car conversations. He'd always felt they had a patient, meandering quality. Silences were more natural, and allowed space for thoughts to grow. Besides, he'd had no one to talk to but his dad for almost a week. A new audience might be refreshing. His mom had a certain distance from his life that his dad didn't have. He knew he needed to talk about everything, and his mom was probably the better choice.

Not that he was keen to jump right into it—"So, Mom, I think I might have screwed over everyone I care about for nothing. Whaddya think?"

And he was sure she probably had a thing or two she wanted to talk about. She was probably itching to ask about his plans for university, now that his racing career had literally hit a wall.

Once they were underway, he checked his phone to buy some time. Everyone had been messaging him like crazy over the last few days. His dad had let the school know what happened, and he'd even talked to Leah several times while Teddy was still drugged out of his gourd. Once reacquainted with consciousness, Teddy had sent a few texts to let everyone know he was fine. But he'd skirted their requests to call him, using fatigue and roaming charges as excuses.

Allison was the most worried. Teddy's dad had had no reason to think she'd appreciate a phone call too, so she knew less about how he was doing than anyone. Teddy had texted her a few details but not much. He was still working out what to say to her. Until he talked to Leah in person, he figured it would be better to say too little than too much. And as he scrolled though the group chats and messages he'd missed, he realized that he didn't know what to say to anyone right now. The crash had kicked him out of the others' orbit and now he was drifting on his own, looking back at them from a distance. He chose to send a picture instead. He held his cast up to his frowning face and commented: "One-handed texting is the second-worst thing about a broken arm."

His mother hummed along to the radio while he texted. But the second he put away his phone, she turned down the volume.

Uh-oh.

"Teddy, I wanted to ask you about something."

OK. I guess we're blowing right past the small talk.

Teddy steeled himself.

I made a promise. I can't go back now. Not that I have anything to go back to.

He turned to her. "Look, Mom. If you're wondering what I'm going to take in university, I haven't decided yet. OK?"

She blinked a few times.

"What? No. That's not . . . Teddy, that's fine. We don't have to talk about that right now."

"Oh. I just, OK. Well, what's up, then?"

Red alert.

She cleared her throat. "Well, I was wondering if you wanted to talk about Graham." She paused and snatched a glance at Teddy. "Your dad told me that you guys didn't talk about him in the hospital and I guess I just sort of wondered if . . . because of the crash."

Stunned, Teddy stared out of the windscreen. Every feeling, every thought that had consumed him the day before came rushing back. It was like she'd pushed him off a cliff.

He told her everything. Every detail. Things he would never have dreamed of sharing with her twenty-four hours earlier. He couldn't have stopped himself if he'd wanted to. By the time he was done, he was shaking. His heart beat faster than a cheetah on Adderall. He wished the pills they'd given him before he left the hospital had been stronger.

She's going to think I'm a monster, he thought.

"Teddy, it's going to be OK."

And with that simple comment he deflated into his seat. Empty, spent.

Teddy woke late Saturday morning. He'd slept for almost twelve hours straight. A deep, dreamless sleep. He stumbled into the kitchen. The dishes from the night before were still piled up in the sink.

"Ah, it lives. How are we feeling this morning, champ?" His dad was dressed and sitting at the kitchen table reading the paper.

Teddy plonked himself in a chair and ran a self-diagnostic. His head was still a bit foggy, but he felt better than he had in a while. His injuries offered dull reminders of their presence, though nothing he couldn't handle. What he noticed most was the quiet. For the first time in months, his mind wasn't nattering. The whispering anxieties had fallen silent. It was like he'd been stuck in a room with a leaky faucet and someone had finally fixed it. He took in the smell of his dad's coffee, the sound of the birds in the backyard, the sunlight warming the kitchen table. He remembered what soft, lazy Saturday mornings felt like.

"I'm good, actually. Really good."

"Well I'm glad to hear it. Because I've got a surprise for you."

Teddy laughed. *Just one day. Can't I have one freaking day?*

"Of course you do."

"Huh?"

"Nothing." He smiled. "What's the surprise?"

"I got a call this morning. From Greg. He heard about the accident and was hoping he could come and pay a visit this afternoon."

Teddy perked up. "That sounds awesome."

"Maxim, too."

Yes! "Even better."

"Also."

The tone put Teddy on alert. The skin under his cast started to itch.

No, no. No "also." This is an "also-free" zone.

"Alex."

What? Teddy was certain he hadn't heard right. He searched his mind for alternatives. *Alec? Alice? All eggs?*

"Alex? Le*Guivre*?"

"The little dragon himself."

"But . . . wha . . . who . . . how . . . ?"

The birds weren't chirping. They were laughing at him.

"I'm as surprised as you are."

Unlikely.

"Seems he called up Greg a few days after your crash."

"This was *his* idea?"

"Well, I think Greg and Maxim were planning to come anyway. They just invited him along. What do you say?"

"Hard no."

"Aren't you curious?"

I'm curious about what it feels like to be eaten by a shark. But I'm not throwing on my swimsuit, am I?

Teddy noticed his dad's expression. He narrowed his eyes. "You already said yes, didn't you?"

"Well it was getting kinda late, and you were sleeping, so . . ."

"Uh, yeah. Car crash." Teddy held up his cast and waved it around.

"I knew you'd see it my way. They'll be here after lunch."

"Hey, did you hear the one about how I'm never talking to you again?"

"Don't tease. It was so peaceful down here a minute ago."

Tell me about it.

Teddy headed upstairs to get ready. Because of the cast, he had to shower with a bag over his arm and try to keep it out of the stream.

OK, this is worse than one-handed texting.

He couldn't think of a single reason LeGuivre would want to visit him.

I haven't even seen my friends yet, for crying out loud.

He scrubbed himself awkwardly with his good hand.

This is nuts. This is just nuts.

But the longer he thought about it, the more his frustration gave way to curiosity. He started to conjure up explanations for the visit.

Maybe he knows something about the crash. Maybe he saw something no one else did. Maybe it wasn't my fault after all.

He had a flash of hope. It was quickly extinguished when he remembered its source. Attaching positive thoughts to LeGuivre felt unnatural. He scrubbed himself a little harder.

Probably just has another conspiracy theory about the twins.

Teddy was standing in the kitchen inhaling a bowl of Chex when the doorbell rang.

"Gentlemen!" His dad welcomed them inside.

Teddy peeked into the hall. The sight of Greg and Maxim sent a jolt of glee through his body. For an instant, he thought they'd changed their minds and left LeGuivre behind.

Maybe Maxim pushed him out of the car on the way.

But after his dad had shaken their hands he reached between them and they parted, like a curtain in a circus creep show. LeGuivre stepped forward and took his dad's hand.

"Mr. Clark," he said. "Nice to see you. Hi, Teddy."

Teddy jumped, and stumbled into the hallway.

"Easy there, Chex. You've only got the two arms," said Greg, stepping forward and pulling him into a quick hug. "You're looking all right. How are ya feeling?"

"I'm good, thanks. Hey, Maxim." He swallowed and nodded at LeGuivre. "Alex."

"Chex, your eyes are dark," the Russian said. "You should eat green beans."

"I—uh, OK."

"Well we don't need to stand in the doorway," said his dad. "Come on in. I'll grab some drinks."

Everyone moved into the living room.

Maxim reclined on the sofa, his legs spread wide. LeGuivre sat next to him. He looked uncomfortable, fidgety. He kept adjusting his position, as if trying to create more distance between them without making it obvious. Greg and Teddy sat in a couple of easy chairs opposite them.

"So how was the drive?" Teddy asked.

"Effortless. Beautiful day for it, too," said Greg. "Bet you had some fun, eh, Alex?"

Teddy frowned. *Why? Maybe Maxim only tried to throw him out of the car.*

"Did something happen?" Teddy asked.

"What? No. I mean Alex's new ride. It's something else. You should check it out."

"You guys didn't come together?"

"I wish. Maybe Alex will let us switch cars for the weekend? Eh? Whaddya say?"

LeGuivre wore an expression that suggested Greg had just pulled a gun on him. He forced a laugh. "I'd love to Greg, but, you know, insurance and stuff."

"Oh, sure, sure. Seriously, though, you should take Chex outside and show him."

LeGuivre leaned forward and rested his elbows on his knees with his hands locked together. He looked back and forth between Teddy and Greg, his legs bouncing.

"Yeah, OK. Sure."

Maxim gave Teddy a look that seemed to say, "Better you than me."

He followed Alex out to the driveway. Next to his dad's BMW was Greg's car, a dark-blue Audi sedan. Behind them sat a steel-coloured Mercedes AMG C 63, its high buff glinting in the sunlight.

"It's like a German invasion out here," said Teddy.

LeGuivre smiled. "Ha. Yeah."

"Just gorgeous," Teddy said, as they approached the car. His hand instinctively reached out to touch the body, to feel its lines. The moment his finger made contact he recoiled. "Oh, sorry, do you mind?"

"Sure, go ahead."

Teddy circled the car silently, taking in its shape, sensing the raw power housed within. When he reached the driver's side he paused and peeked through the window. He could almost smell the polished leather through the glass. *I wonder how much this bad boy cost?* He'd read enough car blogs to have a pretty good idea, and it wasn't as if he'd never seen an expensive car before. His dad's car would have been almost as expensive when it was new. What stuck in his mind was the thought that it belonged to someone his own age. He straightened and looked across the car's roof. LeGuivre stood on the opposite side, watching him with a passive, almost curious expression.

"You want to get in?"

Hell yeah I do. Are you freaking kidding me?

Teddy shrugged. "I mean, sure. Since we're out here."

LeGuivre reached for the handle on his side. The doors unlocked automatically.

Teddy placed himself in the driver's seat, careful not to brush his cast on anything. He wasn't even thinking about his arm. He just didn't want to get any plaster on the interi-

or. The seat seemed to wrap around him, to welcome him. It wasn't like the Formula cars. Sitting in them felt like wearing a suit of armour—powerful, but utilitarian. This felt luxurious, like . . .

He snapped out of his reverie, suddenly remembering who was sitting next to him. "Why are you here?"

LeGuivre was silent for a minute. They both stared out of the windshield.

"Oh, you know," he hesitated. "With your accident and all. Just wanted to check up on you. We drivers have to stick together, right?"

"Cut the crap, Alex," he said, glancing at him out of the corner of his eye. "We've never been in anything together."

Another moment passed.

"I guess . . . I guess I wanted to tell you that I get it. I get what you're going through."

What is he talking about? "You mean your accident? Thanks and all, but I don't remember you missing any races, let alone the whole season."

"It's not the *whole* season. It's only—"

"*Not* the point, dude."

"I mean about the other stuff." LeGuivre looked out of the side window. "The stuff about your dad. Uh, your birth dad."

Teddy dropped his shoulders. *Huh.* His mind flashed back to day of the crash—to when Nick had come up to him at lunch. *"The sons of legends."*

Alex continued. "Other people don't get it. Not really. They think it must be awesome to have a famous-driver father."

Teddy raised his eyebrows and looked at Alex.

Is he . . . blushing? "Seems pretty awesome."

"You know what I mean."

"I'm not sure I do, actually." Teddy knew exactly what he meant. But after everything LeGuivre had put him through, he was delighting in making him squirm. Part of him knew he was being a jerk. He ignored it.

LeGuivre shifted in his seat and looked forward again. "You know my dad isn't even all that crazy about me driving?"

Why? Is there someone who is *crazy about you driving?* The joke almost leaped from Teddy's mouth. The opening was too good. But something stopped him. It occurred to him that he *did* know that. At the shootout, his dad had spent some time with the Dragon. Teddy remembered that after the race his dad had told him the same thing LeGuivre was telling him now. He didn't think it was right to reveal that now, though.

"I didn't, no. Why not?"

LeGuivre seemed to consider his answer carefully. "I think for the same reason any parent wouldn't like it. 'Cause it's dangerous."

Sounds like your dad would get along with my mom.

"But your dad did it."

"Yeah, and it was even more dangerous back then. I guess he just thinks that, well, that I could do anything. My grandparents came from France with nothing. Making it big was, like, really important to them. Don't get me wrong. He didn't just do it for the money and stuff."

No. You don't last long racing if you're only in it for the money.

"Sure. It's like Greg says. 'Drivers are wired funny.'" Teddy looked at LeGuivre, who smiled.

"I've never heard him say that. Sounds about right, though."

Teddy felt as if he'd been the recipient of some secret wisdom. He tingled with pride.

"Anyway," LeGuivre continued. "I guess he thinks that I have more opportunities than he did, so why take the risk?"

"Yeah, but he must get it, right? I mean, if you've got the bug, it's not even a choice."

Teddy didn't doubt for a second that LeGuivre should be racing, despite the issues he had with him as a driver. He wished he could still feel that kind of certainty about his own life.

But what does this have to do with Graham?

"For sure, he gets it. And I'm not saying he's not supportive. But, it's like . . . everyone else is going to compare me to him. Whatever, I can handle that. But, like, I've gotta prove it to *him*. Not prove that I'm great, or as great as he was, but that I'm good enough to belong there. That I'm not better off, I don't know, as a lawyer or something. That I'm not just wasting everyone's time. You know?"

It was like a grinding gear had finally slid into place. LeGuivre's words gripped Teddy's mind and sent it spinning. He remembered every race. Every encounter they'd had on and off the track. Every insult they'd slung at each other. Every cruel thing he'd said about Alex behind his back. He'd been watching a 3D movie and only just put on the glasses. It didn't change what he thought of LeGuivre. Not exactly. He wasn't about to forgive him for all the crap he'd put him through. But he saw something now that he hadn't before—something he recognized in himself.

I've been dealing with this for less than a year. This guy's had to deal with it his whole life.

Then he had a thought that disturbed him to his core.

If Graham had raised me, would I be more like Alex? Would I even want to race?

He didn't know the answer. And he didn't know what to say. But he realized he didn't need to say anything. LeGuivre was explaining this to *him*.

If anything, he thought, fighting the urge to gag, *I could learn a thing or two from this guy.*

Silence filled the car.

Teddy cleared his throat. "Yeah, sure. That makes sense. Should we go back in?"

"Yup, sounds good."

Outside the front door, Teddy paused. "Thanks. You know. For coming."

"You bet. And hey, don't give up. It's just one season. There's always next year, right?"

"Heh. Yeah. Sure."

Teddy clenched his jaw. *For you maybe.*

Back in the living room, his dad and Greg were laughing about something. Maxim hadn't moved an inch since they left. His beer though, Teddy noticed, was empty.

"There you are!" His dad was suspiciously perky. "You won't believe this. Greg, tell him."

"OK, OK. Well, Chex, look, there's another reason we came out here. We wanted to give you the news personally."

Teddy's stomach turned. It was clear from their expressions that they thought this "news" was good. But he'd developed an allergic reaction to the word.

"You know Carter Adams?"

"Sure." Carter and Teddy had gone through the academy together at Motown.

"Well, he's going to be taking your seat in the series while you're recovering."

Huh. I guess that's good news.

"Cool. How'd he swing that?"

Teddy didn't want to say it, but he could tell everyone knew what he was thinking. Carter was a decent driver, but he wasn't an obvious choice by any stretch.

"No idea. Dan Williamson called me up the other day and asked if I thought he could hack it. Sounded like it was all but a done deal already. They just wanted my stamp on it or something."

"Well, good for him, I guess."

There's something else. There's no way they're this excited about that "news."

"But that's not all. You know how your series mechanic quit? What's his name? Travis?"

The silver lining? How could I forget?

"Trevor. Sure."

"Well, guess what? They've asked if I can spare Maxim for the rest of the summer. It seems he impressed Dan at the shootout last year."

"Plus, there's no one else available midseason," his dad said teasingly.

Teddy felt his eyes bug out, and he snapped his head towards Maxim.

"What the! Why didn't you say something sooner?"

Maxim tilted his head and shrugged. "And interrupt male bonding time?" He waved a finger at LeGuivre.

Teddy stared at the Russian. *This. Guy.*

"I am not certain I will take job," Maxim said. "Students are good to work with. School drivers are good. Professional drivers? They are difficult. Complain lots."

Teddy was almost bursting with glee.

"Cross my heart, Maxim. You won't hear a peep from me."

"I believe when I see, Chex."

Chapter 29

Teddy rushed into the school. His backpack flopped awkwardly and slid off his shoulder as he reached to open the inner doors with his good arm. Other stragglers were dashing down the hallways.

"O Canada" suddenly blared over the PA system. Teddy froze at attention.

Damn.

He was supposed to meet with Mrs. Reynolds before class, but he hadn't yet mastered his morning routine one-handed.

She's gotta cut me a little slack, he thought.

He knocked on her office door.

"Come in." Her voice sounded sweetly condescending.

Or not.

"Oh, Teddy. I was worried you'd forgotten."

"Sorry, Mrs. Reynolds."

Is that a new cat picture? Is that a new cat?

"Think nothing of it," she said.

Teddy imagined her saying to herself, "I, after all, think nothing of you."

"How are you feeling?"

"Much better, thanks."

"I'm so very glad to hear it."

I'll bet you were dizzy with concern.

"Well, I don't mean to be abrupt," she said, "but I'll get right to the point. You really shouldn't be missing any more class, especially given the purpose of this meeting."

Teddy leaned forward in his seat. He was far more anxious about learning this "purpose" than he was about missing class. All his dad had told him was that the school wanted to discuss the rest of his term with him.

"You've missed quite a few days this term, and while your teachers say you've done a decent job of keeping on top of things, that was before your accident."

His heart sank. *I should have figured.*

"I'm sorry, Mrs. Reynolds. I'll work extra hard—"

She raised a hand. "Teddy, you don't need to apologize for anything. I'm sure you didn't *mean* to crash your car."

Oh, well I'm glad you're sure about that.

She continued. "But the fact is that you're now a week behind and exams are right around the corner."

Teddy had a sudden, terrible thought. *She's not going to make me repeat the term, is she? Or worse—summer school!*

"I've also had a call from your mother." Mrs. Reynolds's voice took on a bitter tone.

Teddy tried not to smile. He'd seen his mom go to battle with petty officials, salespeople, and customer service agents. Her opponents usually left the exchanges with deep emotional scarring.

"She tells me your arm won't be healed before the exam period. And since it's your writing hand, she has insisted that some sort of"—she cleared her throat—"exemption is in order."

Did she say "exemption"? As in, "no exams for me"? I'll take option B, please.

"Now, I understand that you've already received a conditional offer from McLachlin University."

"Uh-huh."

"Yes. Well. I asked your teachers, and, after some discussion, they agreed that, if you can catch up with your assignments and finish the rest of term strong, they're willing to assign you a mark based on that. A mark that will satisfy your offer."

Teddy couldn't process what he was hearing. He scanned the room for hidden cameras. *Is this a joke? When did this become a joke?*

"Teddy, did you hear what I said?"

"I—uh, yes. Yeah. Thanks. That's . . . this is just great."

"I'd say so. You're a very lucky young man."

"Lucky" didn't cover it. He didn't have to write exams *and* he'd still get into university?

Is Mars in transit through my star sign? Is this karma for the crash? Do I have to sacrifice a goat or something?

"Do you have any questions for me?" asked Mrs. Reynolds.

"No. Thanks. Thank you."

"All right. I guess you'd better get to class, then."

Teddy floated out of the office.

No exams. It's like I'm basically done high school.

The thought made him giddy. It was almost enough to squash all the disappointment he felt about his lost season—his lost career. Almost.

Two weeks of hard work. I can do this.

He stood outside the classroom door, put on an easy smile, and prepared his apology for Mrs. Gottlieb. When he entered, the teacher stopped talking. Everyone in the room looked at him. Richard was sitting at the back, next to Teddy's empty chair. Teddy's stomach clenched. Between rushing to school and what Mrs. Reynolds had said, he'd forgotten all about the other important meeting he had that day. But when he saw his friend's smiling face, he could suddenly think of nothing else.

He still had to talk to Leah.

"Ah, the wounded warrior returns," said the teacher. "Good to have you back. Take your seat, please."

Teddy managed to mutter "thanks" as he made his way to the back of the room. Richard pointed at the cast, grinned, and gave him two thumbs up.

Despite his new motivation to be a model student, Teddy barely heard a word his teachers said all morning. His thoughts ping-ponged between the news about exams and what he would say to Leah. By the time the bell rang for lunch, the world was spinning.

He'd considered waiting until the end of the week to have the conversation. Even the end of the day. But putting it off would be torturous. He'd see her every day at school, and there was no way he'd be able to hide that something was up. Plus, the whole reason he'd decided to tell her in the first place was that he couldn't live with any more secrets. He'd only held off this long because he wanted to tell her in person.

She deserves that much.

There was no way around it. He had to tell her now.

Leah was waiting for him and Richard outside the cafeteria. She rushed forward with her arms wide open. He fought the urge to bolt. His broken arm wasn't in a sling, but when she moved in to hug him he instinctively raised it in front of him as though it were, and leaned his shoulders forward to leave a safe space for it between them.

"Hey! How was your first morning back?" She pulled away and looked at his arm. "Does it hurt? What is that?"

Teddy followed her eyes. Greg and Maxim had both signed his cast. Greg had written "Speedy recovery," with "speedy" underlined. Maxim had written something in Russian. He'd told Teddy it said, "Pain is weakness leaving your body." But for all Teddy knew, the string of Cyrillic letters was a recipe for borscht.

"Oh," he said. "Maxim and Greg visited on Saturday." He left out the part about LeGuivre. He figured now wasn't the time to get into that.

"Aw, man. I'm sorry I wasn't there for the welcome-home party." She hugged him again.

"It's cool. I was pretty tired all weekend."

Well at least that's not a lie.

"How was the cottage?"

"Super gross. A whole family of mice decided to camp out in the sofa over the winter. Completely destroyed the cushions. Left poop everywhere." She frowned. "There was even a dead baby mouse shoved in behind one of them."

"Mmm. Anyone else starving?" asked Richard.

"You're disgusting." She slapped him playfully on the shoulder.

Teddy felt his face redden.

"Nope. I'm just a growing boy. You guys coming?"

Leah started to follow Richard towards the serving area. Teddy reached for her arm.

"Hey wait," he said.

"Oh." She paused. "OK."

Richard kept walking. "I'll see you in there. I'm wasting away!"

"What is it?" she asked. "Are you feeling OK? You look weird." She put a hand on his forehead. He swatted it away a little more aggressively than he meant to.

"Sorry. I'm fine. It's just . . . it's a nice day. I thought maybe we could eat outside."

"Just us?"

"Yeah."

"OK." She smiled. "But we still need to get food first."

"Oh yeah. Right."

I'll take the rat poison, please. No sides.

They walked towards the soccer field behind the school. Leah was asking him about the accident.

"Your dad sort of explained it, but I think he was trying to make it sound like it was no big deal for my sake. Were you scared?"

On a scale of one to right now?

"I don't remember it that well.

"Oh god. Did you get a concussion?"

"Not a bad one."

They took a seat on the bleachers. Leah unwrapped her sandwich and started to eat. Teddy left his sitting on the bench beside him. The day was sunny and warm, but he felt cold. Not the sharp cold of an icy winter blast. Nor the foggy, sleepy cold he felt when he was sick. This cold felt hard and airless, like the frigid, twisted remains of some satellite that had crashed on the dark side of the moon. A metallic taste filled his mouth.

"Are you sure you're feeling all right?"

"I think we need to talk," he said. His voice was scarcely louder than a whisper. He kept his gaze on the field but watched her out of the corner of his eye.

Her chewing slowed. "OK."

His mind went blank. He didn't know how to begin.

Just say something! Start talking!

"When I was in the hospital . . ." He trailed off.

"Yeah? Teddy, what's going on?"

"I've been lying to you."

Leah stiffened. Her hands, still holding the sandwich, fell into her lap.

"About what?"

"About Allison."

She let go of the sandwich and crossed her arms. "Uh-huh." She bit her lower lip.

"I . . . She . . . She knows about Graham."

Leah relaxed. Her expression softened. "Teddy, I know that. You told me, remember?"

"I'm not finished. She knows about Graham because it was her parents who crashed into Susan. She was in the car when it happened." He turned to her.

She looked confused and concerned. She swallowed and took a breath. "OK. Why didn't you tell me this before?"

You can still get out of this! cried a panicked voice in his head. *Stop here. Make it about Graham and Susan and the accident. Don't tell her about the kiss.* He shut it out. *No. I have to keep going. I need to get it out. All of it.*

"We kissed. I kissed her."

Leah's lips tightened. She inhaled sharply through her nose. Teddy felt the heat of her gaze.

Keep going.

"In Indianapolis. After the race. She placed first and I placed second and we were hugging and I don't know it just sort of happened."

No! It didn't "just happen." I wanted it to happen. I made it happen.

Leah stood. He met her stare. Her face reddened and her whole body quivered. And then, before he could register what was happening, she wound up and hurled her sandwich at his face.

Teddy winced and brought his arms up, too late to do any good. He yelped as a bolt of pain shot up his broken arm. He felt a piece of lettuce sticking to his cheek. He wiped it off and got to his feet. Leah had already picked up her bag and was hurrying away.

"Wait, Leah. Can we . . . please. I'm sorry—"

She spun, dropped her bag, and stormed back towards him. "No!" she screamed, thrusting a finger into his face. "You don't get to say you're sorry. You've been sorry more times this past year than I can count. You don't get to be sorry anymore!"

Adrenaline surged through him. The world fell away. Time slowed. All he could see was her face. The face he'd known since kindergarten. Except he'd never seen it like this. Her cheeks flushed with anger. Her eyes glistening with tears. Her lips trembling with hurt and disappointment.

She's right. She is so, so right.

"That's it, Teddy. I'm done. We're done. You . . . You're a selfish piece of crap!" She pounded a fist on his chest. Tears rolled down her cheeks. He wanted to reach out, to wrap his arms around her. But he was frozen. "You have no idea what it's like. No freaking idea. I've tried, Teddy. I've tried to be there for you. I've forgiven you. I believed in you even when you didn't believe in yourself. I put up with . . . And you! You just . . ."

"Can I at least explain?" His words were barely a whimper.

"No." She wiped her face and grabbed her bag. "I don't want to hear it. I don't want to hear another lie come out of your mouth. Good luck, Teddy. I hope it's all worth it."

Teddy watched as Leah walked away. He couldn't move. The world rematerialized and he became aware that his heart had been beating like a snare in a drum line. His legs wobbled, and he sat down to keep himself from falling over.

The truth was all out there now, but he felt no relief. He felt nothing but emptiness. A deep emptiness that was slowly filling up with sorrow. He'd known all along that things could go this way. And yet . . .

What did I expect? That we would stay together? That she would forgive me? Again?

But part of him *had* expected that. That was the problem. Leah *had* always been there. He'd taken that for granted and she'd finally called him on it. She'd warned him before. She'd warned him when he told her about the shootout. She'd warned him again when she found him Skyping Allison in the gym. This was strike three. He was out.

What stung most was realizing that he wasn't the only one who'd been holding something back. All her anger, all her frustration—she'd been hiding it from him, bottling it up. The difference, though, the thing that melted his guts into bile, was that she'd kept her secret to protect him, and he'd kept his to protect himself.

I'm a monster.

Chapter 30

Teddy couldn't remember a time when he'd felt lonelier. The last two weeks of school were hell. It hadn't taken long for the gang to learn what had happened. None of them had wanted to take sides. He knew there was nothing he could say in his defence. Even if he'd wanted to. Instead, he isolated himself.

It's better for everyone right now.

He fell back on the tactics he'd used before Christmas—he'd duck off to the library at lunchtime and use homework as an excuse to dodge invitations from Richard or Tom to go out on the weekend. He did have a lot of work to catch up on, though. And because of his arm, his progress was slow. It was the price he had to pay to earn his exemption from exams, and it would have been that way even if his blowout with Leah hadn't happened. He took some comfort in knowing that at least he wasn't lying.

Allison had stopped texting him, too. At first, he thought she was just reacting to the coolness in his responses to her after the accident. He tried to reach out and told her what had happened with Leah. Her reply was brief: "Sorry, dude. That really sucks." Maybe she thought he regretted kissing her, like he blamed her for the break-up. Maybe she regretted kissing him back.

Maybe it has nothing to do with me and she's just focusing on her own damn life. Which is exactly what I should be doing.

It bugged him not knowing what she was thinking. But he was also relieved that she wasn't forcing him to talk about it. His world had exploded in that crash, and he'd just taken a sledgehammer to the remains. He'd need time to pick up the pieces. For now, he knew it was best to focus on what was right in front of him.

On the last day before exams, Richard begged him to hang out with them and celebrate.

"I checked with Leah," he said. "She's cool with it."

Teddy felt even worse. Either she was again proving herself to be the bigger person, or she'd already gotten over him. And he hated the idea that Leah and Richard were talking about him. Jealousy gurgled up inside him, singeing the back of his throat like acid.

"Thanks, but I'll pass. I'm not feeling so hot."

Wow, telling the truth is easy when you feel like garbage and have nothing left to lose.

That evening, his dad suggested they go out for dinner at The Keg.

"We have to do *something* to mark the occasion," he said.

When they arrived, Matt was waiting for them.

"Surprise! Guess who's here for the weekend?"

He was happy to see his brother but was sure the timing wasn't a coincidence. Thankfully, neither Matt nor his dad asked him why he wasn't out with his friends that night.

They sat in a booth that was all dark wood and over-stuffed leather. As usual, the three of them ordered the same thing: Caesar salad, bacon-wrapped filet mignon, and potato wedges. And, as usual, his dad made a joke to the server about good taste being genetic. When they'd finished eating, his dad reached into his pocket and pulled out an envelope.

"I know it's a couple of weeks early, but I wanted to give this to you now so you didn't make other plans." He passed the envelope to Teddy. Inside were two passes to the Am-Run Pro Toronto Grand Prix. "Since the race weekend falls on your birthday this year, I thought, 'What better way to celebrate?'"

Teddy studied the passes. They were different from the ones he'd seen in previous years. They were silver and shiny and along the bottom they read, "Guest of Dreyfus Minerals."

His eyes widened. "These are pit-lane hospitality suite passes." Teddy turned them over in his hand as if they were made of porcelain.

"Yup. This year we're doing it in style. You'll be able to see right down into the pits—"

"While Dad is busy schmoozing at the open bar," Matt said, winking.

"But what's Dreyfus Minerals?" Teddy asked.

"A big mining firm based in Toronto. Silver mostly. I met the owner, Reg Dreyfus, at a dinner with one of my clients. It's a long story. He's sponsoring a team for the Toronto race and when I told him about you he said we absolutely had to come along."

"Dad, this is incredible."

Teddy had been anxious about going to the race this year. He'd actually considered skipping it altogether. Formula Firebrand would be racing that weekend, too, and he wasn't sure he'd be ready to go back as a spectator by then. But he hadn't missed this race since he was old enough to walk.

"Thanks," he said. "This is awesome." His dad and Matt looked at each other and grinned. "What? What is it?"

"There's something else."

"Two things, actually," said Matt, clearly excited.

His dad put a hand on Matt's arm, as if to settle him down. "The first thing is a bit serious actually." He cleared his throat. "Like most drivers, Graham had a substantial life insurance policy. Since Susan passed away, too, everything was left to you."

Teddy looked at Matt, whose grin had become a permanent fixture on his face. "You're rich, Brony Stark."

I'm what?

His dad held up a hand. "Well, hold on, not exactly. We're not talking Richie Rich money, here. And the money is held in a trust. Your mother and I have been receiving an allowance from it each year to help finance your upbringing."

Finance my upbringing? What does that even mean?

"According to the terms of the trust, you don't gain control until you turn twenty-five. The idea was that, should anything happen to them, Graham and Susan didn't want you to suddenly have a huge chunk of money. They wanted you to finish school and work for a few years *before* you inherited anything."

Did he say huge *chunk?*

"But, they also didn't want money to be a problem if you wanted to go to university," he continued. "So, on your eighteenth birthday, a certain amount will be released, enough to pay your way at pretty much any school you want to go to. It's more than enough to cover four years tuition and expenses at McLachlin.

"Jeez, Dad, get to the point already," Matt said, fidgeting with glee.

Wait, what! That wasn't the point?

"OK, fine then, you tell him."

Matt reached into his pocket and fished out a round plastic bauble on a silver wire loop. He tossed it at Teddy. A key fob. For a car. The logo was unmistakable. Stylized wings and a circle with the word "MINI" inside it.

This isn't real. This is not *real.*

"It's for real, kid."

Get out of my head!

"I'm calling you Mini-Me from now on."

"Wait. Matt, did you . . . ? Is it . . . ?"

"In the parking lot? Right here? Right now? There's only one way to find out."

Teddy leaped from his seat and dashed out of the restaurant. He started pushing buttons on the fob, listening for the sound of a door unlocking, or—

Ah! Turn it off! Turn it off!

The horn blared a few rows from where he stood. He could see the lights flashing. Finding the panic button, he pushed it before running in the direction of the noise. He stopped next to it—the car from the dealership. At first, he thought it looked funny sitting there between two vehicles twice its size. Then he shook his head.

No. It's perfect.

Teddy stood there admiring it long enough for his dad and brother to come sauntering up behind him.

"He knows how the door works, right?"

"Doesn't look like it. Here, sport, better let me have that key back."

Teddy snapped out of his trance and stepped towards the car.

"Not a chance."

He slid into the seat. It felt just the same as it had the first day he saw it. He popped the key into its slot, put in the clutch, and hit the ignition button. He revved the engine a few times. Outside, he could see his dad and brother giggling and clapping. He didn't care. He took his feet off the pedals and let the engine idle. Its gentle rumble vibrated through his body. It felt soothing, comforting. He thought about Susan and Graham.

This is their gift to me. Not the car or the money. But the feeling that they were still looking out for him. Still supporting him. It was almost too much to take. He shut the engine off and opened the door.

"Hey, not so fast!" called Matt. "You don't expect *me* to drive that thing home, do you?"

Chapter 31

Teddy and his dad arrived early Sunday morning. Parking near the track would be almost impossible to find by midmorning. Plus, they wanted time to wander through the paddock before the crowds showed up.

While his dad paid, Teddy waited by the car and looked across the street at the Princes' Gates, a monumental arch flanked by columns. It stood at the end of the track's front straightaway. Though it wasn't even a hundred years old, far from the oldest structure in Toronto, it was one of the few things in the city that felt ancient. Teddy thought about all the times he'd approached that gate in his video games— he'd watch it grow from the size of a thumbnail into a towering colossus on the screen. The track took a hard right just before the gate's opening. He'd often wondered what it would be like if the barriers weren't there, if he could drive a race car right through the arch at top speed. Perched on top of the gate was a sculpture of Victory, a robed goddess standing tall, her arm raised high and holding a maple leaf. Seeing it filled him with a kind of regretful patriotism.

A Canadian Victory, he thought. *Wouldn't that be nice.* It pained him to know that it wouldn't be him. Not this year. Not ever.

They crossed the street and entered an enormous convention centre, the gateway to the track grounds. A long,
high-ceilinged hallway stretched out in front of them.
Floor-to-ceiling windows lined one side of the hallway. Beyond them, glimpses of the track peeked through openings
in the bleachers set up for the weekend. The other side was
a massive brick wall punctuated at regular intervals by sets
of double doors. Above them hung signs for Exhibit Hall A,
Exhibit Hall B, and so on. He knew that beyond those doors
there were no "halls." All doors led to a single room the size
of a commercial airplane hangar filled with show cars, dis-
plays for all sorts of car-related products, and trailers
belonging to the teams in the lower series. It was where he'd
find the Firebrand paddock.

The whole drive into the city, he'd wondered whether
he should insist that they walk straight down the hallway
and leave the doors unopened. Seeing the trailers and the
cars would be nothing less than torture. But there were
people on the other side he was desperate to see. Maxim,
for one. And Allison. They hadn't talked in weeks. And
while he hadn't yet figured out what he wanted to say to
her, he felt enough time had passed since his blowout with
Leah that he could handle seeing her without collapsing
into a puddle of guilt. He was even eager to see Carter
again, to find out how he was getting along with his car and
his mechanic. His dad stayed quiet as they walked, as if
sensing the battle raging within Teddy. But by the time they
reached Exhibit Hall D, the pull had overwhelmed him.

"We should probably check in on Maxim," Teddy said.

"Seems only polite."

They walked through a labyrinth of stalls, trying to get their bearings. The setup inside the convention hall was a little different every year, so it was impossible to know where the Formula Firebrand paddock was without a map.

Teddy spotted a familiar figure storming through the centre of it all.

"Hey! Alex!" he shouted. His voice echoed off the trailer walls before evaporating into the yawning space above.

The other driver slowed his pace and looked around for the source of the voice. Spotting Teddy and his dad, he stopped.

"Oh, hi guys," he said, smiling.

"Hey." Teddy waved and smiled back.

OK. We're smiling now. This is totally normal.

"Looking for the paddock?"

"It's a bit of a maze in here," said Teddy's dad.

"Yeah. Come on, I'll show you. I'm heading there anyway."

Teddy walked beside LeGuivre. It felt awkward but not in a bad way. It was like walking on a trampoline. There was tension beneath each step. *Let go, have fun, bounce*, it seemed to say. But they weren't there yet.

"How's the arm?"

"It's good, thanks. A few more weeks."

"That's great. So you'll be back for Laguna?"

"That's the plan. How was your race yesterday?"

The tickets for Mr. Dreyfus's suite were only valid for the day of the main race. Teddy's dad had offered to buy some general admission tickets for Saturday, but Teddy had told him he didn't have to. He didn't know how he would react to watching his own car from the stands. *What if I can't handle it? What if I don't want to come back the next day?* The suite passes were too good—he couldn't take the chance.

"A battle. This track is tough. Came third behind Kayla and Kyle."

Teddy sensed the anxiety in LeGuivre's voice when he said their names. He was about to ask "What's the deal with you guys?" but held it in. To his surprise, the idea of tugging on LeGuivre's nerves was less appealing to him than it used to be.

"Well, congrats. Good to have a Canadian on the podium at the home race."

"Thanks. Well, I'm over here," he said, indicating to the right. "I think your guys are over there."

"Great. Thanks."

"No prob." LeGuivre nodded at Teddy's dad and walked away.

"And good luck today," Teddy called.

Without turning, LeGuivre raised a hand over his head and waved.

His dad turned to him. "Well, that was—"

"Weird."

They found their way to Carter's trailer. Maxim was closing up the car. Teddy paused as his stomach twisted. He felt jittery all over, and he fought the urge to jump into the car and drive off with it.

Maxim looked up and then checked his watch.

"Ah. You are early worm."

"I'm what?"

"He means early bird, sport."

"Do I?" Maxim cocked his head. He put down his tools, walked over, and pulled Teddy into a big hug.

"It is good you came. I was not sure you would. That would have been mistake. This your race, whether you drive or not." He slapped Teddy on the back. The force shook loose all his apprehensions about being there, like dust beaten from a rug.

Carter stepped out of the trailer. He looked thinner than Teddy remembered, like a long-distance runner.

Or one of those rock stars who survives on whisky and cigarettes.

Slight bags hung beneath his clear blue eyes, and a layer of dark scruff on his cheeks and neck made him look at least five years older than he was. When he saw Teddy, he lit up.

"Hey man!"

"Morning." Teddy smiled.

"Ugh. Tell me about it. Not a fan of this AM stuff."

"Rough night?"

"What? No. Of course not. I'm just more of a night owl." He looked at Teddy's arm and started to fidget. "So, how's the old . . ." He raised his eyebrows, frowned, and nodded at the cast.

"It's fine, thanks."

"Tough break. Er. I mean—"

"It's OK, I know what you meant." Teddy clapped him on the shoulder. "I'm just glad they found someone to keep my seat warm for me."

"Ha. Well, I'm doing my best."

Teddy heard a wrench drop. He looked to see Maxim stoop to pick it up.

Maxim dropped a tool?

"Oh yeah? How was yesterday?"

"Didn't finish." He said this so matter-of-factly, Teddy was sure he'd heard him wrong.

"You didn't finish?"

"Nope." He smiled.

"What happened?"

"Made contact with, uh, what's his name, the young one? The prodigy? Steven?"

"Simon?"

"That's the one. Had the inside going into Turn 7. He came around the outside. A bit aggressively if you ask me. Forced me into the wall. Didn't crash or anything but messed up the wheels on the right side a bit. Had to come in. Coulda happened to anyone, I suppose."

Bang. Another tool had fallen.

Teddy smirked.

"Oh, sure. Absolutely. Well, better luck today then."

"Thanks, man." He checked his watch. "Ah! Gotta run. Catch you later." He reached out and slapped Teddy on the arm, just above his cast. "Oh, shoot. Sorry." His face went beet red.

"It's fine. Go."

When Carter was gone, Teddy turned to Maxim.

"I cut cast off now, maybe?"

Teddy laughed.

"I don't think the cast is the problem. I'd still be a one-handed driver."

Maxim huffed.

"You would still drive more than five laps I think."

Five laps! Poor Carter.

"Now, we must go. Morning practice starts."

They started to wheel the car down to the track. It dawned on Teddy that he wouldn't get to see Allison now. She'd already be in her briefing and then heading straight to the track.

Maybe I can sneak back before the race.

On the way to the pit suite, Teddy and his dad walked through the pro paddock. At ground level, the morning air felt thick and heavy. The sky was bright and clear. *It's gonna be a sticky afternoon*, Teddy thought. *Brutally hot for the drivers.* But right now, all he could feel was anticipation. It hung like a mist—like little drops of moisture charged with electricity. They zapped him as he passed through them. He shivered with excitement.

It was still early, but they were far from alone. Streams of people trickled through the rows between the trailers, poking their noses as far as they could over the barrier ropes to get a closer look at the cars. Dozens of mechanics were hard at work, but there were no drivers to greet the eager fans. They'd be in the briefing rooms with their engineers, discussing the upcoming practice session, how the weather that day might affect performance, how their quali-fying position or yellow flags would affect their fuel and tire strategies for the race. He'd had a taste of the planning that went into every race, but AmRun Pro was on a different level altogether. The Firebrand races were too short to need fuel stops, and accidents weren't common. If you had to pit for any reason, your race was probably finished. In AmRun Pro, stopping for fuel and tires was part of the game, and yellow flags often happened several times in a race. A driver could lead almost every lap only to get stuck at the back if an accident occurred at the wrong time. More than once Teddy had seen drivers who would have struggled to make the top ten take the podium because of when the yellow flags fell.

They made their way to pit lane. A row of luxury suites stood high above, supported by a huge scaffold. As a kid, Teddy had thought it would make an excellent jungle gym.

A chain-link fence surrounded the scaffold at ground level. The only way in was through a little tent, which was manned by a handful of cheery-looking people in matching bright T-shirts who asked to see their tickets. Teddy and his dad held up the passes dangling from lanyards around their necks. "Enjoy the race," the ticket-checkers said, waving them through.

"I don't know why," said his dad, "but I always get nervous with things like that. Even when I know I'm in the right place. You know?"

Teddy nodded. He looked up from the base of scaffold.

The right place. Sure.

They climbed a metal staircase. At the top was a walk-way that ran behind the suites. The whole thing was essentially one long tent, open on all sides. Each suite was divided from the others by a white plastic fence, with white plastic tables and chairs to match. As they traversed the walkway looking for their suite, Teddy noticed that they weren't all the same. Some of the tables had flimsy plastic checkered-flag tablecloths; others had real black-and-white linens. Several were decorated with checkered-flag bunting or company branding. They all had food, but it ranged from baskets of granola bars and fruit to full breakfast buffets served from steaming silver chafers. He wondered which sort of suite they were heading for. They reached the end of the walkway.

"This is us," his dad announced. "Great spot! Pole position!"

Teddy looked around.

Definitely not the right place.

It was one of the nicest suites: fresh linens, a fully stocked bar complete with bartender, and a food table even more elaborate than Firebrand's. Ceramic plates were stacked next to a basket of steel cutlery wrapped in cloth napkins. And then there was the full hot breakfast, fresh pastries and rolls, and rows of bottled juices laid out tastefully on a bed of crushed ice.

Teddy saw his dad eye the coffee station and fight the temptation to run straight there.

"We should probably see if our host is here first," he said. Teddy wasn't sure if he was talking to him or to himself.

A tall, serious-looking man standing with two shorter but equally serious-looking men noticed them and walked over.

"Steve, so glad you could come." His tone was strong but restrained. It was like he was forcing himself to whisper because his natural voice was too much for mere mortals to bear. He offered his large hand to Teddy.

"And you must be Teddy. So good to meet you. Your father has told me all about you."

I hope not.

Teddy watched his hand disappear inside the man's fist. He began to sweat.

"It's good to meet you, too, Mr. Dreyfus. This place is great. Thanks a lot for inviting me."

"Teddy, it's my pleasure. And please, call me Reg. I'd say that my father is 'Mr. Dreyfus,' but since he passed away fifteen years ago, I can hardly use that old joke, can I?"

Teddy put on his best smile. "I guess not."

"But lucky for you, you won't be Mr. Clark for quite some time."

Teddy shifted his weight. *Does Reg know about Graham?*

"Fingers crossed!" His dad slapped Teddy on the back.

"Well, look, I'd very much like to talk more with you Teddy, but for now why don't you get yourself some food. I want to introduce your father to a few people. I'll find you soon."

"OK. Thanks."

Teddy noticed his dad toss a longing glance at the coffee as Reg led him away.

He grabbed some food and headed towards the track side of the suite. The main area gave way to three tiered rows lined with more chairs and long bar-style tables. Teddy walked down to the bottom tier and peered over the edge. He could see right into the pits. The pro teams' equipment sat locked up. The tall chests and little tents full of computer screens waited patiently while the Firebrand teams prepared their cars for practice. The first two stalls, the ones he had the best view of, were the twins'. He watched as they got into their cars and fired up the engines. The sound hit him like a punch in the gut. His appetite vanished.

Practice itself was uneventful. Even so, Teddy was on the edge of his seat. He followed the timings on a TV mounted on the scaffolding inside the suite. Allison wasn't posting great times.

Doesn't mean anything, he thought. *She could just be taking it easy.*

He wished he'd had a chance to see her. He started to worry he might not be able to sneak out as easily as he thought.

The schedule that day was tight. There were a lot of series racing besides AmRun Pro. After only a short break, the cars went out again to begin qualifying.

Teddy perched on his seat. His gaze flipped back and forth between the screen above him and the track below. It was odd, having the cars right there in front of him but finding his attention constantly drawn back to the screen. The suite was filling up, but everyone stayed at the top. He wasn't surprised. No one was as invested in what was happening on track as he was.

His heart fluttered as Allison set the fastest time and then stalled when Kayla replaced it a few seconds later. Now LeGuivre and Kyle were on the track, and Allison's time dropped down again. She took another fast lap—back into third. Then Simon, who'd been setting times below the top ten, suddenly leaped to the top of the board. Teddy clenched his fists. His feet twitched. Despite all the movement at the top, Carter stayed fixed in twelfth place.

Not bad, he thought. *All things considered.* Part of Teddy was rooting for Carter. If he did well, he could earn himself a place in the series next year. *It's not like we're competing for the same seat—not anymore.* And even though he wasn't driving it, it still felt like *his* car. He found it frustrating not to see it crack the top ten.

The session ended. Simon, Kayla, and Kyle made the top three, with Allison and LeGuivre behind them.

Well, this should be interesting.

Teddy stood and leaned over the railing, trying to catch Allison's attention as she got out of the car. *Crap. She doesn't see me.* After a brief chat with her engineer she headed out of the pits.

His dad came up behind him. "So, how does it feel being on this side of things again?"

Teddy struggled to find the words. *Like watching an ice cream cake melt in front of me, knowing I'm not allowed to eat it.*

"I'd rather be down there."

"I hear that. Don't worry, son. Laguna will be here in no time."

Sure. My grand finale.

Reg joined them.

"So, this is the series you race in, is it?"

More like "raced in." Past tense.

"Yup."

"Cars don't seem much different from the big boys', do they?"

His dad had warned him that Reg wasn't really a race fan. To him, the weekend was a promotional activity for his company, a chance to impress clients and reward his top employees. Still, when Teddy thought of the money that he must have spent on the suite, never mind sponsoring a car for the race . . . He couldn't wrap his head around it.

How could anyone spend so much on something they don't know anything about?

The thought fired him up. He looked at Reg, this man who'd seemed so intimidating an hour ago. He realized that despite the luxury around him, this was *his* turf. In a suite full of successful men and women several times his age, *he* was the expert.

What the hell, he thought. *Let's geek out.* Teddy launched into a lecture. He explained the similarities and differences between Firebrand, AmRun Light, and AmRun

Pro, between open-wheel, stock-car, and sports-car racing, between the international series and the North American ones. He went full racing nerd. Reg nodded along as he spoke, and seemed fascinated by every word.

Maybe he's just wondering, "Who the heck is this kid who won't shut up?" But Teddy didn't care. Talking about driving felt almost as good as driving. When he finished speaking, they both sighed.

"Well, I must say, I didn't realize there was so much to know. I think you've given me a new appreciation of the sport, Teddy. I'm getting quite excited now." He looked at Teddy's dad. "Quite a boy you've got here."

"You can say that again."

"Well, look, I'd love to hear more but I'm afraid I'm neglecting my other guests. And if I'm not mistaken, it looks like they're getting ready for your race."

Teddy turned back to the track. The cars were pulling out of the pits to start the warm-up lap. He felt as if he'd just snapped out of a trance.

"We'll talk some more later, I hope."

"Me, too. I mean, thanks. I mean, OK." Teddy blushed. Reg chuckled and started back up to the top level. He stopped halfway and turned. "Oh, I do have one question for you."

Teddy's heart rate jumped. The confidence that had possessed him a moment ago fled. His mind went blank.

Uh-oh.

"Who should I be rooting for?"

Teddy's mind flashed back to Indianapolis. To the pits after the race. To the kiss.

"Allison," he said. "Allison Reading."

"Reading, eh? A Canadian, I hope?"

"Yes, sir."

"Good. Always good to cheer for one of ours."

One of ours.

Chapter 32

Teddy's heart pounded. The cars pushed around the final turn and formed up for the start. He leaned over the railing to watch them power down the front straightaway. Heady fumes wafted up from the pits. He felt lightheaded.

The green flag dropped.

His head whipped back and forth as the cars flew by, jockeying for position as they screamed towards the Princes' Gates before disappearing around the first corner. He jumped back to look up at the TV screen once the last of the cars had passed. The live feed flipped from corner to corner as the cars travelled the course.

Everyone had made it through safely. *So far so good.*

Simon was fighting hard against Kayla's advances. Turn after turn, her attack was relentless.

He's not going to last long, he thought.

Teddy thought about the season's first race. He'd been reminded then how qualifying well on an empty track was one thing; holding your own against other drivers was something else.

Simon's quick, but Kayla's too much for him to handle.

Kyle, Allison, and LeGuivre stayed right behind them. By the end of the second lap, a gap had already started to emerge behind LeGuivre.

I guess all the action's going to be up front.

Five laps in, it was clear that Kayla was wearing Simon down. She stalked his draft coming out of the final corner and then moved wide and sprung up alongside him, as though she'd activated a rocket booster. She was already a nose ahead of him as they crossed the start-finish line. Teddy had no love for Kayla, but he couldn't deny her skill. He found himself cheering her on as she moved far enough ahead to dive back onto the line in front of Simon, just in time to make the turn. He was so fixated on their battle that he forgot to look back as Allison and the others approached. He checked the screen.

No change. Man, those times are close.

Mere hundredths of a second separated the top-five drivers. The cars were evenly matched.

This is going to come down to skill, he thought with excitement. *And luck.* He looked back to the top of the suite.

No one's even watching!

He thought about running up there and dragging Reg down.

See! he wanted to shout at him. *This is what it's all about!*

"Yellow flag." The voiced echoed across the track and bounced around the sparsely populated bleachers.

Teddy's head snapped back to the screen.

Oh no.

The picture on the screen showed two cars stuffed into the tire barriers at Turn 6.

Who is it? Who is it?

He waited anxiously for the drivers to get out of their cars, for the screen to show the new running order, for the field to make its way back to the front straight—anything that would reveal who had crashed.

The screen changed. A slow-motion replay began. Teddy watched as Kayla safely made it through the turn. Simon soon followed, though there was already space between them. Kyle was hard on him, and halfway through a pass attempt. Whether it was panic or just bad driving, Teddy couldn't tell, but Simon adjusted his course, knocking Kyle's car to the outside. The force pushed Simon towards the wall on his right. He cranked the car back to the left to avoid it, ramming into the back of Kyle's car again in the process. They both slid off the line, leaving just enough space for Allison and LeGuivre to squeak through.

Whew! That was close.

Teddy cheered loudly as Kayla, Allison, and LeGuivre led the field across the start-finish line. A few people from the top of the suite came down to his level to see what the fuss was about.

The accident wasn't serious, and both cars were restarted and allowed to rejoin the field. But now they were a lap behind everyone else. They'd still get to finish the race, but as far the championship was concerned, their day was done.

The pace car pulled into the pits and racing resumed. Teddy banged the railing with his good hand as they whizzed by. For the next ten laps, Teddy couldn't stand still. First, LeGuivre got around Allison. Two laps later, Allison retook her position. Even though Allison and LeGuivre were battling for second, Kayla struggled to gain any distance. Teddy almost jumped the railing when Allison overtook Kayla on lap twenty, stealing the lead.

"Is that our girl?"

Teddy hadn't noticed Reg beside him. Almost every seat in the suite's tiered section was now occupied. *Half of them are probably more interested in the crazy guy waving his cast around than the race itself.* But he didn't care.

"Yup," he said. "She's the one."

Pride surged through him. Pride and something else. Something he couldn't name. Something warm and pulsing that made his heart race and his body tingle.

"How much longer to go?" asked Mr. Dreyfus.

Teddy checked the screen. "Only a few more laps."

"I think I'd better stick in, then." The man took a seat next to him. Even seated, he was almost as tall as Teddy was standing. He turned back to the others. "We're cheering for the leader, everyone!"

They all raised their cups and glasses and hollered. And when Kayla overtook Allison on the next lap, they booed and jeered.

But Allison wasn't beaten. On the second-to-last lap, she pulled out from behind Kayla as they soared down the front straight. The white flag dropped. Everyone in the suite got to their feet. Teddy could almost hear the collective gasp as Allison inched her way forward. But it wasn't enough. She had to slide back in behind Kayla before the turn. Everyone went silent and stared at the screen. Teddy couldn't remember feeling this tense in his life.

C'mon, Allie. You can take her.

"She's running out of time, I'm afraid," said Reg. "But this is very exciting."

She only needs one chance. Just one.

Kayla was doing everything she could to hold her off, but Allison wasn't giving her an inch. She moved to pass once, twice, three times.

Just hold on. Don't give up. A little luck, that's all you need.

They entered the final corner. Allison didn't hesitate. She didn't even wait until they were on the straightaway. She pulled to the outside and launched her attack.

The start-finish line was fifty yards behind the front of the suite. Everyone was on their feet now, silent. Those who could bent forward over the railing to watch the final push. The others, unable to see that section of the track, glued their eyes to the screen. The cars seemed to move in slow motion. Every second felt like a minute. Even so, Allison's advance was relentless. With every breath she gained another foot. They approached the line side by side. The checkered flag dropped.

Did she do it? Was she in time?

The people behind him erupted in cheers and applause. Those watching the screen had seen what he hadn't. Allison had won the race.

"Ah, well! That was fantastic. What a wonderful finish, eh?"

Inside, Teddy was exploding with joy. "You're telling me."

Reg laughed. "Oh look, they've just served lunch. Won't you come and grab a plate with me? I'd love to continue our conversation from before."

Lunch? Now? All Teddy wanted to do was rush out of the suite, run to the podium, grab Allison in a hug and tell her how proud he was. Tell her how much he'd missed her. He hadn't even realized how much until that moment.

But he couldn't turn down his host. He turned to Reg and tried to make it seem that the smile stretched across his face was because of his delight at the invitation.

"Sure," he said. "I'd love to."

They sat with their food at one of the tables at the top of the suite. His dad and a few other guests joined them. Despite wanting desperately to be elsewhere, Teddy was so pumped about Allison's win that it wasn't really that hard to get into the conversation. Everyone was grilling him about what it was like to be a driver. Several people admitted that they'd never given the sport much thought before that day.

"Of course, any sport's more fun when you have someone to root for," said one woman.

"Which reminds me," said Mr. Dreyfus. "I thought we could do a pool for the big race. Everyone throws in five bucks and randomly picks one of the drivers from a hat. Should make things interesting."

"Come on, now, Reg. Ten bucks at least if you want to make it interesting," said another man.

"I'd like to play for a week at Reg's place in Muskoka," said the woman, laughing.

Teddy started to lose interest as the conversation turned to what they should wager.

Maybe this is my chance to excuse myself.

"Well, we'd better make up our minds quick," said Mr. Dreyfus. It looks like they're getting ready. What do you say, Teddy? I could really use your expert commentary. As you know, I've sponsored the number 10 car today. You can let me know if it was a good investment."

The others laughed.

Nope. No way out of this one.

"Absolutely," he said. "My pleasure."

It was an exciting race, Teddy had to admit. A crash on the very first turn took three cars out right away. Another two were collected during the restart. In the end, the Dreyfus Minerals car finished third. Teddy was happy for Reg. He didn't have the heart to tell him that the driver he'd sponsored was middle-of-the-pack at best. This was his best finish that season.

With the race finally over, he hoped Reg would turn his attention back to his hosting duties. He looked over at his dad and gave him a plaintive look.

"Reg, I insist you let me buy you a drink," his dad said, taking the hint and gesturing towards the bar area. He winked at Teddy.

Reg laughed. "How very generous of you."

Teddy waited a minute or two, so as not to be obvious, before quickly and quietly exiting the suite. He bolted down the stairs and jogged across the grounds. The covered bridge that arched over the track was the only way to leave the infield and get to the convention centre. With the main race over, many of the spectators were making their way back to their cars. The bridge was packed, a seething mass of sweaty flesh and merchandise inching its way through the passage like toothpaste through a crusty tube.

When he finally exited the bridge he broke into a trot. He didn't stop until he arrived at the Firebrand paddock. *Where's her trailer?* He snaked through the rows looking for her car, her team—anything that would tell him where she was.

"Teddy!"

His heart leaped, and he spun around. Allison ran up to him. She looked as if she was about to hug him and then stopped short. He could tell from her expression that she wasn't sure how he would respond to a hug.

Come on, Allie, he thought. *Why do you think I'm here?*

He quickly closed the distance between them and wrapped his arms around her. She squeezed back. His heart continued to race.

"Hey," he said, still holding her tight.

"Hey yourself."

"Good job today."

"Ha. Thanks. Kayla's pretty steamed."

"Meh. I'll save my tears for Kyle."

"Or Carter."

"Poor Carter."

They separated, laughing. Their hands rested on each other's forearms.

"Look, I've got to tell you something," she said. She had a strange look in her eye.

Should I be worried? Oh, no. Is Chet here?

"What?"

"Here." She led him into her trailer and closed the door.

"Before you say anything, can I just tell you how much—"

She interrupted him. "No, I need to go first."

"OK."

She took a deep breath.

"Chet and I broke up."

Teddy stepped back and almost tripped over her gear bag. He caught himself on the workbench and tried to pass it off as if he'd meant to lean against it. He tried to read her face while his own thoughts ran wild.

Is this good news? This is good news, right? Except it isn't. I mean, I'm the reason they broke up, right? Wait, did she break up with him? Did he break up with her? Does this mean that she . . . blah.

"Teddy, say something."

"I'm really sorry."

She smirked. "Well, don't say that. You don't mean it."

Touché.

"I sort of mean it. I mean, breakups are hard is all." *I should know.* "I just . . . what do you want me to say?"

She looked away. "I don't know."

Teddy was desperate to find out more but didn't know how to ask.

"How are you? I mean, how are you feeling about it?"

Allison sat down on a footstool.

"All right, I guess. I mean, things weren't great even before . . ." She looked at Teddy, holding his eyes. "You know."

He could feel his cheeks burning. He looked away. "Yeah."

"But it's good."

Teddy perked up. "Yeah?"

"Yeah.

"It frees me up, you know?"

Frees her up!

"Yeah?" His voice wavered.

"To focus on racing."

Pin, meet balloon.

"Oh. Sure." His chin dropped to his chest.

Allison moved her head to try to catch his eye.

"Hey, Teddy. I hope you didn't . . . It's just things are really complicated right now."

Seems pretty simple to me.

"You understand, right? I don't regret what happened. I just need to focus on the season. I mean, I still don't even know what I'm doing next year."

Teddy felt his arm start to ache inside its cast, taunting him. "I understand." He rubbed his wrist. "Perfectly."

"Hey, I didn't mean . . . God, I'm sorry, Teddy. I didn't think." She stood up and stepped towards him, taking his good hand in hers.

"The season's not over yet. You're still coming back for Laguna, right?"

"That's the plan."

"Well, there you go. Something to look forward to. And, hey, it's like Greg always says. It's racing. Anything can happen."

Except that sometimes "anything" means "nothing."

Chapter 33

"No, I'm telling you, I need less downforce. The whole back half of the track I'm climbing a hill."

Maxim crossed his arms and glared at Teddy. "And then you come down again. Into difficult corkscrew. I give you less wing, you fly off track."

It was Saturday. The final race weekend. Laguna Seca. Teddy's first day back in the car since the accident. His only day. Tomorrow, instead of a race, there would be a banquet for everyone involved in the series. The season's champion would be announced. Trophies would be handed out to the top finishers. Teddy would have nothing to do but watch. *Today is all that matters. It's all I've got left.*

Teddy put his hands on his hips. A slight ache throbbed in his right wrist. He looked at Stewart. "Help me out here."

Stewart raised his hands as if to say he wanted no part of the discussion.

"Stew, come on," Teddy said. "You can't not have an opinion. You're the engineer for crying out loud."

Stewart chuckled. "Oh, I have an opinion. I'm just enjoying the show. You sure you guys have worked together before?"

Teddy huffed. "Just show him the telemetry. I told you guys during the session, I'm slow through 5 and 6. But you didn't want to try. And now I'm starting P7."

"I need no telemetry."

Teddy threw up his hands.

"OK, OK." Stewart turned to Maxim. "He's not wrong. He's behind the curve on those turns."

"See!"

"But Teddy, Maxim's right. The corkscrew is tricky even with full wing. You're making those turns while accelerating downhill."

"Exactly," said Maxim.

"No, *exactly*," echoed Teddy. "I'm *accelerating*. I'm not at top speed until I'm through them. More to the point, *I'm* making those turns. Not you. And *I'm* positive I can handle it."

"Look, guys," Stewart said, adopting a more serious tone. "We can't argue about this anymore. We don't have time. At the end of the day, you're both right. But if Teddy says he can handle it, I say we give it a shot."

"Thank you." He glared at Maxim. "Besides, it's not like I have anything to lose. This is my last race, probably forever. If you think I'm going to go down without a fight, you're out of your mind."

"Well, I'm glad we settled that," Stewart said. "Now, Teddy, why don't you leave us to it. We'll see you in the pits in an hour. OK?"

"Perfect," he said, in a clipped tone. He turned and started to walk away.

He regretted getting short with Maxim. It wasn't his mechanic's fault. The truth was he'd been psyching himself out since before he even boarded the plane to California. This was Laguna Seca. His white whale. His nemesis. He wanted to apologize but didn't know how to explain why he was on edge without sounding like a dork. *"Sorry, guys, I'm just haunted by the ghost of Video Games Past."*

"Chex. Wait."

Teddy stopped and took a breath before turning around to look at his mechanic.

"Yeah."

"You passed."

"I what?"

"I give you test. You passed. You have laid aside your fears. You are free now just to drive."

Teddy smirked. Then he started to giggle. Within seconds, he was bent over, heaving with laughter.

"Oh. Oh, thank you Maxim. I needed that."

The Russian's eyes were a cocktail of confusion and embarrassment garnished with a dash of anger.

"Why do you laugh? Tell me."

"You, you . . ." Teddy tried to catch his breath. "You really are a horrible loser. Has anyone ever told you that? I love you."

"You are strange man, Chex."

"I might be, Max." He started walking away again and pumped a fist in the air. "But I have 'laid aside my fears'! Classic."

Teddy was still chuckling when he approached Allison's trailer. She was standing outside talking to her team. She waved and moved towards him.

In the weeks since the Toronto race, things had slowly settled back to normal between them. The news that she'd split from Chet had sparked a universe of possibilities in his mind. But it was just a flash—bright but brief. She seemed clear on what she wanted, and that was that. Soon after, they started talking regularly again. She would give him race reports and he would fill her in on his recovery. Her stories were way more interesting. His hand and forearm had weakened considerably inside the cast, and his daily regimen of strengthening exercises made for boring conversation.

"Hey, guess what?" Her face was all smiles.

"Oh, hang on. I can get this. The twins were disqualified from the series because aliens aren't allowed to compete?"

"God, you're *so* funny." She punched him lightly on the right arm. "What's up with you? You seem giddy."

"Oh, it's just something Maxim said."

"Maxim said something funny?" She would have looked less skeptical if he'd said that Maxim had adopted a harp-playing dolphin.

"Not really. He lost an argument and tried to play it off as a teaching moment."

She looked confused. "Uh-huh."

"Anyway, so, what's your news?"

"You won't believe this, but Rachel *Windermere* called me this morning."

"As in . . ."

"As in Rachel Windermere Racing. She asked me if I wanted drive AmRun Lights for her next year."

Teddy pretended to consider this news for a moment. "And what did you say?"

She punched him again in the right arm.

"Hey. Wounded warrior over here."

"Oh, shoot, sorry." She punched his left arm. "Better?"

"Much. No, but seriously, what did you say?"

"Oh, you know. I said I was thinking about taking some time out of racing to go to university, study business, maybe learn French."

Teddy gave her a pained look. "Low blow, Reading. Low blow."

He'd accepted the offer from McLachlin University a month ago. It had been one of the worst days of his life. "You're making a mature decision," his parents had said.

He'd laughed without humour. *What decision?*

Signing those forms had felt like gouging out his own eyes at gunpoint.

Allison had helped talk him through it. "There are tons of series you can still drive in during the summers," she'd said. "As long you're racing, right?"

Sure. Right. As long as I'm racing.

"Maybe I'll follow in my dad's footsteps and go into real estate," he'd said, shrugging.

"You could open a car dealership or something."

"Actually, Greg said he might need help with the business side at the academy in Motown. He said I could even help out with some of the instruction if I wanted."

"Well, that's awesome!" she'd said. "You might get to be the fastest one on the track for once."

He pushed away these thoughts and smiled at Allison, feeling truly happy for her. He pulled her in for a hug. "I'm really proud of you. That's great news, Allie."

"Thanks. It really is. Except . . ."

"Except?"

"Well, Rachel said something that made me . . . I don't know. It set me on edge."

Teddy raised an eyebrow.

"RWR is a small team. They normally only run a single car in Lights. They're adding a second car just for me."

"That sounds even better. Doesn't it?"

She frowned a little. "It's just that the reason they can afford to is that they got a new sponsor. She said they were really keen to support female drivers."

"Well, if it's between you and Kayla, they clearly made the right choice."

Her frown deepened. "That's not the point."

Crap! Teddy wished he could suck the words back into his mouth.

"I'm sorry. I get it."

She gave him a look that said, "Oh, really?"

"I mean, I don't 'get it' get it, but like . . . look. You know as well as I do that half the drivers here wouldn't be here if they hadn't been born into rich families or car families. That's the luck they were born with and they used it. I promise you, they don't sit around wondering whether they earned their place." Teddy thought of LeGuivre, and their conversation in his driveway. "Most of them don't, anyway."

"I guess."

"Allie, you're fourth in the championship. Depending on what happens this weekend, you could easily end up in the top three. You're an amazing driver and you know it. I say, embrace the good luck, wherever it comes from." He waved his right hand. "You never know when the bad luck's coming."

Allison was quiet for a moment. He hadn't convinced her. Not entirely.

I shouldn't have mentioned my accident. That was stupid. Selfish. She's going to feel guilty now.

"You're right," she said finally. "I appreciate you saying that."

Teddy exhaled softly, relieved. "Anytime."

"In a way it's a shame though," he said.

"And why is that?"

"Because I really want to hear you speak French."

She smiled and shrugged. "Meh. The most useful words are just like the English ones anyway."

"Name one."

Her eyes narrowed. "*Idiot.*"

Chapter 34

Teddy entered the pits, his helmet dangling by his side. His heart fluttered like a piece of paper stuck in a desk fan's grate. Each step sent a shock through every nerve in his body. He crept towards his pit stall, scanning the area as though he were looking for a place to hide—or waiting for something to jump out at him.

He focused on his breath. *This is it. This. Is. It.* He repeated the words in his mind like a mantra, using them to deflect the other thoughts pounding for his attention.

Don't . . .

(this is it)

screw . . .

(this is it)

up.

(this is it)

Without so much as a nod to Stewart or Maxim, he entered his stall and hopped the barrier. He laid out his helmet, gloves, balaclava, and, this time, his phone. He inserted his earbuds, hit Play, and closed his eyes. It was a new addition to the ritual. The Spencer Davis Group. Graham's song. It was the missing piece. Especially today, he wanted Graham here with him. The music grabbed hold of him from the inside out. It seized his heart and squeezed it to the tempo. The first organ chord vibrated along every nerve, shaking out the tension and flooding him with adrenaline. His heel bopped against the pavement. Soon his hips, shoulders, and head joined in. He began to hum along. He let it all flow through him, taking slow, deep breaths.

If this is it, he thought, *I'm damn well going to enjoy myself.*

With one last exhale he opened his eyes, a wide grin on his face.

He froze. Stewart and Maxim were staring at him. He felt the blood rush to his cheeks. He cleared his throat and, as quickly as he could, replaced the phone's earbuds with his radio earpiece and slipped the balaclava over his head.

Balaclava—check.

Teddy eased through the warm-up lap, swerving left and right to put some heat into his tires. He knew it was impossible at this speed to sense the effect of the car's lower wing angle. Still, he imagined he could. The car seemed to skate over the asphalt. It felt loose in the corners, just as he'd expected. But on the straightaway the car wanted to fly.

The cars passed through the corkscrew and entered the last few turns of the track. Teddy counted the cars in front of him to bring his mind into focus. Allison was two cars ahead of him, in sixth. LeGuivre was in front of her. In fourth was Pete Hardwick. Simon had continued to qualify well all season. Today, he was starting second, stuck between Kyle on the pole and Kayla behind him. The most important person for Teddy right now was beside him in seventh, Neil Burton.

Obstacle number 1.

He took his position and accelerated. The marshal released the green flag, weaving a frantic figure eight in the air.

Let's go!

Teddy floored it. He began pulling ahead the second they crossed the start-finish line. The first corner was so gentle that Neil's inside advantage was minimal. By the time they reached the turn, he had more than enough speed to take him on the outside.

Too easy.

He slotted himself into seventh just in time to slam on the brakes and drop into third gear. The next turn was a hairpin. He knew he could be cautious without risking a pass from Neil here. But he wasn't eager to give the other driver a chance to catch him on the exit, and he stomped on the accelerator earlier than he should have. He felt the back of his car wriggle out from beneath him. It was a minor slip but enough to send a shock through his system.

Woah. Take it easy. Nothing fun about spinning out on the first lap.

He set his sights on Allison.

No mercy. He smiled.

He'd seen how Allison had flown through Turns 2 and 3, which were sharp and close together. He suspected that she was running with more downforce than he was. But the next four turns were each separated by long stretches of straight road. *That's where I'll get her,* he thought.

Allison hit each corner perfectly. Teddy couldn't help but admire her skill. She'd enter a turn and pull away from him on the exit, but by the time she reached the next one he'd be right there shoving his nose cone into her again. *I wonder if she's enjoying this as much as I am.*

They exited the sixth turn and climbed the hill. The triple-turn corkscrew waited for them on the other side. It was clear that gravity had a firmer grip on Allison's car than on his.

He debated making a move before the crest of the hill. *No. Fun—not reckless. Wait to see how it handles on the other side.*

He checked his mirrors. He'd already gained a decent lead on the cars behind him.

Good. A little breathing room. All right, into the corkscrew.

Right, left, right—barely a car-length between the turns. He fought to keep on the racing line and had to slow much more than he'd expected. Neil suddenly filled his mirrors again.

It's OK. It's OK. Still good. Still good.

He held his ground through the last three corners. There was enough space between them to push his advantage and keep Neil at bay, but Allison was slipping away.

Gotta catch her on the front straight.

He roared past the start-finish line. Allison's car inched closer, like a fish on a line. He kept his foot on the gas through the soft first turn, but it wasn't enough. They entered the hairpin and she began to sneak away again.

The next two laps were déjà vu. Teddy couldn't catch her.

Just keep pressing. She's gotta slip up eventually.

He entered the front straightaway for a fourth time.

"Change up front," said Stewart over the radio. "Simon's dropped down one. Kayla's in second."

Teddy had barely registered Stewart's words when Allison moved off the racing line.

She's gunning for Pete.

Her pass was flawless. She glided into P5.

Nice job, Allie.

When Allison had moved off the line, Teddy had managed to snatch a look at the situation up front. Kyle and Kayla had already vanished into the hairpin. Simon had LeGuivre and, now, Allison right on his tail.

Simon's holding them up, he realized. *He must be defending like crazy up there.*

They moved through the hairpin. Right away, Teddy could see that Pete wasn't going to prove as challenging as Allison. His turns weren't as clean as hers, and he couldn't pull away from Teddy as easily as she had.

He pushed Pete through Turns 4, 5, and 6. The ground rose beneath them. Pete drifted to left, following the racing line. Teddy plowed straight through, letting the line move out from beneath him. He sailed past Pete's right side, rejoining the line and bouncing his wheels on the curb inside of Turn 7.

Woah, woah, woah.

He scrambled to control the car as he wound through the corkscrew, desperate not to let Pete retake the position. His heart thumped as his guts sloshed around inside him. At the bottom of the corkscrew, he found himself staring once again at the back of Allison's car.

Round two.

There was hardly any space between him, Allison, LeGuivre, and Simon. Even from sixth, he could see Simon fighting hard to keep them off his back. They exited the final turn. LeGuivre made his move. He popped out from behind the young driver and pushed up beside him. Simon must have decided he couldn't fight him anymore and shifted slightly off the line. It was the right move, but it cost him. Allison seized the opportunity, whipping her car into LeGuivre's draft on the front straight. LeGuivre was past Simon before they crossed the start-finish line. By the time they reached the first turn, Allison was half a car-length ahead. She held the outside line. They approached the hairpin. Allison edged in front of Simon and dove hard in front of him. Simon slammed on his brakes. Teddy reacted quickly, braking and dodging to the outside to avoid smashing into him.

Way too close!

Simon was clearly rattled. He took the hairpin even slower than Teddy had been until now. *Hope he doesn't recover his nerve before we get to the hill.* But now Pete had caught up again. Teddy's muscles started to twitch when he realized that he'd be trapped between the two of them through the part of the track where his setup was weakest.

I can't wait for the hill, he thought. *I've got to make a move now.*

They exited Turn 4.

I wonder if . . . The fastest route between the turns went to the right side of the track first, before swiping left at the last minute. Teddy imagined what would happen if he just kept to the left the whole way. As Simon drifted to the right, he'd leave Teddy with a clear shot down the inside. It was a risky move. He'd be taking a slower line, and he couldn't be sure his low wing angle would give him enough of advantage to make up for it.

Let's roll the dice.

He hammered the gas pedal. His car launched forward, leaving his heart and guts in the rearview. Simon stuck to the line, and the track opened up in front of Teddy.

Come on . . . come on.

He was gaining ground but running out of space. He didn't need to clear Simon entirely to claim the line when it veered left again into the next turn. But he needed to be far enough ahead to force Simon to concede it to him. He counted each inch he gained.

Side by side. Just a little more.

The turn was coming up fast. He took a deep breath and entered the braking zone.

Now!

It was enough. He decelerated sharply and pulled left. The turn was his.

Whew! All right. Now we're moving.

"Teddy—you know there's a racing line right?" He could hear the smile on Stewart's face through the radio.

"Sometimes, you've gotta make your own line," he said, panting.

"Fair enough. Just keep it on the track."

"I'll do what I can."

Allison was now three car-lengths ahead of him, still hot on LeGuivre's tail.

OK, Allie. Nowhere left to hide. Just gotta catch you first.

She didn't make it easy. Three, four, five laps went by. There seemed to be nothing Teddy could do. Without Simon in their way, LeGuivre and Allison flew around the track with flawless technique. Teddy was fighting as hard as he could just to keep up with them.

"We've got about five more laps, Teddy," said Stewart.

"I know, I know. I just can't catch them!"

"Keep on it. There's still time."

I don't need time, he thought. *I need a miracle.*

Twice more they passed the start-finish line.

A memory flashed in Teddy's mind: sitting in his dark basement, his fingers cramping as he pounded the controller. His right arm started to ache.

Stop it! he commanded. The pain vanished.

He passed through the hairpin. He was already picturing the hill in his mind.

There's got to be a way to gain some ground.

Leaving the line wouldn't help. Not with the distance between him and Allison. If anything, he had stay as close behind her as possible, to try to pick up some advantage in her draft.

The engine whined as the track rose beneath him. He kept his car squarely behind Allison's.

Was that an inch? Maybe two?

He blinked and her lead vanished. He slammed the brakes.

What the—!

They crested the hill. A marshal outside the barrier wall was frantically waving a yellow flag.

Stewart's voice crackled in his ear. "Caution! Caution! Caution!"

Teddy followed LeGuivre and Allison through the corkscrew.

Huh. You don't see that every day.

The twins were stopped halfway down the hill. Kayla's car was pointed backwards, while Kyle's was butted up alongside hers, locked together like an automotive yin-yang symbol.

Teddy smiled and turned his head as he passed by them.

Aw. That's kinda cute. Brother and sister. Better luck next time.

They completed the lap under yellow. By the time Teddy reached the corkscrew again, the twins' cars had already been pushed clear of the track by the safety crew.

"OK," said Stewart. "We're green on the next lap. Also, white. Last lap, Teddy."

"Thanks." *No pressure.*

Teddy checked his mirrors. Pete was still behind him.

Forget about Pete. Eyes forward. You've got one foot on the podium. Just gotta climb the steps.

He took a deep breath and tried to visualize the restart. He pictured the field exiting Turn 11 and forming up. LeGuivre would take a line just left of centre. Allison would stick close to him on the right and try to pass on the outside of Turn 1. For Teddy, the smart move was obvious: glue himself to the back of LeGuivre and follow him through the inside. If Allison couldn't get around LeGuivre on the first turn, she'd be forced to fall in behind Teddy at the hairpin.

Or . . .

They hit the straightaway. LeGuivre snatched the middle of the track before they even reached the line.

Cheeky.

Allison didn't budge. She held fast on his right, their wheels an inch apart.

Teddy could smell the exhaust of LeGuivre's car as he got right up behind him.

"Hold your line, Teddy," said Stewart.

That's the plan.

The tower loomed. The marshal leaned over, his arms a blur of green and white.

Now or never.

The instant LeGuivre crossed the line, Teddy pulled to the left. He planted his foot so hard on the gas he thought he might break the seat with his back.

He tore down the straight. LeGuivre drifted a little to the right, clearly focused on pushing Allison farther off the line. It was like he'd opened a door.

Why, thank you, Alex. I guess we drivers stick together after all.

By the first turn, they were running three wide.

He tried to imagine the look on LeGuivre's face when he pulled up along his left side—and kept going.

This. Is. It.

Teddy was almost a full car-length ahead at the next turn. He let off the gas. His back end started to slide. It didn't matter. The turn was his.

Yes! Yes! Yes!

He checked his mirrors.

No way!

Allison had forced her way between him and LeGuivre. And she was positioning herself for another attack.

No way . . .

Teddy slowed for the third turn, but Allison had the grip to stay on the gas a fraction of a second longer than he could. They took the corner side by side. She started creeping forward. Teddy had the line in the next turn, but Allison held fast. He recovered the distance on the way to Turn 5, only now Allison was on the inside. Once again, Teddy had to slow earlier, and she took the lead.

NO. WAY.

He shadowed her all the way through Turn 6. Her line was perfect.

Which is perfect for me.

As they climbed the hill she moved to the left. Teddy powered straight.

I've got her.

He crested the hill first and claimed the entrance to the corkscrew. He accelerated through the bends, gravity pulling him like a skier through the slalom.

Just three more turns.

Allison was almost shoving him from behind.

Two.

She moved to the outside.

One.

He glanced to the side. Allison was right there beside him.

And then he stared down the straightaway. All he saw was the checkered flag.

Chapter 35

"Well, if that's not a happy ending I don't know what is."
Dr. Miller smiled warmly from his chair across from Teddy.
The sun filtered through the office blinds. A band of light
landed on Teddy's eyes. He leaned forward on the sofa so
he wouldn't have to squint.

*That's one way to look at it. I might have gone with "a
slap in the face."*

"Sure," he said with a shrug.

"You don't seem that happy about the win."

"Oh, no, don't get me wrong. It . . ."

It had been the happiest moment of his life. Getting out
of the car. The cheers, the applause. Maxim's bear hug. "I
always knew you could do this, Chex. But good mechanic
helps, no?" Running up to Allison in the pits, grabbing her,
squeezing her. The look she gave him. One that sent fire
through every vein in his body. His heart pounded, his skin
burned. He wanted more than anything to kiss her again.
But he didn't. He'd learned his lesson. He wasn't going to
risk ruining that moment. It was already perfect. The feeling lasted all the way to the podium. They clasped hands,
raised them high in the air, and turned back towards the
crowd. His dad clapped and shouted like a madman. He'd

done it. He'd proven he could do it. And at Laguna Seca, of all places.

It had started as a whisper in the back of his mind. *This is it*, he'd thought. *I'm done. This is as far as I go.* His happiness flickered. He looked at Allison. The tears of joy began to dry on his cheeks. *But not her. She's moving on. I don't know when I'll even see her again. Or if . . .*

"The win was great. But—"

"But it feels like the end."

It is *the end.*

"McLachlin doesn't offer a course in racing."

Dr. Miller chuckled. "No. No it doesn't." He shifted in his seat. "But that doesn't mean it's all over, does it?"

Teddy remembered his conversation with Allison.

"I mean, there's other series and stuff, sure. I don't know."

"Teddy, I know things must feel pretty dark now."

"No, not dark." *He thinks I'm giving up.* He sat up straight and looked Dr. Miller in the eye. "More like the flag's dropped. The race is done. My race is done. I gave it my all. I really believe that. I'm not saying I was perfect or anything. It's just, well, it feels settled now. You know?"

Dr. Miller nodded. "I think I do. There's no 'reverse' in a race car."

"Exactly."

"I see."

"I've been really lucky. To get as far as I did. Even in that last race, if Kyle and Kayla hadn't spun out, would I have had a chance? No way."

"But you were on the track?"

Huh? Of course I was on the track.

"What do you mean?"

"I mean you weren't watching in the stands. You were on the track. The luck didn't fall into your lap. You drove into it."

Oh. I get it.

"I see. 'You miss 100 percent of the shots you don't take'—is that what you're saying?"

"Bingo. The Great One said it best."

"Yeah, well. I had a lot of luck before that."

Teddy thought about his dad and their weekends up at Motown. *If dad hadn't wanted to race himself, I probably never would have started go-karting. I never would have met Greg, or Maxim. Never would have had a chance to race the shootout.*

"I get what you're saying. But there's more to it."

Dr. Miller leaned back in his chair. "Oh, I get that, Teddy. There isn't an athlete who walks through my door who hasn't had a hundred lucky breaks just to get their shot at the big show. It doesn't matter the sport. No one gets there alone. I understand that perfectly. But I'm not entirely convinced that *you* get it."

Teddy frowned and crossed his arms. *How can I not get it? I'm the one who just said it.*

Dr. Miller glanced at his watch. "I'll tell you what, you think about it. I'm afraid we've already gone over and my next appointment is probably getting impatient."

Wait, what? Oh come on.

"Um, all right."

They stood and shook hands.

"Can I just say it's been a real pleasure working with you, Teddy. I hope this isn't our last meeting." The look on his face told Teddy he meant it.

"Uh, yeah. Me too. Thanks."

"Would you mind sending in my next victim on your way out? I need to jot a few things down before he comes in."

Ugh. Great. Probably some Olympic wrestler.

"Sure." Teddy turned to leave.

"Oh, one more thing."

He looked back.

"Yeah?"

"I hope you don't mind my asking, but what about your other . . . personal issues? I'm guessing by your performance at Laguna that you sorted them out? Or at least found a way to manage them?"

Teddy half-smiled. *How much time you got?*

"A bit of both," he said.

Dr. Miller winked. "That's the ticket."

As Teddy walked down the hallway, he thought again about what Dr. Miller had said. *I'm lucky. I've had help. I'm not alone. What am I missing?*

He was still in his head as he entered the waiting area. When he looked up he almost tripped over his own feet.

"Alex?"

LeGuivre stood up. He hesitated then took a step forward. "Oh, hey man. You were just with—"

"—Dr. Miller, yeah."

"Yeah. Sure. It's his office."

"Right."

"Right."

They both shoved their hands in their pockets and started to sway a little where they stood.

"So, Spartan-Taylor, eh?" Teddy had heard that LeGuivre had received an offer to drive in AmRun Lights the following year. "Good team. Congrats."

"Thanks."

Teddy pulled out one of his hands and thrust it towards LeGuivre, who shook it.

They stood another moment in silence.

"I guess I should . . ."

"Yeah, you should probably . . ." Teddy turned towards the exit.

"Hey."

Why can't I ever just leave a room?

"Yeah?"

"It, uh, it won't be the same without you."

Teddy studied his face. *Holy crap. He means it.*

"Thanks, man."

He left the office. A strange feeling came over him. *Am I . . . uh-uh. No way.* He tried to push it away but found he didn't really want to. *I'm actually gonna miss that guy. The world is officially bonkers.*

Chapter 36

Stay cool. Just breathe. You got this.

It was the first weekend of September, but the summer was still going strong. Even in the cool shade of the doorway, Teddy's shirt was moist with sweat. He lifted an arm and stuck his nose into his armpit. He took a whiff. *At least I don't reek. Yet.*

He pressed the doorbell. The sound triggered a jolt of adrenaline.

This is a mistake. I still have time to bolt. His leg muscles twitched.

The door opened.

Too late. Damn.

"Hi!" His voice was about a hundred notches more enthusiastic than he'd meant it to be. He raised his hand as if he were swearing an oath, or greeting new arrivals from Mars. *What are you doing!* The arm snapped back to his side. "Hey."

Leah looked like she was about to burst out laughing. She smirked, snorted, and then managed to contain it, giving him a tight smile.

Please let me die of heatstroke. Spontaneous combustion. Anything.

"Hello to you, too. Come on in. Everyone's out back already. You can keep those on," she said, pointing at Teddy's flip-flops.

Maybe if I click my heels together a few times . . .

He followed her through the house, walking as slowly as he could to maximize his exposure to the air conditioning. They entered the kitchen. Leah's dad was sitting at the table. He looked up from his paper and raised an eyebrow. "Oh, hello *Teddy*. I didn't realize *you* were coming."

Teddy scrutinized his tone, his expression.

He hates me. Of course he hates me.

"I . . . Leah invited me." Even though Leah's dad always told her friends to call him Mike, Teddy threw in a "sir" for good measure.

"Dad, come on. I told you he was."

"Hmph." He looked back at his paper. "Well have *fun*."

What's that? "Take a deep dive in the shallow end" you say?

They stepped through a sliding door and onto the patio. The gang was already gathered around the pool. Richard sat on a lounger, plucking lazily on his guitar. Justin reclined in the lounger next to him flipping through a magazine. Ben and Tom horsed around the pool while Zana sunbathed on a towel. Beside her sat a cooler and a portable speaker hooked up to a phone.

It had been weeks since they'd all been together like this. Not since before the breakup. Teddy's stomach twisted.

I can't do this.

He stopped and reached for Leah's shoulder. His hand grazed her skin and then shot back. He felt as if he'd stuck his finger in a socket. "Hey, hold up."

She turned and gave him a puzzled look.

"What?"

"I just . . . Are you sure about this? We haven't really, I dunno, talked or whatever."

"Yeah, well, I guess talking was never really our thing, was it?" Her tone was biting but playful at the same time. He could tell she was trying to hide how she really felt.

"Look, if you want me to go . . ."

"Just stop, OK?" She sighed. "I won't pretend I'm not still angry. Don't think that for a second." She spoke in a loud whisper so the others wouldn't hear. "Honestly, part of me wants to drown you in that pool right now."

More than part of me wants to let you.

"Well, then why—"

"Wake up, Teddy. This isn't just about you and me. Justin and Zana are moving to Kingston next week. You and Tom are moving to Hamilton. The rest of us are moving downtown. Who knows when we'll even see each other again?"

Teddy fidgeted. "Well, we all have to come back at Thanksgiving. For commencement."

Her eyes flared. "You *know* what I mean. Everything's changing. I—*we* all just wanted one last chance to hang out."

Last chance. Teddy almost threw up in his mouth. He'd worked so hard the last few weeks adjusting to the idea that he might never race again, he hadn't given much thought to what would happen with the gang in the fall. Even when he'd hung out with Tom or Richard or Ben, no one had talked about it.

Or maybe I was too busy talking about myself and my precious lost career that I didn't hear them.

"I guess I just thought . . . It's not like we're moving to different countries or anything."

She crossed her arms and tilted her head. "C'mon, Teddy." Her tone softened. "Obviously I want us all to stay friends." His eyes widened when she said "all." "I can't imagine not having you guys around." He started to speak but she cut him off. "Don't. Don't even. I meant it before. I'm still—" She closed her eyes and took a deep breath. "Here it is. Whatever happens next, we got this far together. All of us. I'm not going to pretend you don't exist, or let this thing between us ruin everything for everyone. I'm willing to do my best to put everything to one side, just for today. I hope you'll at least try to do the same."

Teddy smiled. Then he started to laugh.

Leah's pleading expression twisted into one of puzzlement. In fact, she looked a bit annoyed.

"What?"

"You're asking me to compartmentalize."

"I'm what?"

"Hey, is that Teddy!" Tom shouted. He waved his arms over his head, sending a spray of water in Zana's direction. "About time! Get in here!"

"Seriously, Tom? Are you kidding me right now?" Zana barked. "Leah, your parents are insured right? For accidental deaths and stuff?"

Looking exasperated, Leah spun and walked towards the pool. "I'm surrounded by children. Every one of you. Children."

She started to laugh. The sound melted every knot in Teddy's body.

I can do this. He thought. *This is what I do.*

He'd taken two steps towards the pool when his phone buzzed. He pulled it out of his pocket.

"Just got a call. We need to talk. Dad"

I've got to get him to stop signing his texts.

He continued walking as he typed.

"Can't talk now. Home later." He smirked. "Teddy." *No, wait.*

"C'mon man, put that away," said Richard.

"Hey, when a man needs to text . . ." said Justin.

"Just a sec, it's my dad." He deleted the last word and typed a new one: "Chex." "Sorry. Well," he said, turning to Richard. "C'mon, let's see what you got."

Richard grinned and began strumming.

His phone buzzed again. He glanced at it.

"Urgent. Dad."

He pursed his lips. His thumb reached for the call button. He stopped and looked up. Then he tossed his phone on a folded towel next to the cooler.

Right now, so is this.

Chapter 37

It was dusk by the time he left Leah's. He hummed as he strolled home. It was one of the band's songs. The others must have sung it a dozen times that afternoon, but Teddy still didn't know the words. He walked to the beat, his flip-flops squishing along to the tune. The air was cooling quickly, but he could feel his skin glowing hot from the sun.

I'm probably redder than a lobster. He smiled. *Covered in ketchup.*

He walked through the side door so he wouldn't track dirt into the front hall.

"Hey, Dad!" He entered the hallway, still humming. "Sorry about earlier. I was, uh, tied up. So what's the big—"

His dad stormed down the stairs. "What is the point of having a phone if you—you know what? It doesn't matter. Hurry up. Get changed." He looked Teddy up and down. Then he checked his watch and grunted. "No. Strike that. Shower. Then change."

"Um, I was planning on it. We're all going to the movies tonight. Richard's coming to pick me up in an hour."

"Are you even listening to me?"

"Are you even saying anything? What is going on!"

His dad clenched his jaws. "Well, if you'd call me when I ask, you'd know."

This is going nowhere.

"Dad. OK. I'm s-o-r-r-y."

His dad seemed to relax. "You'll never guess who I ran into at the Queen's Head today."

Probably not. So . . .

Teddy leaned forward. His eyebrows made an impressive attempt to touch his hairline.

"Reg Dreyfus."

Why is this earth-shattering news?

"The suite guy?"

"The suite guy." His dad looked at him as if he'd just shared the secret to curing cancer.

"Right."

His dad started to bob his head slowly.

Either I'm missing something or he's lost everything.

"Cool story, Dad."

His dad frowned. "Teddy, you're being thick."

Teddy huffed and folded his arms. *What could be so urgent about Dad running into some rich dude in a—holy crap.*

His dad smiled. "Oh, he gets it. Hallelujah."

"You mean . . . he wants to . . ."

"AmRun Light. Full ride."

Full ride. Hallelujah. His knees started to tremble.

"He's only in town for the night. Wants to have dinner. So go wash your . . . everything."

Teddy bolted up the stairs. *Omigodomigodomigod.*

"And polish off that winning charm of yours while you're at it. I don't know what you said to him at the race but, well, a little more of that couldn't hurt."

Teddy jumped into the shower. His hand was shaking so hard he kept dropping the shampoo.

This doesn't make any sense. This can't be real. This can't *be real.*

He ran a comb through his hair.

This isn't how this works. I didn't win the series. I missed half the races.

He stumbled trying to put on his shorts and fell onto his bed. He didn't even bother standing up to finish the job. The framed gloves above his bed caught his eye.

"How is this happening?" he said. He stared at them for a minute. Then two.

Are you expecting them to answer? Keep moving!

"Teddy, let's go!"

This is happening too fast. I'm not ready.

"I'm not ready!"

He looked at the gloves again.

"Well, *be* ready, sport. Like it or not, we've gotta go!"

He grabbed the cleanest shirt he had, the one he'd worn for his interview with *Road & Race*. He was still buttoning it as he blundered into the front hall.

"Dad, this isn't right. I'm not ready. I didn't win the series." He buttoned up his top button. Then unbuttoned it. "It doesn't make any sense." He unbuttoned the next one. "I only won the last race because of luck. I—"

"—hold it right there."

Flashes of Dr. Miller's office.

"I know, I know. The luck only worked because I was on the track to begin with."

"Well, yeah, but that wasn't what I was going to say."

"All right, well?"

His dad clasped Teddy's shoulders. "This is the off-season, son. Nothing makes sense. That's why it's called—"

"—the silly season."

"Bingo."

Teddy looked into his dad's eyes. They shone with pride. He felt his cheeks flush and pull back into a grin.

"All right, Dad. Let's go be silly, then."

"That's my boy." He gave Teddy's shoulders a squeeze before releasing him.

Teddy turned and opened the front door.

"Oy!"

He looked back.

"You really are being thick tonight." His dad threw something at him. Teddy almost tripped on the threshold trying to catch it.

He looked down at the key fob for his Mini and then back up at his dad.

"You're driving."

Thank You

Thanks for reading. I really hope you enjoyed the book. I'd love to hear what you thought of it. Why not visit the *Chasing Checkers* Facebook page and let me know?

I also hope you'll consider leaving review at your favourite online bookseller. It's a huge help to me, and to others who are looking for their next great read.

If you want to hear about special promotions, book signings, and future books, visit **chasingcheckersbook.com** and join my mailing list.

Finally, if you liked the book, don't forget to tell your friends about it!